TO DIE FOR

HIDDEN NORFOLK - BOOK 9

J M DALGLIESH

EXCLUSIVE OFFER

Look out for the link at the end of this book or visit my website at **www.jmdalgliesh.com** to sign up to my no-spam VIP Club and receive a FREE Hidden Norfolk novella plus news and previews of forthcoming works.

Never miss a new release.

No spam, ever, guaranteed. You can unsubscribe at any time.

TO DIE FOR

PROLOGUE

THE DOOR CLOSED and the latch clicked as it dropped into place. He looked across the room to the figure standing resolutely at the door, one hand resting on the frame, head bowed. The footsteps on the decking faded as the last guests walked to their cars. The only sound was the ticking of the clock mounted above the fireplace; a monotonous staccato as the hand moved around the face. He watched the movement, sitting bolt upright on the sofa, hands on his knees, for almost a full revolution until it hit twelve and the minute hand passed effortlessly to midday.

His brother sighed, drawing his eyes to him as he came to the centre of the room, breaking his concentration. He didn't speak in reply to the gesture, which was undoubtedly his brother's intention when making the noise, but he merely followed the younger man with his eyes as he first loosened his tie, unbuttoned his shirt at the collar, and then sank into the armchair to his right shaking his head slowly. His brother looked at the clock.

"It's been a long day."

He nodded briefly but still said nothing.

"And it's only lunchtime."

His brother stared hard at him, his eyes narrowing, their gaze fixed on one another.

"Do you... think we should have done more?"

It was a curious question. Open ended. He shrugged, unsure of what he was expected to say. This was one of the things that regularly irritated him about his sibling, this innate need to analyse every detail, to explore the possibilities of what has happened, could happen or would happen in any given scenario. What did it matter? What was done was done and couldn't be revisited. His brother misinterpreted the movement.

"About holding a wake, I mean?" he said, running the palm of his hand slowly back and forth across his chin. "It's one thing to have a handful of people back here but..."

He cocked his head to one side.

"But what?"

"We could have done more, couldn't we?"

The suggestion irritated him but he didn't know why. His brow furrowed. The expression appeared to please his brother for some reason because a half-smile crept onto his face.

"So, you are still in there then."

The irritation grew.

"I wasn't aware that I'd ever left."

His brother sighed again, lowering his head into his hands. He ruffled his hair before sitting up.

"I think it's time we talked, don't you?"

"About what?"

"Well..." he looked around. "This place for starters."

He followed his brother's eye around the room. Everywhere he looked reminded him of their mother. The pictures on the walls were all her choices. She was obsessed with the southern Mediterranean, the mountains of Spain, the vineyards of Bordeaux and the rolling hills of Tuscany, all reflected in her choice of painting or framed photography. They were all prints of course. She'd never been to any of them. In fact, he couldn't remember her ever having left Norfolk, let alone ventured abroad. So, what was it? The exotic implication of faraway lands? He didn't know. There was every chance his mother didn't know where any of these places were. It didn't matter. Not to him anyway.

"So, what do you think?"

The tone in his brother's voice suggested this was a repeated question. He met his eye.

"About?"

"Keep or sell? The land is probably worth more if we parcel it up and the house," he looked around again, almost like he could imagine an estate agent appraising the value, "would fetch a tidy sum if we fixed her up a bit."

"It's not for sale."

"Excuse me?"

He licked his lower lip. It felt as dry as his mouth.

"I said it's not for sale. I'm not selling."

"But that's what we need to talk about—"

"No." He shook his head, rising from the sofa and crossing to the sideboard; opening the top drawer. Picking up an envelope, he returned to stand in front of his younger brother and handed it over. His brother took it from him and lifted the flap. He returned to his place on the sofa and sat back down, once again resting his palms on his knees. Looking back at the clock, he watched the second hand begin another pass of the clock face as his brother flipped through the pages nearby.

"B-But... this has to be wrong—"

"It's not wrong," he said, eyes fixed on the clock. "Read it for yourself—"

"I have read it." There was tension in his voice, more than merely displeasure. Shock, maybe? "I can bloody read! I just can't believe she... why would she do this to me?"

He turned away from the clock to observe his brother who was staring at the pages in his hand, lips parted, eyes wide.

"Like I said. It's not for sale. None of it."

"But she can't do this!"

"And yet she has."

His brother lurched to his feet, scrunching the paper in his grasp and brandishing it before him as he came to stand over him, glaring down at him.

"This wasn't what she said she'd do."

He shook his head. "It doesn't matter what she said. It is what it is."

"And you're happy with this, are you?"

It was disbelief. That was what he'd heard in his tone before, disbelief at the decisions their mother had made towards the end of her life. He thought his younger brother a little odd at that moment, but that wasn't for the first time either. They'd always been different as far back as he could remember. Their approach to life, friendships – parents – were vastly at odds with one another and noticeably so to the point, that if they didn't look so alike one might conclude they were of different parentage.

He shrugged. "Like I said. It is what it is."

"You did this!" His brother shook the paper in front of him and then, having not elicited the expected response, threw the papers in his face. The disbelief was gone now, replaced first by indignation and now by fury. "I'll not take it lying down."

He angled his head to one side, pursed his lips and looked up at his brother. The skin of his face was blotchy, turning that pinky-red colour it does when frustration gets the better of you. A flash of anger that must be kept in check no matter what. The alternative was to lose control. That was something else his brother was good at, losing control. He was one of the most undisciplined people he'd ever known. Most people would feel vulnerable at this point faced with such a combustible individual but he remained calm, unfazed. His brother was many things, many of them bad, but violence had never been a thing up to this point in his life at any rate.

"There are things I can do... people I can go to... solicitors and stuff."

He shrugged. "Do what you feel you have to—"

"I'm entitled to what's mine, damn you."

"That's not what Mum thought."

"You did this to me, didn't you? Staying here, working on her day after day? You did this."

He shook his head. "We didn't talk about it, not until near the end. It is what she wanted, not me."

His brother was furious, his hands by his side, fists balled and hands shaking.

"So, what are you going to do? How will you manage?"

"I will… somehow."

His anger seemed to dissipate then and he threw back his head and laughed. A dismissive sound, hollow and artificial.

"You'll manage! Have you seen all these?" he said, marching over to the kitchen table and returning with a stack of envelopes, many unopened and stamped on the exterior with red ink, and hurling them at him. The envelopes bounced off him harmlessly and he ignored the confrontational gesture, turning his gaze back to the clock. "If Mum and Dad, with your help, couldn't make this place work how the hell are you going to go it alone?"

"I'll manage," he said slowly, a smile crossing his face.

He didn't watch his brother leave or listen to what he was mumbling, no doubt curses…. The next he heard was the door slamming shut. The sound of footsteps on the decking receded and he looked around the family home, picturing the memories: children, fun and family occasions. His eye drifted to an old grainy photograph taken on the beach barely a quarter of a mile from where he was sitting, the two boys in dungarees, smiling, each holding a mother's hand as they paddled in the gentle surf. They couldn't have been more than five or six years old that day. Days like those would return.

He would find a way. What else did he have to do?

CHAPTER ONE

THE CAR BOTTOMED out on the unmade track up to the house. The driver winced. Not because of the sound of the sump grating against the loose stones and the frozen earth, but the dark look on his wife's face.

"I know, love, I know."

The admission did little to lighten her expression.

"I was supposed to be there by now. You know what my mum is like when I'm late—"

"Two minutes, no more. I promise."

"Honestly, Gary. Why couldn't you just phone him."

He sighed. "I *have* phoned him... several times but he's not picking up."

"Maybe he doesn't want the work."

Gary laughed, the car jolting on the uneven surface as they bounced along. The access track to the property could do with some tender loving care, that was for certain.

"Since when have you ever known Billy to turn down work? Particularly when it's cash in hand?"

His wife, Jenny, thought about it as she firmly grasped the door handle and muttered a curse under her breath as they lurched to the left.

"Ill then?"

Gary inclined his head, still focussed on steering the car via the path of least resistance. "Yeah, maybe." He looked over at her. "But, again, when was the last time you remember Billy being sick?"

She tutted. "What do you think I am, his secretary or something? I've barely spoken to the man."

Gary glanced sideways briefly at her but said nothing. They reached the five-bar gate at the entrance to the property, a timber cabin in the centre of a clearing some four hundred yards from the highway along the unadopted road. He stopped the car. The place was in darkness. That in itself wasn't necessarily unusual as it was mid-afternoon, but the day was overcast even for mid-March. Spring seemed tantalisingly close but was yet to assert itself. There was still a chill wind coming in off the sea, winter's last gasp; an attempt to hold onto them before allowing the onset of warmer weather. The least he'd expect to have seen though, was a curl of smoke drifting up from the chimney but, aside from the branches of the surrounding trees swaying in the breeze, everything in the yard was still.

"Do you think he's home?" Jenny asked.

Gary leaned forward over the dashboard, squinting as he scanned the outside of the property. The cabin was a single-storey affair, dilapidated and in need of repair with the exterior cladding rotting in places and two of the windows had obvious cracks in them. Besides the main residence there was a collection of outbuildings, although the term was arguably at odds with the reality, for they were little more than an ageing mix of haphazardly placed sheds incorporating several makeshift lean-tos. A three-berth caravan was set to the right of the furthest one on the far side of the yard. It was once white but was now faded to a grungy tone of cream tinged with a strange green growth across the exterior including the windows which were themselves shrouded by dirty old curtains anyway. Moss grew on the roof and the tyres were flat. The caravan hadn't moved in years.

"His car is there," Gary said, pointing to a small blue Nissan hatchback parked to the side of the cabin. "And his tractor is there as well."

"Geez... does that thing still move?"

Gary smiled. She was right. It was an ancient Ford model that predated the current safety regulations for agricultural machinery, it didn't even have a cabin. It was an agricultural relic, but Billy somehow managed to still keep it running. That was testament to the man's skills.

"Come on. Let's go and give him a knock."

Jenny didn't speak as he pulled the car into the yard. Two spaniels appeared from their makeshift kennels and ran to the boundary of their chain-link fencing, excitedly barking at them and jumping up against the barrier.

"Well, he wouldn't go on holiday without asking someone to have the dogs," Jenny said, absently watching their frantically wagging tails as Gary brought the car to a standstill.

"Billy go on holiday? As if he would," Gary said, cracking his door open. "And he wouldn't agree to the work if he knew he was going to be away, would he?"

Jenny shot another dark look in his direction and internally Gary regretted being so dismissive. She was already annoyed and he should know better than to poke the beast inside her.

"I just meant he's not the holiday-taking kind, is he?"

"He used to go away though, didn't he? A while back, I mean."

Gary held the door open with his hand but didn't get out, a cold draught passing over him as he thought about it. She was right, again; Billy used to go away for a couple of weeks every year, but that was some time ago now, although he had been away the previous year for a few days but he couldn't remember where. He'd forgotten about the annual breaks Billy used to take. He never said where he was going. He shook the thought away and got out.

"Two minutes!"

He smiled at her. "You don't fancy coming in then?"

She shook her head. "Nah. Gives me the creeps."

Gary looked over his shoulder at the cabin. "It's not that bad."

"Not the house – *him*."

He waved away her comment and shut the door, approaching the steps and mounting them up onto the decking. There wasn't a doorbell, just an old-style brass bell with a cord hanging from the clapper to the right. He glanced back at Jenny watching him intently from the car. She raised her hand and pointedly tapped the watch on her wrist. He looked away and rang the bell. The dull sound reverberated in his head and set the dogs barking again.

There was no movement from within and Gary leaned closer to the pane of glass in the door and tried to peer through the netting hanging from the other side. He could just about make out the interior but there was nothing of note. The car horn startled him and he jumped. Spinning around, he glared at Jenny whom he could see laughing. Dispensing with the bell, he rapped his knuckles on the glass door and called out.

"Billy! Are you in there?"

He waited. Still, there was no response. He tried the door, finding it unlocked. He cracked it open and called out again.

"Billy! It's Gary!" He poked his head through the gap and glanced around. There was nothing untoward that he could see, the place was clean and tidy, but he'd never been inside before. Billy was always pretty coy when it came to letting him in, always keeping him outside on the rare occasions he stopped by for help fitting something to his car, to borrow a tool or give him a lift to work. He'd never taken offence, assuming Billy just liked his privacy more than most. It was true that he seldom spoke of his personal life, Gary presuming he didn't have anything of note to speak of.

"What's going on?"

Gary looked round to find Jenny standing behind him. He was expecting another admonishment but it didn't come. She didn't seem ready to hassle him.

"I don't know," he said.

"Blimey. What's that smell?"

Gary hadn't noticed it, but then again his sense of smell was underdeveloped. Jenny's on the other hand was finely tuned. "I don't know," he repeated, frowning. "But come to mention it, something is a bit off."

"Does his place always smell like this?" she asked as he pushed the door open further.

"No idea. I've never been inside."

The rush of air pulled from indoors carried the pungent smell to them, only this time it was far stronger. Jenny brought her forearm to her mouth using the sleeve of her thick woollen jumper as a mask. Even Gary cupped his mouth and nose with his hand. He took a step inside.

"You coming?" he asked.

Jenny shook her head. "Told you, he's creepy. And the smell... it must be minging in there."

He dismissed her protests and entered. Despite her reservations, Jenny hovered at the threshold, peering past him as he walked across the open-plan living room, scanning the interior as he went and on towards the kitchen. The smell was growing stronger and Gary swatted away several flies buzzing around him as he approached the kitchen. His eye was caught by an old shoe box sitting on top of a large rustic wooden dining table with the lid upturned alongside it. He peered inside and his eyes widened. Turning to summon Jenny, he hesitated, his eye drifting to the floor.

"What is it, Gary?"

He remained still. He'd heard the question but didn't react, his eyes focussed in front of him.

"Gary?"

This time he did look back and there must have been something in his expression that conveyed far more than the words that stumbled out of his mouth. "I... I... it's... Billy."

Jenny hurried over to where he was standing, disregarding the unpleasant smell and coming alongside she grasped his forearm, gasping as she looked down. Putting a hand across her mouth, she felt her stomach lurch and she gagged before turning and running from the cabin for the sanctuary of the outdoors.

Gary didn't flinch, his eyes transfixed on the scene before him, fear rooting him to the spot.

CHAPTER TWO

THE BAND WAS in full swing. The dance floor was peppered with excited children and those who had made the most of the complimentary table wine through dinner. There were ten of them seated at the table but conversation was sparse. Beyond the person sitting immediately beside you, it was almost impossible to hear. Tamara Greave often found herself nodding and smiling appreciatively without any clue as to what was being said or if her mannerisms were appropriate.

Eric and Becca appeared at her shoulder, the recently married Mr and Mrs Collet were grinning At least Becca was; Eric still looked rather like a rabbit caught in the headlights, the expression he'd adopted for the entire day. The lady sitting next to Tamara, who'd been speaking extensively about greenhouse maintenance as far as Tamara could tell, stood up and hugged both of the newly-weds in turn and sauntered off to find another victim to talk to. Tamara waved and smiled as she left, thankful of the respite.

Becca slid into the recently vacated seat and took Tamara's hands in her own, Eric standing behind her and placing his hands gently on his bride's shoulders. Becca leaned in so that she wouldn't need to shout to be heard.

"Thank you so much for everything you've done to help this week."

Tamara smiled. It had been a pleasure. Becca was an only child and came from a small family which seemed to be at odds with most of the people she'd come across since she'd arrived in Norfolk. Becca needed to hear a voice from outside the family, and her relationship, turning to Tamara and Cassie for that support. One of the ushers approached Eric and whispered something in his ear and Eric leaned into Becca, excusing himself. Cassie came across and sat down with the two of them, nursing a glass of wine.

"You go easy with that, Detective Sergeant Knight," Tamara said, eyeing the glass in Cassie's hand. "You've got work tomorrow, remember?"

"It's sparkling apple juice," Cassie said, smiling. She seemed to recognise Tamara's sceptical expression. "I swear! I'm the designated driver. I lost out to Lauren seeing as she's got tomorrow off."

"Turned out well then."

Becca looked around, seeing Eric was deep in conversation with his uncle on the other side of the room and definitely couldn't hear her, she frowned at Tamara. It was the first negative look that had crossed the bride's face all day.

"Thank you for helping with Eric's... mistake as well," Becca said.

Tamara was momentarily thrown but then she realised. "Oh, the annual leave mix up?" Becca nodded. "That's okay. It's not a problem."

"What have I missed?" Cassie asked. Tamara wasn't going to elaborate but Becca did.

"I gave Eric one job to do for this wedding, besides showing up obviously. One job," she said raising a pointed finger. Tamara grimaced because she knew what was coming, Cassie leaned in attentively. Tamara had the impression Becca had been easing the stresses of the day with liquid lubrication.

"What was that?" Cassie asked.

"To book the honeymoon," Becca said, sitting back in her chair and throwing her hands theatrically in the air.

"And?"

"And he fluffed it," Becca said, shaking her head. Cassie glanced at Tamara who bit the outside of her lower lip and raised her eyebrows. "He got the dates wrong. Can you believe it?"

"So, that's why he's still rostered on this week?" Cassie asked. Tamara nodded. "When are you going?"

"A week tomorrow."

Cassie smiled. "Well, that's not too bad. My youngest sister had to wait nearly a year for her honeymoon," she raised her eyebrows whilst looking at Becca whose jaw dropped, "but that was because they were skint."

Tamara felt hands on her shoulders and looked up to see her mum's smiling face. She turned and Francesca stepped back.

"What is it, Mum?"

"I've got someone I want you to meet, Tammy darling."

"Really? Now? We're just in the middle of—"

"Becca, love, I think someone needs their mummy."

They all turned as Becca's mother joined them, a crying George in her arms. She passed the two-month-old infant to Becca and the baby settled almost immediately, heading off the potential grizzling episode.

"How are you, my little man?" Becca said tapping her forefinger near to George's chin and he opened his mouth to suck on it. "I think someone's hungry."

Cassie leaned over to get a better look, smiling at the child. Francesca did likewise. Tamara admired from a distance.

"He was so good during the ceremony, wasn't he?" Cassie said. "We barely heard him."

"I'd better go and feed him."

Becca slid out of her seat, heading off to find somewhere quieter to sit.

"Come, come, come," Francesca said, clearly not taking no for an answer and levering her out of her seat and guiding her away. Cassie smiled and stood up herself as Tamara was led away.

"Seeing as you have me here," Tamara said as she was speed-marched along the edge of the dance floor just as the band took a break and the brief interlude of silence was broken by a song aimed at the children. She caught sight of Tom Janssen being led onto the dance floor by Saffy, his partner Alice's daughter although Tom was as close to a father as she was ever likely to have or need. Alice was clapping along to the rhythm of the music with the others at the table, one allocated to those guests with similar age children, as the dancers began a sequence of moves that must accompany this particular song, one that had happily passed Tamara by. But it was a lovely sight. "I was wondering if Dad was coming up again this weekend?" she asked, framing the question as casually as she could.

"Oh, I think so, yes."

Tamara glanced sideways at her mother who was staring at her, a knowing look in her eye.

"That's okay, isn't it?"

There was an edge to the reply. Tamara realised she had to tread carefully. Her mother's impromptu arrival on her doorstep, unannounced, over four months previously had been unexpected, as was her revelation that she'd left her husband, Tamara's father. Since then, the two had taken great strides towards a reconciliation, something that had gathered pace in the last couple of months but still her mother hadn't sought to return to the marital home in Bristol.

"Yes, of course." She did her best to sound genuine and it was, to a point.

"Then why does it not sound like it is?"

Tamara stopped in her tracks, turning to face her mother. She took her hands in her own, squeezing them tightly and offering an earnest expression.

"*It is fine*, Mum, honestly. I don't mind at all. I think it's great that Dad is making the trip... what is it, every couple of weeks now?"

"Every weekend this past month," Francesca said, beaming.

"E–Every weekend, right. I was just thinking... you know... just off the top of my head, if you might be going back with him this time?"

Francesca's eyes narrowed. "So, it *is* a problem?"

Tamara saw the hurt in her mum's face and moved to assuage it, firmly shaking her head. "No. I mean it, it's not a problem at all. I know we don't talk about... relationship type things and I was just wondering, that's all."

"Really? You don't mind?"

Tamara smiled supportively and Francesca relaxed, the evident tension in her shoulders visibly dissipating as she smiled.

"Yes, you can stay as long as you like."

"That's wonderful, Tammy." Tamara silently bit her tongue at the use of her childhood nickname, one she had never cared for, returning the smile. "Come on, I want to introduce you to someone." Francesca resumed her walk at a swift pace, taking a firm hold of Tamara's arm and dragging her along beside her. "I'm so pleased you said that, Tammy, because your father was thinking he'd stop for a few weeks this time so that I can properly show him the sights."

Tamara, unseen by her mother, rolled her eyes as they walked. She didn't have time to formulate a reply as they quickly reached their destination. Francesca pulled out a chair at one of the tables in the second row back from the dance floor, ushering Tamara to sit down. She repeatedly tapped the shoulder of the man who was in the next seat with his back to them, currently in mid-conversation with two other people. He glanced around and Francesca warmly smiled. He returned it.

"Conrad, this is my daughter – the one I was telling you about, Tammy."

The man looked from her to Tamara and back again, momentarily thrown, before he smiled politely and nodded at Tamara.

Turning fully to face her, he offered his hand and introduced himself.

"Conrad Reardon."

Tamara, self-conscious, hesitated before taking his hand and smiling.

"Tamara."

"Conrad works in finance, Tammy. In the city," Francesca said, tapping her palm on Tamara's shoulder, "don't you, dear?"

"Ah... yes, yes I do."

Tamara felt her embarrassment growing. Conrad seemed unfazed, though. Inclining his head and adopting a natural smile. "And I forget what it is Francesca said you do, Tamara."

"I'm a—"

"PR consultant," Francesca said, bending over and putting her head between them as she interrupted, turning her face so only Tamara could see and nodding furiously with her eyebrows raised. Tamara eased her mother aside, nodded and smiled. Francesca, grinning, righted herself. "I'll leave the two of you to get acquainted."

She skipped away and Tamara smiled awkwardly at Conrad. For his part, he seemed to take it in his stride. Her mother wasn't very subtle but she did appear to have good taste. Conrad was a similar age to Tamara and clearly spent time in the gym on a regular basis. He was athletic, had a strong jaw line and sculpted cheekbones, a full head of hair that had the tiniest speckling of grey to its blond colour. He didn't dye his hair yet, she could tell. And he had the most natural, winning smile. The song that was playing ended and the lead singer of the band asked for everyone's attention.

"Ladies and gentlemen – the ladies in particular I should imagine – it's the time you've all been waiting for. It's time for the bride to throw the bouquet!"

A loud cheer went up accompanied by much applause. Tamara sat back in her seat and exhaled, pleased for time to gather her thoughts.

"You're not going up?" Conrad asked as the women gathered at the end of the dance floor furthest from them, Becca walking forward with her flowers in hand.

"Not my thing, really," Tamara said, smiling.

"Really? My wife's always the first one up there."

Tamara frowned. "Your wife?"

"Yes, that's her," Conrad said, pointing to a woman in a pink dress in the thick of the group. Tamara nodded glumly. *Call yourself a detective,* she thought eyeing the gold wedding band on his left hand. As if she'd been waiting on a prearranged rescue signal, Alice appeared next to her, placing hands on both Tamara's shoulders and encouraging her to join the forthcoming melee. Tamara didn't argue as she allowed herself to be guided onto the dance floor.

"He looks nice," Alice said in her ear.

"Yes, so does his wife."

"Shame."

Tamara leaned in as the two of them took positions slightly off centre in the group as Becca turned her back to them and readied herself to launch the bouquet. "If it comes near us I'll give you a hundred pounds if you make sure you catch it!"

"Deal," Alice said, laughing.

The audience cheered as Becca hurled the flowers up and over-head. They arced through the air and the group all tried to track the route. One woman slipped and fell taking two others with her to the floor and despite her best efforts, Alice missed the flowers and instinctively Tamara caught them as they came to her. Everyone cheered and Tamara caught her mother looking at her, grinning. She winked and Tamara ignored her, smiling at those around her, noting the peculiarly dark look one young woman in particular was sending her way.

She put her hand out and helped Cassie to her feet, as she was one of those who'd fallen.

"I didn't think this was your thing, Cass?"

Cassie shrugged. "Lauren bet me a tenner I couldn't get it and I hate to lose."

"Here you go," Tamara said, thrusting them into her hands. "If she didn't specify exactly how and when you were to get the flowers, then you might still win... in a roundabout sort of way."

"I like your thinking," Cassie said, throwing an arm around her shoulder. Tom came across to speak to them, his expression serious.

"What is it, Tom?" Tamara asked as Alice slipped her arm around his waist. He looked into Alice's eyes and winked, clearly he wasn't bearing good news.

"Just had a call," he said glumly. "A body's been found."

Tamara could read the unspoken words in his expression. "I'll come with you."

He shook his head. "No there's no need. I can take a look—"

"I'm coming," Tamara said, catching sight of Francesca heading their way, Saffy in tow. The little girl ran ahead, slipping in between all the adult legs and threw her arms around Tom's, smiling up at him. He ruffled her hair. Tom looked at Alice, grimacing.

"I'm really sorry."

"I can run you guys home whenever you're ready," Cassie said to Alice. "It's not a problem"

"Can you drop my mum off as well?" Tamara asked as Francesca joined them.

"Palming me off already?" Francesca asked playfully.

"Duty calls, Mum."

"Oh blast. That's such a shame."

"Yeah, tell me about it," Tamara said. She looked at Tom. "We'd better have a word with the bride and groom, explain."

He nodded, leaning down and kissing Alice. He then scooped up Saffy and she threw her arms around his head.

"Do you really have to go to work now?"

"Afraid so, munchkin," he said, smiling glumly. "Got to catch the bad guys."

Saffy's brow furrowed, fixing a stern look on her face well beyond her years. "Don't they *ever* take a day off?"

"It doesn't feel like it, does it?" She shook her head. "So, it's a good job I'm very good at catching them then, isn't it?" She nodded.

"Can I dance with Eric?" Saffy asked.

"We'd better check with Becca," Tom said. "Come on."

"Or I could dance with Becca."

"I imagine so, yes," Tom said, walking off to the newlyweds with her still in his arms.

Francesca took hold of Tamara's forearm as she made to follow, drawing her a half step away from the others.

"So, what do you think of Conrad? He's quite a catch, isn't he?"

Tamara nodded. "I dare say his wife thinks so, yes."

She unhitched herself from her mother's grasp and hurried over to where Tom was saying his goodbyes, leaving a rather perplexed Francesca behind.

CHAPTER THREE

TOM JANSSEN PULLED up to the entrance to the yard and was met by a uniformed constable standing at the gate with a liveried police car parked to the left of the entrance. He recognised both Tom and Tamara, waving them through. Tom lowered his window and the constable suggested they park on the left of the yard because the main crime scene was in the cabin behind him. Tom looked over and saw a red Audi that he knew belonged to Dr Fiona Williams, their local forensic medical examiner, parked alongside the forensics van. Beside these two vehicles was a CID pool car. Beyond these was another police car with two civilians talking with a uniformed constable who had his back to them and Tom couldn't see who it was.

They were met on the decking by PC Kerry Palmer, usually a uniformed constable who was undertaking a temporary sidestep into CID as part of a personal development plan. She was covering this particular day because the team's caseload wasn't too demanding at present and everyone was in attendance at Eric's wedding to Becca.

If Kerry was at all fazed by the two senior ranks' arrival then she didn't let on, greeting them with confidence.

"Sir, Ma'am," she said. "I'm sorry to call you away from the celebration."

Everyone at the station knew Eric was finally walking down the aisle, delayed somewhat by his recuperation from a stabbing the previous year and his fiancée's subsequent pregnancy. Becca made it clear she didn't wish to look like a *whale in a wedding dress* in their photo album. And so it was an early spring wedding and the collection gathered for the newlyweds totalled just over a thousand pounds, not including the gifts from those attending the ceremony. This was a reflection on just how popular DC Eric Collet was.

"No problem," Tamara said. She looked across the yard at the man and woman talking to the police officer and nodded in their direction. "Who are they?"

"They found the body, Ma'am."

Tamara nodded, turning back to Kerry. "One ma'am is enough per day, Kerry."

The young PC flushed with embarrassment but she didn't have time to dwell on it as Tom looked past her and into the interior.

"Have we been shut out?" he asked. Kerry nodded.

"Yes, sir. The crime scene photographer is just squaring everything away and then we'll be clear to go in."

A flash lit up the interior as if to emphasise the point and Tom could see individuals clad in white coveralls moving around.

"What can you tell us, Kerry?"

Tom had been the one who selected Kerry Palmer as the officer he wanted to gain experience. She was intelligent, committed and took an incredibly diligent approach to her work. A number of eyebrows were raised when he put her name forward, not that she wasn't believed competent or capable, merely that there were other officers with far more experience who felt they should get the nod ahead of her. That wasn't how Tom saw it at all. His own experience when he left Norfolk for the Met taught him that age and *years in* were not the greatest measure of ability and competence. As much as experience in the service was essential, in his mind it was often the knowledge, character and intelligence that made the officer.

The members of his investigative team needed to complement one another, the blend of the team members being greater than the sum of its individual parts and the selection of Kerry Palmer would provide balance to Eric's commitment, Cassie's tenacity and his own methodical approach. So far, he'd been impressed with her in the brief stints on operations where she'd been involved, but those occasions were few and far between and she'd never been first on call in a situation such as this one. That was the thing about a regional post such as this; Metropolitan Police officers might deal with a number of cases in one month that a coastal Norfolk officer would only come across in an entire career. He was keen to see what she made of it.

"We had a call from a member of the public," Kerry pointed to the couple across the yard, "earlier this evening and uniform attended. They then called me." She opened her notebook and scanned her notes. "Inside is a deceased male, aged approximately forty to forty-five years of age. The couple who found him are friends and they have identified him as Billy Moy, a local man who has lived here since he was born." She waved the pen in her hand around in a small arc in front of her. "This place is registered to him. It has been the family home as far back as his friends can remember. I only spoke to them briefly, but they were expecting him at their place – Heacham Way – to take down a tree in their garden and he never showed."

"Is he a tree surgeon?" Tom asked, looking around and seeing a large pile of split logs, probably three or four tonnes' worth at the far end of the yard. A thick layer of sawdust lay on the ground nearby.

Kerry shrugged. "Not primarily, no. I think he's a *jack of all trades* as far as I can tell."

"What happened to him?" Tamara asked.

"The FME is inside but I think the cause of death is quite apparent," Kerry said, glancing over her shoulder as another flash lit up the kitchen. "He was found lying on the kitchen floor with a knife sticking out of his chest."

Tom sucked air through his teeth, raising his eyebrows. "Evidence of a struggle?"

She shook her head. "Not that I could see. The place is neat and tidy, no furniture overturned, broken crockery or anything like that. Likewise, no sign of forced entry. I had a brief look over the victim and couldn't see any defensive wounds or grazing to the knuckles to suggest he'd been in a fight for his life." She frowned.

"What is it?" Tom asked.

She looked uncertain for a moment and then shook it off. "I'm not convinced he saw it coming, even though his attacker must have been standing right in front of him. Single blow, straight to his chest and I wouldn't be surprised if it went straight through his heart. The amount of blood that came out, and the deep colouration of it, implies a major organ was struck... it's almost as if..."

"As if?"

She smiled. "As if it was a lucky strike..." she shook her head again. "Sorry, just speculating."

Tom smiled approvingly.

"Then there's the weapon itself," she said, reading through her notes to make certain she'd not missed anything, "I don't think the killer brought it with them. There's a carving knife missing from the chef's block on the worktop and the handle of the blade in his chest matches."

The front door opened and Dr Williams appeared. She took her mask away from her face and dropped the hood of her coveralls, smiling at Tom and Tamara in turn.

"You two can come in now, if you like," she said, then eyed Tamara up and down. "Somehow, I don't think you're quite dressed for the occasion."

Tom looked at Tamara, Fiona Williams had a point. Tamara was wearing a free-flowing green dress, the cut of which hung almost to the top of her high heels. Tom was also still in his best suit but the plastic boot covers would protect his finest leather footwear.

Tamara smiled sheepishly.

"Come on," Fiona said to Tamara whilst handing Tom pairs of gloves and boot covers, "I have a set of wellies in the car and I'm pretty sure we can hitch that dress up so it doesn't drag into anything it shouldn't. How was the wedding anyway?"

Tamara gratefully accepted and the two of them descended the steps to make their way across the yard to Fiona's car deep in conversation about the day's events. Kerry Palmer watched them go and then turned back to face Tom who was busy donning the covers and tying them off at the ankle.

"How did Eric get on today?" she asked, seemingly somewhat bashful in Tom's opinion.

"He coped really well, I thought he was going to stumble on a couple of his lines but he carried it off."

"I'll bet he looked handsome in top hat and tails."

"He did, yes. They made quite the couple. Becca wore a shoulderless dress, or at least I think that was what Alice called it—"

"Strapless?" Kerry said.

Tom righted himself, checking his covers were on tightly enough. He nodded. "Yes, no straps over the shoulder, and a thin, fancy head-thing through the hair holding her veil in place."

"*Fancy head-thing?*" Kerry asked, struggling not to laugh. "I think you mean a tiara."

"Yes, I reckon that's probably it," Tom said, with a sideways smile. "Me and clothes, fashion... don't mix."

Kerry pushed the door open and held it with the flat of her left hand. "After you," she said. Tom entered, stopping one step inside and looking around the room. The decor was simple and unfussy. The furniture was old and mismatched without any particular style or trend, checked blankets were thrown over two sofas and a slightly tatty rug was set out before the wood-burning stove set into the hearth against the far wall.

Each wall had pictures or framed photographs hanging on it but again, there didn't appear to be a theme; each frame was a different size, style or colour and those that weren't personal photographs looked like reprints you could pick up in high street shops at minimal cost. Overall, the room appeared tidy and well kept if in need of a little general cleaning. He looked at Kerry standing alongside him.

"Is he married?"

She shook her head. "According to the friends he's a confirmed bachelor, lives here alone."

"Doesn't look like any bachelor pad that I've ever known."

Kerry smiled. "Maybe he was connected to his inner female."

"I'll have you know some of us men are fastidiously clean and tidy, too, you know."

"Sorry, sir."

Tom laughed. "The victim?"

"Through there," she said pointing to the kitchen area where a forensic officer rose from where he was kneeling. They made their way over, watching their footing as they stepped into the kitchen. Tom had the same first impression that Kerry Palmer had described. The blood loss was severe, the pool of blood growing around the fallen man. It was drying now, thick and congealed, soaking into the tongue-and-groove floorboards. The crime scene officers had placed transparent stepping plates around the room in order to aid them in traversing the space without treading in the blood and contaminating the crime scene. Tom and Kerry would need to do the same.

"Are we clear?" Tom asked and the officer nodded.

"Yes, we're done here for now. Once you're happy then the body will be removed and we'll sweep the entire place for fingerprints and start bagging everything up."

Tom thanked him and tentatively stepped up onto the first crate. He'd done this before, many times, but he often thought they'd give way under his weight. Being comfortably six foot three and a powerfully-built man, he thought the plastic wouldn't hold, but it did. Two crates next to the body were placed in close proximity to one another to make it easier to assess the victim closely, Tom dropping to his haunches, Kerry standing off to his right.

Billy Moy looked older than his years. He was a similar age to Tom but could easily pass as ten years older. His hair was thinning and receding, shot through with large streaks of grey. His skin, even taking into account that he was dead, appeared dry and deeply lined. A quick glance at the man's hands told him that he spent a lot of time outdoors, working tough jobs. One hand was upturned and the skin of the palm, as well as the fingers, was coarse and ingrained with dirt. He was an outdoor man. Despite his physical stature being quite slight, Tom figured he was in decent shape. His upper body didn't carry an ounce of fat and the muscle tissue of his arms, visible from the edge of his T-shirt, was well toned. He was probably quite capable of wielding an axe to cut that wood outside with great proficiency. Kerry seemed to notice and must have thought similarly.

"You see what I mean about how it went down?"

Tom glanced at her and nodded, returning his gaze to the body and then around the kitchen. There were items on the worktops, appliances, boxes of food and crockery. None of it appeared to have been disturbed. There was nothing on the floor either, which one might expect if there was even the briefest of struggles before the fatal blow was delivered.

"It does look like it was a single strike," Tom said, his brow furrowing, "and I dare say he—"

"Knew his killer," Kerry finished for him. Tom looked up at her. She smiled apologetically. He waved it away.

"Exactly right. Whoever was with him wasn't threatening, and they were able to get close enough to dispatch him with one blow... unless there are other injuries we can't see."

"Not that I've found, Tom," Fiona Williams said, entering the kitchen with Tamara beside her. It wouldn't be appropriate to comment in front of the assembled junior ranks but Tom found Tamara's get-up to be incredibly comical. She was still wearing her wedding outfit, which she wore beautifully, her hair tied up in a stylish design with make-up and jewellery to complement it. In fact, Tom had never seen her look so beguiling as she did that day.

However, the ensemble took on a very different style when the dress was gathered together and crudely tucked into the top of a pair of wellington boots.

Tamara caught his eye and one look convinced him he was right not to draw attention to her look. Dr Williams offered her thoughts.

"I'm sure you've already noted the likely cause of death. I should imagine the knife was driven into his chest at close quarters, the killer standing directly in front of the victim. The blow has most probably penetrated the heart due to the amount of blood loss we can see here, which also confirms the stabbing was pre-mortem rather than post. The pathologist will confirm but I can say with a degree of confidence that this will be the cause of death. If he didn't die immediately from the blow itself, then it was more than likely that he bled out in a matter of minutes."

"Any other injuries, or just that stab wound?" Tamara asked.

"His T-shirt is white and although it has soaked up a great deal of blood, I haven't been able to find any other penetration to the material, so I think it is just the one wound. Usually, at this point I would ask for you to help me lever him up so we can have a look at his back, but I think on this occasion we will have to wait. Otherwise we'll be standing in this poor chap's blood and traipsing it throughout the crime scene. We'll just have to wait for the pathologist to confirm if there are any other wounds, of the stabbing variety or any other I'm afraid. I'm sure you've spotted that he is sporting a shiner?"

Tom frowned, scanning the body. Due to the poor lighting in the kitchen, part of the dead man's face was cast in shadow. Tom reappraised him and saw the bruising around the left eye. He nodded.

"That doesn't look fresh to me, too much colouration," he said.

Fiona Williams agreed. "I'd say that's been there for a day or two prior to death but no longer."

Tom looked the deceased up and down once more. He had his shoes on and was dressed in a T-shirt and jeans. It seemed a little cold at the moment to not have thicker clothing on his upper body. He looked around the cabin but couldn't see any radiators. At the centre of the kitchen against the outer wall was an old Aga. He guessed this was not only used for food preparation but also supplied heating and possibly hot water. He pointed to it.

"Is that warm?"

The forensic officer looked over at it and shook his head. Tom realised there was a chill in the cabin and he figured it was so old that the property had little by way of insulation or, if there was, it was grossly inadequate.

"Estimated time of death?"

Fiona Williams looked at the clock. "I haven't been able to do the liver test yet. Rigor has set in and relaxed." She thought about it. "Where are we now, approaching six o'clock? I think he's been dead for a couple of days, but it's been cold inside and out, so I'd expect the analysis to come back with the night before last. Unlikely to be more than forty-eight hours, I'd say."

"Right, thanks. That puts likely death to be Thursday evening or night," Tom said. He looked over at Tamara. "Shall we have a word with the couple who found him?" Tamara nodded. Tom turned to Kerry. "Have you been through the rest of the cabin yet?" She shook her head. "Okay, while we're talking to them can you have a look around the other rooms and see what stands out to you? Anything at all that looks odd or out of place. I'll run through it with you once we're done."

"Will do, sir."

CHAPTER FOUR

TOM AND TAMARA left the house and made their way across the yard to where the witnesses were waiting with a uniformed constable. The yard was uneven, predominantly mud, and this had been churned up by various vehicles over time judging from the ridges and mounds in places. There was also a fair amount of loose straw scattered around and Tom heard animal sounds coming from one of the nearby sheds. They were too small to house a significant number of cattle but goats and chickens were feasible. As if on cue, several hens appeared in view making their way across the yard absently pecking at the ground and paying them no attention at all.

The officer stepped away from the others to greet them and Tom saw the man's eyes drift over Tamara's get-up and momentarily appear distracted, but if he was thinking about commenting he soon dismissed the idea and remained professional.

"Ma'am, sir," he said, gesturing to the waiting couple. "This is Gary and Jenny Bartlett. They found the body a couple of hours ago."

Tom took the lead. He cast an eye over them as he introduced himself, customarily displaying his warrant card as he did so. They were in their fifties, he guessed. The man, Gary, was casually dressed in jeans and a loose-fitting woollen jumper that had seen better days and had some mud visible on it. It still looked damp as if it was recent. For her part, Jenny, was quite the contrast wearing a hoodie and a pair of tracksuit bottoms and wellies. The ensemble was completed by a waxed jacket over the top. The latter was far too large for her, the collars at her wrists covered most of her hands. Presumably, she was wearing Gary's coat to keep her warm. The end of her nose was red, as were her ears, and she was shuffling on the spot trying to keep warm. The day had been chilly anyway but now the sun had set and any notion of early spring forgotten as the feel of winter was very much upon them.

"I'm sure you've already covered this with my colleague," Tom said, "but if you wouldn't mind going back over what you found as well as how you came to be here today?"

"Y–Yes, of course," Gary said, nodding. He glanced at Jenny but she seemed quite happy to let him speak, she was standing along-side him quite awkwardly but Tom couldn't see why that would be so. "Billy," he pointed to the cabin, "was supposed to come over to ours today and do some cutting ahead of spring when everything shoots up again."

"Cutting?"

"Trees… near to the house. They're good for acting as a barrier to the coastal wind but they're blocking too much light coming into the house now. We should have done it last year but," he looked at his partner again, "we never got around to it, did we, love?"

She shook her head.

"You live nearby?" Tom asked, glancing around.

Gary nodded. "Yes, next place over." He pointed in the direction beyond the sheds as if they could see through the outbuildings. "It's a five-minute walk along the track."

"And you walked here this evening?"

"No, but the car is out on the lane. I just washed it today and didn't want to get muck on it from Billy's yard."

"Right. And you said Billy – that's Billy Moy – was supposed to do some work for you?"

"Yes, but he never showed," Jenny said, conversing for the first time since the initial introductions. "Gary called him but didn't get an answer and so we thought we'd stop by just in case."

"Just in case of what?" Tamara asked.

Jenny looked at her, then Tom before her eyes finally settled on Gary.

"To see if he was all right, you know?"

"Any reason why he wouldn't be?" Tom asked. Gary stared at him blankly. "All right, I mean?"

"Oh... um... no," he said, shaking his head and looking puzzled. "Not that I can think of... at first I thought his job at Finney's place must have overrun but then I figured he lives here on his own and he does stuff, you know?"

Tom shook his head. "No, not really. What kind of stuff?"

Gary held Tom's gaze for a moment and Tom thought he could almost see the cogs turning. After a moment of silence, Gary pointed to the tractor and waved a hand around the yard. "He's always up to all sorts is Billy. He works some of his land, although not as much as he used to back in the day. Other times he's felling trees, his own if not someone else's. He sells firewood by the tonne as well."

"I see, so you thought he might have had an accident or something?"

"Yeah, exactly," Gary said. He nodded towards the old tractor. "That old thing he has there is a bloody death trap. If he rolls that over he'd be pinned under it or drown in a ditch long before anyone happened upon him. I keep telling him – kept telling him – to update his kit, buy some safety equipment," his tone softened, "he was always hanging off branches with a chainsaw, not harnessed up... accident waiting to happen."

Tom cast an eye back to the cabin momentarily. "And what do you think happened here?"

Gary shook his head. "An accident?" He shared an exchange of vacant looks with his wife. "At least, I hope it was. A bizarre accident."

Tom didn't comment on the theory. "You said he had another job on, at Finney's?"

Gary nodded vigorously. "Alan Finney. He's a farmer over the way there," he said, gesticulating in the direction away from the cabin. "Billy said he had a week's worth of work over at his place but he'd do ours at the end of the week."

"Okay, thanks," Tom said, making a note. "What was Billy like as a person, as a worker?"

"A top bloke, Billy," Gary said, looking at Jenny again. This time she looked down at her feet. Tom pressed her.

"What would you say, Jenny?"

She looked up and met his eye, her lips pursed. She nodded curtly. "Yeah, as Gary says. He was a nice enough guy. A bit odd sometimes."

"In what way?"

She shrugged. "I don't know really. He was just a bit..." she looked at Gary for support.

"Odd, yeah," Gary repeated. "Billy was a bit of a loner. Lived alone, unmarried. Jenny reminded me that a while back he used to go away on holiday from time to time, alone, so maybe he did like seeing people on his own terms. That all seemed to stop though."

"Why was that, do you think?"

Gary shrugged. "Don't know. Maybe he couldn't afford to travel."

"It was abroad then? Where he used to go?"

"Yes. At least he came back with a tan and it was always the off season if I remember right, so he must have gone abroad to get as tanned as he did. Never spoke about his trips. Not to me at least. I guess that's why I forgot about them until Jenny reminded me."

"Would you consider yourself to be a good friend? Close?"

Gary shrugged. "Not especially. As I said, Billy didn't really seem to do people, you know?"

"So he spent most of his time out here alone?"

"Yeah. I really think he could have done with getting out and about a little more, talking to people and stuff. Then, maybe, he wouldn't have been so... what's the word?"

"Odd?" Tom ventured. Gary and Jenny both nodded.

"I would've gone with weird myself, but odd is probably fairer. Don't get us wrong, Inspector," Gary said. "It's just that anyone who spends as much time on their own as Billy has done these past few years," he waved a hand around in the air in a circular motion, "especially all the way out here is going to be a little strange, aren't they?"

"Right. You say he lives alone now? What about before?"

"Used to be a family-run business going back," Gary said. "This place has been passed down several generations I think, working the land, doing whatever was needed. Billy's dad passed about ten years ago and his mother five, maybe six—"

"Longer, I think," Jenny said, "on both counts."

Gary turned the corners of his mouth down and bobbed his head. "A while back anyway. Since then it's just been Billy."

Tom nodded, making a note. "And did he have any other family or many friends locally?"

Gary's brow furrowed. "I think he's got a brother somewhere, local-ish but don't ask me where. He never visits as far as I know. And there was a sister—"

"But she died," Jenny said.

"Yeah, she died," Gary agreed, frowning. "Shame really. Billy's dad died out in the fields, on that very tractor I think. Heart attack or so Billy said."

"Friends?"

"None that I'm aware of, no. Don't misunderstand, I know I said we weren't especially close but thinking about it, I would consider us – would have considered – us friends. I mean, as friendly as Billy ever got with anyone. Billy really didn't socialise much. As Jenny said, kept to himself."

"Preferred his own company?" Tom asked.

"Yeah, right. That's what I'd say."

"Okay, so you came here this evening... what, knocked on the door?" Gary nodded. Tom encouraged him to elaborate.

"Oh right, yeah. Well, there was no answer, so Jenny wanted to leave," he glanced sideways at her, "didn't you, love? But the door was open... the place was in darkness, though, unlocked. It was strange, so... I went in to check it out. I found him there..." he paused, his eyes glazing over and taking on a faraway look. "He was dead." Gary shook his head.

"Did you touch anything?"

"No, I didn't. I don't think so anyway. I just ran outside and called you lot. I guess I should have checked if he was still breathing and that but, well, he looked too far gone."

"Did you see anyone around or hear anything unusual while you were in the property? Did anything seem disturbed or out of place?"

"No, I can't say I did. Hear anyone I mean."

"What about you, Jenny?"

She looked startled but answered quickly. "I didn't go inside."

"And the state of the interior, is that how it is usually kept?"

Gary blew out his cheeks. "I can't say I'd know, sorry." He looked deeply apologetic. "I've never been inside before. Whenever I've been round here, or given Billy a lift somewhere if his car is broken, he's always met me outside or kept me waiting on the doorstep."

"Why would he do that do you think? It's a bit odd, seeing as you know one another."

"That's Billy," Jenny said with a sideways smile.

"Keeps a tidy home by all accounts," Tamara said.

Jenny scoffed. "I was surprised about that."

"But you didn't go in, did you?" Tom asked, his eyes narrowing.

Jenny's lips parted slightly. "I–I was outside on the porch and looked through the door. Like you say, it's tidy. It's odd."

"Why?"

She shrugged. "Billy... was never one to take much pride in his appearance. He was likely as not to be dressed in oily overalls no

matter whether he was working or doing his evening shopping."
Tom raised a single eyebrow quizzically. "You'd always see Billy up
at the local supermarket around closing time. Every night."

"Regular as clockwork," Gary said. "He always went up for the
discounted bargains. The end-of-life bakery things, fruit and veg
that was on the turn, that sort of thing. I reckon he knew the exact
time of the evening when they put the labels on the products. I
never knew if he was short of cash or just a bit tight."

"And when did you last see Billy alive?"

The couple exchanged another glance. Gary answered. "Probably a couple of nights ago. Wednesday maybe? We saw him at the
supermarket, funnily enough, and that was when I asked if he
could come and hack back some of our trees. He said he would
come round Friday."

"Friday? Not today?" Tom asked.

Gary looked shocked. "I meant Saturday, today. Sorry... it's all
been a bit stressful." He shook his head. "I don't know where I am
at the moment, sorry."

"Quite understandable. Tell me, as far as you know, has Billy
had an altercation with anyone recently?"

"Altercation? How do you mean?"

"An argument, fight... a falling out over anything at all?"

Gary frowned. Both he and his wife shook their heads.

"Billy was a bit strange, but no one had a bad word to say about
him as far as I know," Gary said. "I mean, everyone knows him. The
Moys have been a part of this area for as far back as I can
remember and beyond that, generations. Billy probably did some
work for almost everyone over the years, either fixing their tractors
or cars, delivering them firewood in the winter... all sorts. He's that
type of bloke, Billy, really good with his hands, machinery and the
like. I don't think he even finished school and I never saw him
write anything down, just had a memory for information, dates
and so on. A curious character, not to everyone's liking I'm sure but
I've never heard anyone badmouthing him. Quite the opposite in
fact."

"And what about you, Jenny?" Tom asked, fixing his gaze on her.

She returned his look for a few seconds, appearing far less confident about her husband's statement but she said nothing, breaking eye contact and looking at the ground at her feet, and then shaking her head.

"Okay, we can leave it there for now. I'm sure the constable here has all your details," the officer nodded, "and we will have to have someone call round to see you and take a more detailed statement a bit later, if that's all right with you?"

"Yes, of course, Inspector. Anything we can do to help," Gary said, nodding vigorously.

"You mentioned a brother. I know you said you didn't know where he lived but do you have any idea at all? It might speed up the process and even if they're not close it would be better for him to hear the news from us rather than the media. Do you have any idea at all where he might have moved to?"

Gary thought hard. "Dereham way, I heard someone say once, I think. Not certain though."

"Great, thank you. It gives us something to work with. In the meantime, if you think of anything else we need to know or if you recall something you think might be useful, no matter how trivial, you can give me a call anytime."

Tom handed Gary one of his contact cards and the man eyed it before slipping it into his back pocket. He put his arm around his wife, awkwardly it seemed to Tom, and the two of them made to walk away.

"Oh, and we'll need to take your fingerprints as well, if you don't mind?"

They stopped, Gary looking at Tom fearfully. "W–Why do you need to do that? Have we done something wrong?"

"No, not at all. But you were inside and we'll be dusting the house for fingerprints and will need to rule yours out so as not to confuse things. You didn't seem too sure if you'd touched anything or not."

"Oh, right. Yes, of course." Gary's slightly surprised expression lifted and he smiled. "Should we do that now or..."

"Don't worry about it now. We'll send someone round to yours, Mr Bartlett."

Gary nodded, smiled again, and set off with his arm resting on his wife's shoulder and guiding her over the rough ground. He glanced back at them once more when they were halfway across the yard heading for the gate. Tamara stepped alongside Tom, nudging his elbow, as they both watched them leave.

"There's something about those two," she said.

"Yes, there is," Tom replied. They watched the Bartletts until they reached their car parked just beyond the gate, a battered old Ford Mondeo. They got in, Gary offering them a brief sideways glance before starting the car and driving away. Tom cast an eye up and down Tamara. "You should wear that look more often," he said, smiling. "Suits you."

Tamara rolled her eyes. "Remind me to keep a change of clothes in the car in future."

"But we came in my car."

"In all cars, then," she said, setting off for the cabin without waiting for him. Tom glanced at the constable standing off to his left who was trying not to smile.

"At ease, Constable," Tom said, heading after her. The constable grinned.

CHAPTER FIVE

TOM CAUGHT up with Tamara as she stopped by the steps up to the decking of the front porch dropping to her haunches to examine something. Whatever it was it had certainly caught her eye. He joined her.

"Got something?"

"Maybe," she said over her shoulder, indicating to her right. "What do you make of this?"

He lowered himself to her level and realised she was inspecting a tree stump. It projected barely a foot above the ground with the bulk of the tree having been felled at least a year ago judging by the colouration of the wood, dry, greying and even blackened in places. New shoots were emerging from it. However, this wasn't what Tamara was interested in. A layer of bark at the edge where the trunk met the cut had been torn away along with a chunk of the fresh wood beneath.

Tom took a pocket torch from his pocket and switched it on, angling the beam at the tear. The light reflected off fragments seemingly embedded in the wood.

"What is that, paint?" he asked.

Tamara nodded. "I'd say so. And this is fresh, you can see the paleness of the wood and the edges of the bark haven't been exposed to the air for long."

"I'll make sure scenes of crime document it and take a sample," Tom said, turning the beam away and scanning the ground around them looking for anything that stood out. The ground was still hard. The front of the cabin faced north and therefore received the least amount of daytime sun and although on clear nights the ground still froze with an overnight layer of frost, usually the mud softened during the day. However, here it was still solid and there were no telltale impressions left by vehicles that he could make out. Tamara seemed to share his thinking.

"Make sure they check the yard over as well, try to match any tyre impressions they find to the vehicles we know Billy Moy owned or had access to."

"They'll love us for that," Tom said dryly as he casually widened his search pattern around them with his torchlight.

"Come on," she said, "let's go inside and see what surprises Mr Moy has in his closet. First impression I have is that this isn't a burglary gone wrong and something tells me there's far more to this chap than his friends realise."

"Or are prepared to share with us," Tom said, thinking about Jenny Bartlett's reticence. He saw PC Kerry Palmer moving between the outbuildings on the other side of the yard, choosing to leave her to it and pick her brains later.

Back inside the cabin, preparations were well underway to remove the body from the kitchen. They separated and Tom left Tamara to look around the open-plan living area while he ventured along the corridor towards the rear of the cabin where he expected to find the bedrooms. The first room he entered appeared to be a guest bedroom. There was a ready-made-up double bed, an occasional table and a dresser, with nothing atop it, set beneath a window overlooking the side of the cabin. On the far side of the room was a wardrobe with louvre doors. Inside he found shelving to the left that was empty, and a clothes rail with a number of dresses and blouses hanging neatly that filled the hanging space.

Some were inside plastic covers as if they'd returned from the dry cleaners.

The clothes looked dated to Tom, albeit he would be the first to accept ladies' fashion was not a subject he excelled in. All of the hangers and the shoulders of the material had a film of dust on them. They couldn't have seen the light of day for quite some time. There was an odd smell coming from the wardrobe as well, pungent and artificial. Above the rail was a storage shelf with a number of shoe boxes stacked one on top of the other. He lifted one down, it felt light and he opened it to find nothing inside. Choosing another at random, again, he found it empty. The next box did hold some contents, old photographs. These were not organised or catalogued in any way, just thrown in loosely. Most of them were family pictures, some were in colour whereas others showed their age in black and white. Judging from the clothes people wore or the furnishings depicted they were taken over a number of years, probably depicting multiple generations of the same family. There were no names, places or dates stamped on the reverse of the images to aid in identifying when they were taken. Tom carefully put them back in the box, putting it back on the shelf where he found it. Moving back into the corridor, he approached the next room.

The door to the bathroom opened and he cast an eye around the interior. It was a nondescript room comprising a white three-piece suite with wood-panelled walls and ceiling, pine strips stained in a light oak colour. As he was finding everywhere he went in the cabin, the room was clean and well kept. Towels hung on the rail, folded neatly in place and the sanitary ware, although old and a little tired, was clean and bright. The sealant around the bath had patches of mould growth, to be expected with the passage of time, but the bath had a shine to it aside from the age-old lengths of limescale charting a path into the plug hole.

A small mirrored cabinet was mounted on the wall above the inset basin and Tom opened it, inspecting the contents. There were basic over-the-counter medicines, an unopened box of toothpaste and some assorted toiletries but, curiously, on the other side of the cabinet were two empty shelves. It was as if only half of the cabinet had been used. However, there was some residue present, what one might find accumulating at the bottom of bottles over time, leaving rings beneath them.

Turning his attention to the cupboards beneath the basin, he opened the doors but found nothing to pique his interest: cleaning products, cloths and a few spare toilet rolls. A shower head was mounted above the bath with a corner quadrant basket unit along-side. This had two shelves but all that he found there was a half-empty bottle of shampoo with the cap open and a bottle of shower gel hanging from a hook below.

The next room was the principal bedroom. The bed here was made up as well and Tom found clothes either hanging in the built-in wardrobe or folded neatly on the shelving. It was all very ordered, very precise. The thought occurred that Billy Moy may have spent time in the military, such was his attention to detail. He would certainly pass a barracks inspection on this evidence. There was a laundry basket in the corner of the room and Tom lifted the lid to find it had a few items of clothing inside but, by the looks of it, barely a day or two's dirty laundry. Picturing the same basket on the landing of the house he shared with Alice and Saffy, he could see the contrast, for theirs was forever overflowing even though running the washing machine was pretty much a daily occurrence. Billy Moy clearly didn't have children.

It was a similar story when Tom inspected the contents of the chest of drawers. T-shirts, shorts and underwear were all folded neatly and everything seemed to have a place. It all seemed quite at odds with the description the Bartletts gave of the man. However, if, as they both said, Billy Moy didn't allow anyone particularly close, then they were only guessing and perhaps they didn't know him half as well as they thought they did.

Tamara poked her head into the room. "Tom, come and have a look at this."

She retreated from the room and he followed. She waited for him at the entrance to the next room, stepping aside as he came alongside her. He peered in and could barely see anything in the gloom. Tamara flicked the light switch on next to the door and they were bathed in a soft red light that illuminated the interior in a macabre fashion. In the centre of the room was a trestle table with three plastic trays set out side by side. Lengths of string were tied at one end of the room, crisscrossing from one wall to the other. Metal clips, resembling heavy-duty clothes pegs were hanging in places from the string. Tom glanced at Tamara and entered. Along the length of the far wall was a homemade bench with shelving beneath. On the shelves he found a mixture of unmarked bottles of clear liquid, ranging in size from two litres up to five or more. On top of the bench he found a plastic tub with more pegs of assorted sizes.

"I guess we found his hobby," Tom said quietly. Tamara nodded. "I didn't think anyone still bothered with processing film like this."

"If you enjoy doing it, and have always done it, then why would you stop?"

Tom inclined his head, then looked around. "So, where are all the films... and the developed pictures for that matter?"

Tamara shrugged. "They must be somewhere. Let's face it, with all the outbuildings dotted around this place it'll take days to pick through everything. I wonder what he liked to photograph? I thought in the digital age all of this—" she waved her hand in the air in a circular motion, "—would be in the past?"

"Maybe it's not Billy's hobby at all?"

"Mother or father?"

Tom nodded. "Could be. Is there anything in the living room or kitchen that's interesting?"

"Depends on what you mean by interesting," Tamara said. "I think he'd recently returned from shopping, judging by what's on the work surfaces. Much of the shopping is still in bags and hasn't been put away, even those that needed refrigeration."

Tamara led Tom back through the cabin and into the kitchen. He saw what she meant. Two plastic carrier bags were off to one side, not far from the range cooker. He hadn't noticed them earlier, his attention drawn to the body.

"The bags have been photographed, so we can go through them," Tamara said.

Tom, still wearing his forensic gloves cast an eye over the bags. One of them held mainly fruit and vegetables whilst the other had bread products on the top and canned goods beneath. Kerry Palmer entered through the back door as Tom tentatively began removing items from the bag of vegetables. He found what he was looking for, confirming what the Bartletts had described: reduction labels on almost every item. Some of the produce had been through several price reductions, now costing as little as ten or fifteen pence.

"He certainly did like a bargain," Tom said. He looked at Kerry. "What did you find outside?"

"He was a bit of a hoarder," she said, glancing between him and Tamara. "Or maybe the whole family were, I don't know. The outbuildings are rammed with stuff: old tools and farming equipment I doubt has seen a use in years, all manner of other junk, odds and ends. I found some old storage crates that have years upon years of magazines, farming editions, photography... dating back to the seventies in some cases, as well as stacks of folders of photographs—"

"Home processed?" Tamara asked.

Kerry nodded. "Yes, I think so. A lot of landscape shots. Being a local girl, I'd say they are Norfolk locations as they look familiar to me. I take it you've seen the dark room?" Tom nodded. "Weirdly," she said, frowning and drawing both Tom and Tamara's attention to her, "I can't find any equipment... cameras and such."

Tom glanced around, meeting Tamara's eye. She shook her head as well.

"No electrical items either: mobile phone, television or laptop," Kerry said.

Tom leaned over and looked into the living area. She was right, there was no television. However, the seating in the room was arranged in such a way as to face something in the corner where, now, only a small corner unit stood. There were cables running along behind the unit, disappearing from view. Tom walked over and glanced down the back and found the ends of a power cable as well as a television aerial.

"Well, there used to be one here."

"I also found a mobile phone bill in the top drawer over there," Kerry said, gesturing towards a sideboard. "It's dated for last quarter, so I think there's a fair chance it is still an active account. I dialled the number but nothing rang and it cut to voicemail within a couple of rings."

"Good. Anything else?"

Kerry glanced out of the window. Tom's eye followed but it was dark now and nothing leapt out at him. "I think he had a fire going out there. It was recently, too," she said, gesturing to the yard with a nod, "in a makeshift brazier – a rusty old oil drum with multiple holes punched through the sides to increase the air flow."

"What was he burning?" Tom asked.

She shook her head. "Couldn't tell in this light, but I reckon it'd be worth picking through the ashes."

Tom noticed Tamara had drifted over to the other side of the kitchen and was hovering in front of the fridge. There were a number of sticky notes stuck to the door with handwriting on them. He moved to join her, skirting the pool of drying blood. She was lost in thought and didn't notice his arrival.

"Anything?"

She looked sideways at him, her brow furrowing. "This looks like a diary of sorts."

Tom eyed the notes, some were reminders of things to do, others with specific dates on them and the odd name but nothing further to say what they related to. Either Billy Moy had a remarkable memory for detail or he lived his life in a very haphazard manner. The latter was curiously at odds with how everything else in the cabin was presented where everything appeared well ordered and kept in its designated place.

He looked around the kitchen again trying to get an impression of what had happened in Billy Moy's final moments. Tamara was doing the same, he was sure. Kerry Palmer was the first to speak.

"My first thoughts were leaning towards a burglary gone wrong," she said.

"What makes you think so?" Tom asked openly, ensuring she didn't feel he might be dismissing her theory.

"Well, the shopping hasn't been put away and it looks like he'd just returned with it. Maybe he stumbled across someone in the act, took them on and the burglar grabbed what was closest to hand – the knife from the block – and stabbed him before fleeing."

Tom nodded. It was a theory that fitted some of the facts, but he wanted to test her thought process. "Any issues with that?"

"One or two..." she said, sounding uncertain and looking around.

"Such as?"

"No sign of a forced entry," she said. Tom nodded. "So, if he disturbed a burglar when he came home, how did the burglar get in?"

Tom agreed. "Anything else?"

"Burglars tend to take off if they're disturbed... they don't usually get into a fight, let alone kill the occupant."

"Maybe he was backed into a corner and felt like he had no choice?" Tom said, deliberately playing devil's advocate. The young PC frowned.

"Perhaps. But then they still had the cold-blooded nerve to clear the house of electrical items before leaving and..." she hesitated.

"What is it?"

She smiled slightly, "If so, they're the tidiest burglar I've ever come across."

Kerry was right. Burglars weren't known for carefully going through possessions, prioritising speed above anything else. The less time spent in the property meant the less chance of being caught. An experienced burglar could go through a property of this size in less than five minutes, turning over every room, drawer and cupboard in the process and leave with whatever they could carry in that time. The debris and destruction left behind often looked like they'd deliberately torn a home to pieces which was usually far from the case in reality. She was also right on the violence. Burglars seldom sought confrontation, choosing to do their work on properties where the resident was not home, often when they were out at work. To turn a house over in the evening was unusual, unless they were certain of not being disturbed.

The thought did occur to him though that perhaps Billy Moy's routine was well known to locals and that could lead to someone believing him to be out when they came around. The same person might know how to get in, if Billy left a spare key somewhere or, which was also possible, whether he was prone to leaving his house unlocked. After all, in such an isolated spot, he was unlikely to be the victim of an opportunistic burglar who happened by.

"Lack of defensive wounds as well," Kerry said, almost as an afterthought. "If the homeowner disturbed them and they came to blows, how come he doesn't show any signs of having been in a scrap?"

"Indeed," Tom said, smiling proudly at her.

"Weird, isn't it?" she said.

"A good analysis," Tamara said, joining them. "I agree, this is very strange. I don't think it's a burglary at all."

"Made to look like one by an amateur, do you think?" Tom asked.

"Maybe," Tamara said, then shook her head and sighed. "Something isn't right." She then met Kerry's eye and smiled. "You've done well today, PC Palmer."

"Thank you, Ma'am."

Kerry clearly tried hard not to let her pride show but her chest swelled nonetheless. Tom and Tamara exchanged a glance and Tamara nodded. Tom addressed the constable.

"How would you feel about extending your stay?"

"Extending?" Her forehead creased.

"Yes. This is a murder investigation and Eric will be away from next week and we don't want to be left short."

Kerry's lips parted and she looked between the two senior officers.

"Unless you don't feel up to—"

"No! I do," she said forcefully, finding her voice. "Absolutely, I do. Very much," she said, grinning.

"Good," Tamara said. "I'll square it with your inspector. You'll be with us until Eric returns from his honeymoon."

Kerry Palmer's expression darkened slightly but when she caught Tom watching her the smile returned, although this time he thought it was a little forced.

CHAPTER SIX

Tom looked over to Tamara. "Forensics will be picking over this place for the next day or so. Why don't you take the pool car and Kerry can come with me to the supermarket."

"Agreed. I could do with getting out of this dress."

Kerry met Tom's eye. "The supermarket?"

"He hadn't unpacked his shopping and judging from the sell-by dates, we know he purchased the fruit and veg the night before last."

"So, that was the last time he was seen alive?" she said.

Tom smiled. "Well probably, aside from the person who killed him but let's not get ahead of ourselves," he checked his watch. "They'll be closing up around now and if he's in there every night then maybe the staff are used to seeing him at this time and might have seen him with someone or can at least tell us how he seemed in relation to normal."

"Right, yes. Of course," she said, also glancing at her watch.

"Do you have somewhere you need to be, Constable?" Tom asked.

Her face flushed and she dropped her arm to her side, shaking her head.

"If you need to make a call, let someone know you'll be a bit late home, that's okay," Tom said.

She shook her head again. "Shall we go?"

Tom gestured towards the door with an open palm and they headed out.

"Let me know how you get on," Tamara said. "I'm just going to pick the good doctor's brains about a couple of things."

Tom looked out to where the FME, Dr Williams, was taking off her coveralls as she packed her things away. Kerry gave Tamara the keys to her car and fell into step alongside Tom as they walked to his vehicle.

"That was a strong analysis of the crime scene," Tom said, glancing sideways at her as they reached the car and he walked around the other side, unlocking it.

"Thanks," she said, smiling awkwardly and getting in.

Tom got the impression she found it hard to take praise, wondering if it was a confidence or self-esteem issue. Kerry Palmer excelled in her role as a constable, always the first to raise her hand when an opportunity arose for her to gain experience. She was riot trained, had taken a diplomatic protection course and recently travelled to the other side of the country to assist in the security operation surrounding the G7 summit, hosted in the south-west of England this year. Having hit every target set for her, earning glowing reviews from her supervising officers along the way, Kerry was earmarked as a future sergeant. Not that any of this seemed to cut any ice with her, always remaining humble. He had a decent team around him and Tom figured that PC Palmer would enhance the unit. Popular, intelligent and committed, he liked what he saw in her. She reminded him a little of himself when he was early in his career.

The supermarket, located on the A149, was the largest in the area of nearby Heacham without driving further along the coast to Hunstanton where two of the larger chains also had branches. As Tom expected, the branch was getting ready to close up as they pulled into the car park. Only a handful of cars were still present and most of those were probably staff owned. Pulling up near to the entrance, they got out and approached a man who was busy with a manual pallet truck, bringing stock inside that was on display outside during daylight hours: sacks of coal and logs. Another man disappeared through electric doors pushing a display unit holding spring flowers.

Tom approached the man, who eyed him warily as he jacked up another pallet, reading his name badge and seeing he was a store supervisor. Tom took out his identification, introducing himself and Kerry. His expression softened and he introduced himself as Terry Cole, releasing the handle of his pallet truck and wiping the palms of his hands on his trousers. Despite it being cold now, as it was approaching ten o'clock, he still had sweat on his brow as they gathered in the stock.

"By any chance, do you know a local man by the name of Billy Moy?" Tom asked.

"Billy? Yes, of course. Everyone knows Billy. He's a regular fixture around these parts," Cole said, sniffing hard and looking between the two officers. "Why, what's he done?"

Tom ignored the question for now.

"He comes in your store often?"

Cole nodded. "Most nights. I get the impression he's not a *weekly shop* kind of bloke."

"When was he last in, do you remember?"

His brow furrowed as he thought hard. "Um… he's not been in today as far as I know, nor last night because I'd have seen him but I was off for a couple of days prior to that. Dean will know, he was in."

The electric doors swooshed as the second staff member returned, Cole looking over his shoulder and beckoning him over to them. He approached, curious as to what he was walking into.

"Dean, you were in Wednesday and Thursday back shift, weren't you?" He nodded. "Did you see Billy Moy come in at all?"

"Billy Discount, yeah, he was in both nights." Dean grinned. "Same as normal, doing the reduction dance with Coupon Man."

Cole frowned at him and, reading his supervisor's face, Dean's grin faded.

"These are police officers," Cole said, "asking about Billy."

"Oh, right. Sorry," he said sheepishly.

"Billy Discount?" Kerry asked.

Dean flushed. He was a pale man and he was now beaming red.

"It's the nickname we have for him... because he comes in every night to pick up the reduced-price items, usually doing battle with another customer as to who gets first dibs."

"Coupon Man?" Tom queried.

Dean nodded. "He's a bloke who runs one of the stalls on the seafront promenade up in Hunstanton... always comes in and buys up leftover pastries and rolls and that at discount, sells them for a quid fifty the next morning at his place. The tight git." He caught his boss eyeing him again and screwed his face up. "Sorry. You just get used to people who come in and see them out and about, you know?"

Tom nodded. "And what about Billy Moy? What would you say about him?"

"Nice bloke, Billy," Dean said, inclining his head to one side. "A real character. Everyone likes him. I know we make fun of him buying cheap stuff but... I don't think he has a lot of money, so it's fair enough. He's always quick to say hello, have a bit of a laugh with you."

"And when did you last see him?"

"Thursday, I reckon. I'm sure he didn't come in last night."

Cole nodded his silent agreement, smiling as Dean confirmed his own recollection.

"And how was he?" Tom asked.

Dean shrugged.

Tom persisted. "Was he the same as usual? Quieter, louder... any change at all?"

"To be honest, he was just Billy, normal. We shared a joke about him being late... I mean he wasn't, which was the joke." He smiled, looking at Tom and Kerry in turn, then the smile faded and he seemed embarrassed. "I guess you had to be there."

"Nothing unusual at all?"

"Oh, come to think of it he did have quite a shiner on him."

"A black eye?"

Dean nodded. "Yeah, I asked him who he'd been scrapping with. He laughed."

"Did he say how he got it?"

"No, I don't think he did, not exactly. He just shrugged it off saying he'd had a few too many beers earlier. Reckoned he'd tripped." Dean frowned, shaking his head. "Not that I bought it."

"Why not?"

Dean met Tom's eye. "Well, I didn't smell booze on him and when someone's been drinking a fair bit you can, can't you? Besides, he didn't walk or look like he'd been drinking... and he was driving. His old banger was in the car park when I was closing up. And besides that, I've had shiners before and he must have been sporting that one for more than an afternoon. The swelling wasn't there and the bruising was coming out. Still," he shook his head "none of my business, is it?"

"Anything else you can think of? Anything at all, no matter how small?"

Dean thought hard, his eye drifting across the car park almost as if he was picturing the scene of two nights previously.

"I did see him chatting to someone in the car park as I was bringing the stock in."

"Who was it, do you know them?"

Dean shook his head. "No, not really. He looked a little familiar but I can't say where I'd know him from."

"And what were they talking about?"

"Couldn't hear them to be honest," Dean said apologetically. "I was getting the stuff in and it was midweek, so I was doing it alone. We don't," he hesitated, glancing at his supervisor "we don't have as many staff on during the week."

Cole felt he needed to intervene. "True, we get busier at the weekend and once the season really gets going we'll be looking to take on more staff but as it is now—"

"That's okay, Mr Cole," Tom said, turning his attention to Dean again. "Please go on."

"Um... not much more to say really. They were chatting... it didn't look like they were friends or anything. For a second I thought maybe they'd had a bump in the car or something."

"What makes you think so?"

"I don't know, really. It's more a feeling, body language and all that. Billy didn't look comfortable. He's quite a laid-back kind of guy from what I know of him, but he was kind of rigid when talking to this bloke... and his missus called him away."

"There was someone else there?"

"Yeah," Dean said, nodding. "A woman. She was in the car. I assumed she was the bloke's wife or something."

"Why the wife?" Kerry asked. Dean looked at her confused. "I mean, you said wife. Why not his girlfriend?"

Dean shrugged. "I dunno. Age, I guess. The guy looked to be a similar age to Billy. Same height and stuff as well... and I guess I'm just assuming. I'd say she was a similar age too."

"What happened next?"

"Nothing." Dean held his hands up. "I was getting the stock back inside and when I came back out both cars were gone."

"But the woman called him away?" Tom said. "Do you remember if she used his name?"

"Nah... sorry, I don't remember. I guess she must have, though."

"And you've no idea what they were arguing about?"

Once again, Dean shook his head. "No, sorry. But they weren't friendly, that's for sure."

Tom glanced up at the entrance spying a camera above the door. "Any chance you'll have them on camera?"

Terry Cole was about to answer but Dean cut him off. "Won't do you any good. They didn't come in the shop... the couple I mean. They were parked up outside next to the recycling bins, so they may have been there for that but they definitely didn't come in the store. I would have seen them. It was quiet."

"Right," Tom said, failing to keep the disappointment from his tone. "How about the car they were in? Can you remember that?"

"An estate of some sort... dark blue or black, maybe. It's hard to say in that light."

"Make or model?"

Dean shook his head. "Couldn't say for sure. Probably Japanese... I'd know if it was one of the German ones from the grilles, but I can't say for this one. Yeah, if I had to put money on it I'd say an older Japanese one. Sorry, but I was up against it time-wise and wasn't really watching them."

"Okay, no problem. That's all very helpful," Tom said. "Tell me, you said Billy came in most nights?"

"Yeah, he did. Even if it was lashing down, he'd still be in for his bargains."

"Was he always on his own?"

Dean chewed on his lower lip, thinking hard. He exhaled, blowing out his cheeks and nodding. "Yeah, now that you mention it I don't think I ever saw him with anyone else. Unsurprising really."

"Why would you say so?"

"I don't know... it's just Billy was... a bit odd. I mean, he was a nice enough bloke, always polite and up for a chat. Everyone knew him around here, he's been a fixture in the town since... well, forever. It's just that he was a little strange." Tom watched him intently, encouraging him to elaborate. "Well, he'd think nothing about shopping in a boiler suit covered in oil, smelling of horseshi—"

"Dean!" Terry Cole interrupted him.

"Well, personal hygiene wasn't his thing," Dean said with a shrug, trying to be more diplomatic. He glanced at Kerry. "And some of the women," he looked back at the store behind him, "not that I ever saw any of it myself, mind you, but some of our colleagues felt a bit uncomfortable around him."

"What did he do that made them feel that way, do you think?"

Dean frowned. "I don't think he ever... you know... touched them or anything," he said, his eyes flitting to Cole and then back to Tom. "They said he used to look at them funny, smiling... that sort of thing. A bit creepy, I guess."

"Any unwanted advances that you're aware of?" Tom asked, thinking about a jealous boyfriend or husband.

"Oh no, nothing like that," Dean said. "Billy wouldn't say boo to a goose. He was at ease with me and the guys, but women," he shook his head, "no, like a fish out of water. I expect it was more that he was keen but didn't know what to say or how to approach them. How else could a guy get to his age and not be married or involved with anyone?" Dean shook his head again, this time more forcibly. "Nah, Billy was all right, just a bit of an oddball. You would be, though wouldn't you, living all the way out there on your own."

"So you knew where he lived?" Tom asked.

"Yeah, of course. It's Billy! Everyone knows where the Moys' place is. What's all this about anyway?"

"Thank you both for your time, gentlemen," Tom said. Turning to Terry Cole, he said, "I'd like to send an officer around to see you tomorrow in order to take a look at the CCTV you have in the store, if you have no objections? We would like to confirm timings from Thursday night, to see when he arrived here and what time he left, whether he had interactions with anyone in particular?"

"Yes, of course. I'll speak to the branch manager straight away and I'm sure he won't mind. Is Billy in some kind of trouble?"

"I'm afraid I can't comment on that at this time, Mr Cole. I'll have someone come by first thing tomorrow."

They exchanged goodbyes and Tom walked back to the car with Kerry alongside.

"What do you make of this couple in the car park?" she asked him.

Tom glanced up at the lights illuminating the car park, catching sight of the cameras and following their lines of sight. One of them was overlooking the recycling zone where the bins could be seen.

"Dean could be wrong and they might have been acquaintances just saying a brief hello in passing," Tom said. Nodding towards the cameras, he added, "But it will be interesting to see what was going on."

"I'm curious to know who gave him the shiner, though," she said.

"I think we'd all like to know who would have had cause to put one on him, if that's what happened," Tom said, agreeing as he got into the car and closed the door. For a man who, by all accounts, liked to spend almost all of his time alone and was agreeable to those he did come across, someone took exception to him and it was enough to come to blows over. Would the same person still be carrying enough angst over the confrontation to return two days later and settle the argument permanently?

Billy Moy was a curious character in life, and even more so in death.

CHAPTER SEVEN

TAMARA GREAVE ENTERED the operations room to see Tom already preparing the morning briefing. It was seven o'clock in the morning, a damp and overcast morning which matched her mood. DS Cassie Knight was perched on the edge of a desk deep in conversation with Kerry Palmer who appeared bright and fresh-faced. She must be still riding the burst of enthusiasm that came with the opportunity to step up into CID. It was only supposed to be a brief stint, a couple of days to garner some experience but now she was in the thick of a murder investigation. It would be invaluable experience for her.

Tom smiled as she approached him and reaching to his left he passed her a cup of takeaway coffee, presumably from his usual haunt. She accepted it gratefully, finding the cup warm and the liquid the perfect temperature to drink. Unclipping the lid she sipped at the coffee, casting an eye over the white board which Tom was busy using to detail what they knew about their victim. It wasn't much.

"Forensics?" she asked him.

"Preliminary report will be with us at lunchtime with the full works following tomorrow," Tom said. "Labs are on minimal staffing today, being a Sunday, but have promised they'll throw everyone at it first thing tomorrow. Bit more luck with the pathologist though. He's agreed to complete the autopsy today."

"Can we do that as well, take the weekend off?" she asked. Tom smiled but didn't respond. He must know it was rhetorical. Tamara cleared her throat, drawing everyone's attention. Cassie broke off her conversation with Kerry and the two looked at her. "Right, thanks for coming in so early on what is a dreadful day, even without a dead body to investigate I think I'd be on a downer."

"That's okay," Cassie said, smiling. "I'm feeling good. It's a Sunday and I don't have a hangover despite going to a wedding yesterday. Must be a first."

"The hangover-free Sunday?" Tom asked. Cassie grinned. "How did the newlyweds enjoy the reception?"

"Yes, it went well. Becca had to tell Eric off for holding too tightly when they were cutting the cake. He was so nervous, bless him. It all went off well, though. Both of them looked so happy together."

Tamara noticed Kerry's eyes dip away to the floor as Cassie was talking.

"Thanks for taking Mum home last night, Cass."

"No problem. I love your mum, she's fascinating."

Tamara pursed her lips, Cassie smiling at her. It was well known that the team found her mother interesting and far more enlightening than she cared for. She could only hope her mother hadn't let slip any more information that she'd find embarrassing. She dismissed the thought, thinking Cassie was probably just trying to wind her up as usual.

"Right, any joy with tracing the next of kin?"

"Not yet, Ma'am," Kerry said regretfully. "What the deceased's friends told us panned out and Billy Moy's only living relative is his brother, Simon. However, I haven't been able to find a current address for him. The last known address on file was in Dereham but it was a private rental and he left there nearly five years ago. He's no longer recorded on the Electoral Roll in that area but he might not have re-registered at the new address. I'll keep looking."

"Good, okay." Tamara looked at the white board, Billy Moy's face staring back at her. "Known associations?"

Tom said, "Moy doesn't have a record, not even a speeding ticket. He hasn't come onto our radar at all, so that's a complete blank. I ran down the records of his address and confirmed what we were told out at the cabin yesterday. Haydock Farm, as it used to be known, was owned by Arnold Moy, Billy and Simon's father. Arnold died and Maureen, his widow, took ownership until she, too, passed away. The farm then passed into Billy's hands and he has run things ever since.

The Land Registry shows a change in title, I'm thinking some of the land was parcelled up and tenanted or sold off periodically. Haydock Farm then largely ceased to exist in the form it always had, but Billy still holds title to significant acreage. How much of it he still actually works is up for debate. I had a quick look at the business filings over the past few years with HMRC and the company has been making nominal sums to the point of posting losses for the last two years."

Tamara nodded, frowning. "Do we have any idea who the business passes to now he's dead?"

Tom shook his head. "Not yet."

"Billy never married or had children?"

"No, Ma'am," Kerry said. "Not as far as we know anyway."

Tamara would need to speak to PC Palmer regarding her formality. It was how it worked in most stations but within this team it wasn't how she chose to lead things.

"Okay, Kerry, please keep on trying to track down the brother." She looked at Tom. "Until we have the full forensics and pathology report I think we should focus on building a timeline for Moy's last hours. As it stands right now we have almost a two-day window between when he was last seen in the supermarket car park and when the neighbours found his body."

"Agreed," Tom said. "We're working on Fiona Williams' time

frame of his death likely occurring late on the Thursday evening shortly after his return from the trip to the supermarket. He never got around to unpacking the shopping and some of it was perishable and would have needed refrigerating, so I think it's a likely scenario."

"There was no sign of forced entry, so unless he was prone to leaving his place unlocked when he went out – something to ask the friends about in the coming days – it would be reasonable to assume he either had a visitor that he knew or—"

"Someone was already at home waiting for him," Tom finished for her.

She nodded. "Exactly. It would be interesting to know what he had planned this week, who he mixed with in the days leading up to his death as well. The couple who discovered him, didn't they say he was doing work for someone else this past week?"

"Yes, up at Alan Finney's place."

"Do you know him?"

Tom gently rocked his head from side to side. "Sort of. More by local reputation than in person, although I think I have met him a couple of times in passing. Interesting chap."

"Interesting?"

"A bit full of his own importance," Tom said. "In my opinion anyway."

"I think we need to have a word with him to see if Billy Moy has been at his place, what he was up to, how he was behaving, that type of thing. Maybe Cassie could—"

"I'll go out there after the briefing and have a word," Tom said. He glanced at Cassie. "Alan Finney is the sort to expect to be treated a cut above, if you know what I mean?"

"A lowly detective sergeant wouldn't cut it?" Cassie asked without any hint of irritation.

Tom inclined his head. "Yes, he's a bit like that."

Tamara's mobile beeped and she scooped it up off the desk, opening a text message. She read it and sighed.

"What is it?" Tom asked.

"The local jungle drums are already beating," she said, turning the screen towards him. Tom read the message and rolled his eyes.

"That's all we need."

"Yeah, right," she said, turning to the others. "It looks like local media are already reporting Billy Moy's death—"

"But we haven't officially ID'd him yet," Cassie said, frowning.

"*Local sources are naming him,*" Tamara said. "But they're not describing it as a murder yet, so there's something."

"Our killer will now be aware of our interest, though and they already have a two-day head start on us," Tom said.

"If it's a local then that might play into our hands a little," Tamara said. "They'll have been playing it cool these past couple of days, perhaps growing in confidence that the news hadn't broken of the discovery of a body. They might have become emboldened and this may make them a little twitchy, tip off those around them that they are behaving differently."

"And if it's someone who's already fled the area?" Kerry asked.

"Then it won't make a whole heap of difference," she said. "No reason to alter our approach. Let's start mapping out Billy's life, who he hung out with, where he spent his time. Even loners have to go places other than the supermarkets. If he's as well known as everyone says then he must have interacted with people otherwise he wouldn't be on anyone's radar. Cassie, can you go out to the supermarket and get the CCTV from Thursday?"

"Yep, will do," Cassie said.

"And then make a start on his digital footprint: financial records, bank accounts, credit cards, mobile phone, and put the word out to pawn shops that there might be some cheap electrical items passing their way in the near future if they haven't seen it already. The television was missing but he may have had a mobile or a laptop as well. It could have been a job lot being traded for quick cash. Go as far as you can in every direction. There can't be many businesses converting goods into cash in our coastal towns."

Cassie nodded. Tamara looked at Tom and raised her eyebrows. "Anything we've missed?"

"Not that I can think of," he said. "It might be worth speaking to the Bartletts again, advising them not to speak to the press."

"You think it was them?"

"Perhaps, or at least someone they subsequently spoke to after they left us."

"Good idea. We'll need someone to take a formal statement from them anyway. Kerry, that's a job for you."

She accepted the task with a broad smile. Tom exchanged a look with Tamara and she nodded to say she was done.

"I'll go and speak with Finney and catch up with you later."

CHAPTER EIGHT

TOM'S VOLVO ESTATE car sat low to the ground, a fact he was reminded of as he heard the underside of the vehicle scrape along the ground as he made his way up the uneven track. Ashwood Farm sat at the head of a prominent point above Thornham on the coast overlooking the village from roughly a quarter of a mile up a gentle slope. Alan Finney was one of the largest agricultural land-holders in the area, his family farming the north-west Norfolk region for several generations.

Although Tom couldn't claim to know the man particularly well, he had been made aware in the past that the apple hadn't fallen far from the tree when it came to Alan Junior, the son of a notoriously difficult man who bore the same name. Alan Senior had died unexpectedly in his early fifties and having become a family man quite late in life the working of the business fell to his son, himself barely out of his teens. Alan Junior had easily matched his father's irascible temperament according to those familiar with him. Add to this the power and influence that came from being one of the foremost powerful family names in the area and it was a toxic cocktail, one that the young Alan took to. He was well known for expecting to have his way and more often than not he managed to get it.

The entrance to the property took Tom past several agricultural barns, modern affairs clad in sheet steel and dwarfing the more traditional barns that one could find dotting the Norfolk country-side. Ashwood was a professional and clearly large-scale venture. The farmhouse itself was set apart from the working courtyard and ringed by mature trees, obviously planted many decades previously to offer the residence a natural windbreak from the coastal winds that swept up at it off the coast.

Passing between two ornate brick-built piers, Tom entered the property from the south and followed the driveway around to where it opened up before the main entrance. To his right was a stable block with a manege visible beyond it. He saw several figures moving in and out of the stables as he brought the car to a stop and got out. A woman with blonde hair, tied into a pony tail hanging almost to her waistline, turned to observe his approach. As he drew closer he guessed she was in her early forties, dressed in riding trousers and boots and sporting a green gilet over her navy-blue fleece. She stepped forward to meet him, hands on her hips.

"Good morning," Tom said, smiling. She returned it. He reached for his warrant card and another person emerged from the nearby stable block leading a magnificent-looking horse, a teenage girl alongside him. "I'm Detective Inspector Janssen."

The young girl broke off from the man and horse, coming to stand alongside the woman who slipped her arm across her shoulder.

"Good morning, Inspector. Ginette Finney," she said, smiling warmly and looking at the girl beside her. "And this is my daughter, Kim."

Tom should have realised because the younger woman was the spit of her mother from skin tone and eye colour to hairstyle.

"Whatever can we do for the police on such a dull Sunday morning?"

Tom smiled. "Yes, not quite ideal riding weather, is it?" he said.

"All weather is riding weather, Inspector. Do you ride yourself?"

Tom glanced sideways, taking in the horse being led away across the yard. "Not for a while, but it has been known in the past."

"You can't beat it, can you? Getting out in the countryside, fresh air, great views..." she cast a glance at the heavens "...when the mist and fog clear anyway."

Tom nodded. "True enough. I was hoping to speak with your husband, Alan, if he's around?"

Ginette gestured towards the house. "He's over in the main house. What's this about, if you don't mind my asking?"

Tom glanced at Kim. She must be fifteen or sixteen and although he figured she would be old enough to not be traumatised by the news of Billy Moy's death, he still didn't feel comfortable discussing it in front of her. He looked at Kim and away again. "I understand that Billy Moy has been doing some work for your husband recently."

"Billy?" Ginette said, her expression conveying surprise. She also glanced sideways at Kim, clearly noticing Tom's attention towards her daughter. "Kim, darling, why don't you go and rouse your father from his study and tell him we have a visitor." She smiled at Tom and Kim seemed happy to oblige, smiling awkwardly at Tom before averting her eyes and hurrying off towards the house. Her mother watched her go for a moment before turning back to Tom. "Yes, I think Billy was here in the early part of last week. Why? What's he been up to?"

"Does Mr Moy do a lot of work for you around here?"

Ginette looked around, shrugging. "Billy has his uses. He's quite adept at turning his hand to most things."

"I've heard that." Tom followed her gaze around the stable yard. "Forgive me—"

She met his eye inquisitively, nodding.

"—but it strikes me as a little surprising that an operation such as yours that you have here would be in need of a, how can I put this, a jack-of-all-trades type man as Billy Moy?"

Ginette laughed, looking away. "I suppose that's a fairly apt description for Billy, yes." Her eye was drawn to the main house as a man appeared from the back door. Tom recognised Alan Finney. He was alone. Ginette's laughter was replaced with a warm smile. She was an attractive woman. "By your accent I would say you are from these parts, but have spent some time away. Is that right?"

"Quite accurate, yes." Tom matched her smile with one of her own. "You've missed your calling. I thought I was supposed to be the detective."

She inclined her head slightly. "Then you'll know that those of us who are from here look after one another."

"After a fashion, I would agree."

"The Moys have been around these parts for as long as my family," she said, lowering her voice as her husband approached. "Even longer than the Finneys." Alan Finney came within earshot and Ginette stepped forward, placing a gentle hand on his forearm. "Darling, this is Detective Inspector..." she looked at Tom apologetically.

"Tom Janssen."

"Detective Inspector Janssen, Alan. He's asking after Billy."

Alan Finney's brow furrowed as he looked between the two of them, his eyes settling on Tom. "Whatever do we have to speak to the police about regarding Billy? I thought you'd finally got around to doing something about those bloody pikies!"

"I beg your pardon?" Tom asked.

"Those buggers have been out here coursing again," Alan said, bristling. "Tearing up my land, illegal gambling... I've been on to your chief superintendent and still you lot haven't bothered to deal with it."

Tom took a breath, allowing him to get it off his chest.

"I'm sure that will be looked into in due course, but I'm here on another matter—"

"Yes, Billy Moy. What the devil has he brought to my door this time?"

Tom found that a curious response.

"I'm afraid I have some bad news for you both," Tom said, carefully watching the two of them for a reaction to the news he was lining up. "Billy was found dead at his home yesterday."

Ginette audibly drew breath, putting a hand up to cover her mouth. She looked at her husband who stared straight ahead at Tom. Other than a deepening of his frown, there was no apparent reaction from him.

"Well, that's quite a shock," Alan said after a moment. Tom had the impression he wasn't particularly shocked at all. At least, he didn't seem to be.

"How... I–I mean..." Ginette stuttered. She shot a look at her husband and then Tom. If Alan Finney didn't seem shocked, his wife was at the polar opposite end of the scale.

"I'm afraid Billy was murdered."

Alan's lips parted and Ginette reached for his hand, clasping his in her own. Tom saw him squeeze her hand as his expression softened from stern to sympathetic. "Who on earth would have it in for Billy?"

That was the question Tom planned to ask them.

"Can you tell me what Billy was doing for you here?" he asked, trying to inject some normality into the conversation to help ease the shock.

Alan looked at Tom, thinking hard. "Um... I had some servicing of the equipment that was overdue... getting things ready for the next planting."

"I would have thought you would have contracts for that," Tom said, "based on your size—"

"Yes, well," Alan said, waving the comment away and glancing sideways at his wife, "but Billy is – was – useful at short notice. Cost effective as well."

Tom still found it odd but he didn't press the point. "And how would you describe Billy Moy to someone who didn't know him?"

"How do you mean?" Alan asked.

"As a person for starters. Anything you can think of."

Alan blew out his cheeks. "Nice enough bloke. A bit... out there sometimes."

"Out there?"

Alan shrugged. "Dreamy. That's probably a better word. Wouldn't you say, love?"

Ginette agreed. "He was in his own little world a lot of the time. He has always been that way."

"You've known him a long time?" Tom asked.

"Oh, yes. Billy and I go way back," she said, averting her eye from Tom's. He wondered if Billy's being around the place was some of that *looking after one another* she had spoken of. He was curious as to what she meant by that.

"And what about you, Mr Finney?"

He shrugged. "What about me?" There was an edge to his tone in the reply.

"Do you and Billy go back a long way as well?"

Alan sniffed hard, looking away. "The Moys have been around these parts for donkeys' years, but Billy was a few years below me at school back in the day. I think he was starting as I was leaving. I barely knew him and I can't say I spent a great deal of time with him either back then or now for that matter."

If that was the case, Tom was even more curious as to why Billy found work at the Finneys. It wasn't as if you could see Billy and Alan rubbing shoulders socially or professionally. It was a curious mix, but it was possible he was reading too much into it. Billy Moy had a reputation for being good with most things and maybe it was just as the Bartletts described, Billy was a useful guy to have around.

"When did you last see Billy?"

"That's easy. Wednesday," Ginette said, looking at her husband. "He was here Monday to Wednesday, wasn't he?"

Alan nodded. "Yes, that's right. Billy was here until early afternoon on Wednesday... he left around two o'clock, if I remember right."

"And how did he seem?"

Alan shrugged. "I can't say I spent a lot of time with him. He seemed all right, to be fair. Normal. He was working on the sprayer, over there in the second barn," Alan said, pointing to a structure visible beyond the house.

"The sprayer?"

"Crop sprayer. The nozzles can get blocked and you flush them through. It's a simple enough job but pretty tedious."

"Right," Tom said, looking at Ginette. "And did you see more of him?"

"Why would she?" Alan asked. "I mean, you were about, weren't you, love? But you wouldn't have seen much of him."

"That's right," she said, nodding. "I was pottering around the stables here." She gestured in the air with a circular hand motion. "I didn't really see him."

"Is there anyone else around who may have spoken to him?"

Alan raised his eyebrows. "A number of people, yes." He looked around the yard. "I daresay they aren't here today though. You're more than welcome to come back tomorrow, if you like?"

Tom nodded. "I'll do that. Perhaps you can provide me with a list of employees who were at work last week, highlighting those likely to have had contact with Billy?"

Alan sighed. Tom noticed his irritation and Alan was aware. He didn't seem bothered.

"That's *a lot* of people, Inspector."

Tom eyed him impassively. Alan Finney held the eye contact but Tom was unfazed.

Alan sighed again. "And when would you like this list?"

"Before I leave," Tom said flatly, ensuring he remained polite. He would have been happy to receive the list when they returned tomorrow but something about Finney's attitude made him less eager to accommodate him.

"Fine. I'll get it together," Alan grumbled.

"Thank you. I would appreciate it." Tom smiled at him. "Any time you're ready."

"Right, okay." Alan looked between Tom and his wife. "Now?"

"If it's no trouble," Tom said, his smile broadening. "Unless you have anything else that you think might be useful for me to know?"

Alan looked momentarily uncomfortable, but nodded slowly. "I'll... um... crack on with that list then."

He turned and strode across the yard, glancing back over his shoulder once, frowning as he hesitated but then he continued on. Ginette let out her breath slowly, chewing on her lower lip as she saw Tom watching her.

"You'll have to forgive Alan, Inspector Janssen," she said, "he isn't really a people person... and Billy... wasn't really his type of character."

"Then why have him around?"

She shrugged but this time he didn't let her off the hook so easily.

"Mrs Finney? Why have Billy around at all? No matter how useful he was, your husband can't have need of him, not really."

"No, that's true," she said, pursing her lips. "To be honest, Alan throws work Billy's way because of me."

Now she had Tom's attention. "How so?"

Ginette coughed. It was a dry sound and when she ran her tongue along her lower lip. He figured her mouth and throat were dry.

"Mrs Finney?"

"Billy's mum, Maureen. Do you know of her?"

"Only on paper. She died some time ago I believe."

"That's right," she said, staring into the distance. "A few years back. Maureen was lovely. She worked with my mum," she waved a hand in the air to brush the comment away, "a long, long time ago. She did right by my mum. I had a lot of time for her... and after Maureen passed... I felt like I should look out for Billy. Can you understand that?"

Tom nodded. "I can."

"And for all of Billy's capability, he found the daily grind of life, running a business... functioning in society, quite a challenge. He's not the businessman his father was... and he was nothing without

Maureen behind him picking up after him when he dropped the ball so to speak."

"I see. And Billy? What do you make of him?"

Her eyes glazed over and she found another spot on the horizon to focus on, drawing a deep breath.

"He was a lovely man, Billy. He had so much to give but..." she shook her head.

"But?"

"I don't know. He was awkward... and not everyone understood him. Not that there was anything wrong with him mentally, please don't think that, but the way he was around people... they struggled. He was someone you spent short spells with quite happily but anything beyond that... could be rather trying."

"It sounds like you speak from experience."

She broke her gaze away from the horizon, looking directly at him. She smiled weakly.

"Sort of, yes. I'm a little younger than my husband. I knew Billy from school." She laughed awkwardly. "That was all a long time ago now."

Tom waited to see if she would add to what she'd already said but nothing else was forthcoming and they stood in silence for a minute. A man stepped out from the stables leading another horse. He came to within a few metres of them, drawing Ginette's attention. She turned to him.

"Will you still be riding this morning, Mrs Finney?"

She looked at Tom as if to query if he had anything else to ask her and he shook his head.

"Please excuse me," she said, smiling weakly.

"Thank you for your time, Mrs Finney."

"Ginette, please," she replied, nodding in his direction as she walked away. Tom smiled. "Yes, Frank," she said addressing the waiting man who passed her a riding hat. "I'll take her if you can saddle up Bess for Kim." Ginette glanced back at Tom, still standing in the same place with his hands in his pockets, as she took the reins from her stable hand and the man disappeared back inside the stable block to do as requested.

Tom noted that Kim hadn't yet returned from the main house.

"I'm sure Alan won't keep you waiting long, Inspector," Ginette said as she mounted the horse, settling into the saddle and guiding the animal near to Tom.

"No problem," Tom said, reaching up and stroking its neck. "Magnificent horse."

"My favourite, Inspector" she said, smiling down at him.

"Do you know where I can find Billy's brother?" he asked, almost as an afterthought.

Ginette thought hard. "I haven't seen Simon for years." She shook her head. "I think he came back for Maureen's funeral but I don't recall seeing him afterwards. I'm sorry, Inspector, I'm afraid I don't know where he might be."

"Please call me Tom," he said. "No matter. I'm sure I'll track him down."

She smiled again, dipping her head to him. "Tom."

Encouraging the horse, she moved away, walking it towards the house. Kim appeared at the door with a stern expression on her face. She looked past the horse directly at Tom, and when she realised he was watching her she quickly moved out of his eyeline putting her mother and the horse between them. Soon after, the stable hand reappeared leading another horse, only this one was a chestnut mare and a fair bit smaller than the gelding Ginette was riding.

Kim came out from behind her mother, fastening a riding hat in place, but didn't look at Tom at all, climbing up into the saddle while the hand held the horse steady for her. Mother and daughter then set off trotting out of the yard and around to the other side of the house, presumably starting their route. The man whom Tom had overheard being called Frank was making his way back into the stables when Tom approached him, brandishing his warrant card. He stopped and eyed Tom warily, evidently surprised to find himself speaking to a policeman on a Sunday morning. Tom explained why he was there.

"I can't say I knew him very well," Frank said, speaking of Billy Moy. He looked past Tom in the direction of the house.

"But you've seen him around?"

Frank shrugged. "Yes, of course. It's a small place, you know?"

"And is Billy working here often?"

"From time to time." Frank's gaze narrowed. His guard was up and that intrigued Tom.

"What about last week. Did you see him then?"

"Yeah," Frank raised his eyebrows, "last week... come to think of it that was—"

Frank's eyes moved to the house and he stared at something. Tom looked round to see Alan Finney approaching with a sheet of note paper in his hand.

"That was what?" Tom asked.

Frank shook his head. "Nothing really. Something and nothing."

"Sounds like it might be something—"

"I'd best get on," Frank said, turning and striding into the stable block. Tom watched him go, wondering what the man was about to say but had obviously thought better of it.

"Here's that list you were after."

Tom accepted the piece of paper from Alan, casting a cursory eye over it. There were more than a dozen names on the list. He raised it towards Alan and smiled.

"Thank you for this. We'll be back at some point tomorrow."

"If you must," Alan said, sighing dismissively.

Tom found himself irritated and fixed his eye on Alan who stood his ground. Just as before, he seemed not to be in the least bit bothered being under Tom's watchful gaze. "Yes, we must."

He headed for his car without looking back to see if Alan was watching him leave. He scanned the list of names wondering if one of them might be close enough to Billy Moy to know what he was up to in his personal life. So far, everyone he'd spoken to had a strong view on Billy, where he lived, who his family were and what he was both good and bad at but, crucially, no one seemed to know him at all.

Unlocking the car, he hesitated as his mobile rang and he answered it, looking over at the retreating form of Alan Finney walking back to the house. It was Tamara Greave.

"Hey, Tom. Where are you at the moment?"

There was an edge to her tone but he couldn't determine what it meant.

"I'm still out at the Finneys' place. I'm just leaving now."

"Right. Can you meet me in Hunstanton, down on the seafront?"

"Yes, of course. Why?"

"You'll not believe it," she said, "but something has come in on the tide."

CHAPTER NINE

TOM CONTINUED STRAIGHT OVER at the roundabout on South Beach Road, Hunstanton town centre being off to his right. Where the road skirted the holiday park's static caravans, curving around and back towards the funfair on the seafront, he took the left turn and drove in the opposite direction. The sea defences here protected dozens of homes in the holiday park as well as the line of brick-built residences set further back from the beach, but in the event of a severe storm front striking the coast all of them were low lying enough to be at severe risk of flooding.

The road narrowed as Tom reached the town's boundary, becoming a cracked and broken concrete surface before petering out to little more than a dirt track accessing the holiday homes beyond. These structures were predominantly built on stilts or raised plinths, offering not only better views of the seafront but also protecting them from the potential flooding. The police presence was visible at one of these plots and Tom pulled in through the five-bar gate and parked alongside the liveried vehicle nearest to the entrance.

The constable on duty at the gate greeted him as Tom got out of the car, directing him towards the beach. To the side of this plot was a dilapidated caravan which looked barely serviceable and as Tom drew closer to the bank running up to the sea wall, he spied a dozen or so concrete squares in the ground. They were anchor points for the brick pillars to be erected later and form the base for the house. Grass was growing over and around them. It would appear the preparation for this particular building project had begun but had been halted some time ago.

Looking up and down the line of holiday homes situated between the first line of sea defences and the second earthen bank behind him on the far side of the track, each was in a varied state of repair. Some houses were substantial, modern with aluminium windows and crisp cladding lining the exterior, whereas others looked ready to collapse if a suitable gust of wind struck them. That was deceptive, however, because many of these properties had stood up to the ferocious coastal battering that came their way on a frequent basis, apparently doing so for many years. There seemed to be an acceptance by many of the owners that their location was precarious, a place to be enjoyed when the weather was pleasant but the inevitability that one day it could all be reclaimed by the sea meant they chose not to invest in the buildings too heavily. It was a sensible decision in Tom's mind. He could remember the sea breaching these defences on numerous occasions over the years.

Clambering up the steep bank, Tom could see the activity on the beach beneath him. The tide was out and half a dozen figures were milling around the scene. He stepped onto the promenade and then dropped down onto the sand beyond it moments later. Tamara saw his approach and came over to greet him.

"A dog walker found it about an hour ago," she said, glancing past Tom and gesturing towards a man sitting on the sea wall, a dog calmly lying at his feet, accompanied by a uniformed officer who was making notes as they talked to one another. Tom fell into step alongside her as they crossed the beach heading towards the groyne.

Fiona Williams was kneeling alongside the body as Tom cast an eye over it. He could see why the dog walker had assumed it was a seal. Tom could see it was a man and he was dressed in black jeans and wore a dark T-shirt beneath a black thigh-length leather jacket. By the look of it he had been brought in on the tide and then snagged on the groyne as the water receded. He was facing away from the promenade, strands of seaweed disturbed from the sea floor were caught in his hair, wrapped around the head and draped across the side of the face along with wet sand clinging to both clothing and skin.

Tom moved to his left to get a better look. There was substantial damage visible to the upper body and the left side of the head. Tom grimaced at the sight of it. Dr Williams noticed his reaction.

"Yes, made quite a mess of him didn't they?" she said glumly, looking between him and Tamara standing a couple of steps behind him.

Tom nodded. The man's face – the undamaged part – was pale, veins visible beneath the skin and the latter appeared to have a green tinge to it. Tom thought he looked to be in his late thirties judging by the lack of greying to his hair although it was possible it could be dyed. In contrast, the man's face looked lined, as if he was well travelled, making him appear older. He had a silver stud earring in his left ear-lobe and Tom could see extensive tattooing protruding from the neckline of the T-shirt. His footwear caught Tom's attention, leather boots with a large heel, larger than Tom would ever consider wearing. They were a style statement but he hadn't seen boots like those before. Maybe he was too out of touch with fashion.

"How long has he been in the water?" Tom asked.

Fiona Williams thought about it, screwing her face up. "Four, maybe five days at a push I would say." She looked up and met Tom's eye before looking out to sea. "The temperature of the water has slowed the decomposition. This sea has possibly helped you here. The bloating one would expect with the build-up of gases within the body as bacteria speeds up decomposition would usually have brought him to the surface sooner, but this hasn't happened yet." She looked back at the body. "In warmer climates he would no doubt have bobbed to the surface within a day or so but in this case I can see signs that the North Sea's critters have already set to work on him, crabs and the like, so I reckon he's been on the seabed for much of that time. The tidal current has brought him ashore. Lucky for you really," she said, screwing up her nose as she spoke. Tamara offered her an inquiring look. "I've sailed these waters since I was a child and I dare say he would probably have washed up on some continental beach in northern Europe in a few months' time, if at all, with much of his organic tissue missing, had he not come ashore here and now."

"What do you think did that to him?" Tom asked, tracing a finger in the air and indicating the damage to the chest. The doctor slowly rocked her head from side to side, pursing her lips.

"It is hard to say," she said, her brow furrowing. "Looking at it, I would imagine it is post mortem, likely after he'd already gone into the water judging from the preservation of the tissue. If I had to guess, and I stress it is a guess, it could be the result of an impact with a large, blunt surface."

"In the water?" Tom asked. She nodded, looking thoughtful. "That would be... a collision with a boat or something like that?"

"I would say that is quite likely, yes. However, if you want me to suggest a cause of death, then I would look here," she said, encouraging the two of them to come closer as she leaned over the body, indicating the head. "Do you see this injury," she pointed to a wound above the hairline. It was difficult to see through the matted hair with the detritus of the seabed clinging to it, and therefore make out the detail. "I think this is separate. It looks like a puncture wound to me."

"Caused by what?" Tom asked.

The doctor shrugged. "It looks deep. I don't think it's a blade as far as I can tell because the wound is too circular which is why I described it as a puncture wound rather than a cut. If it was a knife then one would expect the width of the incision to be wider, and indeed narrower – like a slit – as the blade went deeper into the brain."

"How deep is it?"

"I can't tell you that, I'm afraid. You'll have to wait for the pathologist to carry out their examination."

"Okay. Is there anything else you can tell us?"

"I can give you the cursory observations," she said, eyeing the body up and down. "A male, likely in his early to mid-thirties and seemingly in good physical health judging from his athletic build and muscle definition. Somehow, I doubt he'll turn out to be a local fisherman."

Tom smiled wryly, looking at the clothing again. The man looked more likely to be on a night out at a club rather than on a ship at sea. Falling, or jumping from a passing ferry was possible, even potentially explaining the possible collision with the hull of a vessel but the puncture wound was intriguing. He couldn't fathom how such an injury could happen.

"In your opinion, could this be accidental?" Tom asked, already forming his own answer in his head.

"Hard to rule anything out at the moment," Dr Williams said, her brow furrowing. "I can't think of how that head wound in particular could be accidental, but that is speculation on my part."

"I'm thinking the same," he replied, glancing at Tamara who nodded.

"Well, I'm finished," Dr Williams said, standing up and stepping back with a sigh. She looked at Tom and Tamara in turn with a half-smile. "If the two of you could see your way clear to not giving me another dead body for a day or two, then I would be grateful." She looked at the body again, shaking her head. "The poor chap."

"We'll see what we can do," Tom said and the doctor smiled again before departing. He dropped to his haunches alongside the body, cupping his chin with his hand before looking up at Tamara, frowning. "Forensics had better get a move on," he said, eyeing the water. "It'll not be long before the tide comes back in. Anyone been through his pockets for an ID yet?"

"No, but you can," Tamara said. "They've done the camera work."

Tom donned a set of gloves and manoeuvred himself into a better position, bracing himself on the damp, rotting wood of the slippery groyne beside him as he lifted the man's jacket to get access to the pockets of his jeans. The material was sodden and gently patting them front and back revealed nothing. The leather jacket was unbuttoned with no zip, a cut designed for style rather than practical protection from the weather. He patted the inside lining and there was something in the inner breast pocket. It felt slim but firm and substantial. He carefully reached in and withdrew the item. It was a burgundy passport.

Tamara had an evidence bag ready for him to place it into. Despite spending several days in the water it was still in good condition. He looked at the front, not recognising the crest. He read it softly aloud but with difficulty, "Eiropas Savieniba Latvijas Republika."

"Latvia?" Tamara asked.

He looked up, nodding. Tom opened the passport, aware that the internal pages would not have fared as well as the plasticised exterior. He gently thumbed through, but he found very few stamps. Latvia, as an EU country was also a signatory of the Schengen Agreement and travel within the European Union didn't require the stamping of passports.

"What's his name?" Tamara asked as Tom reached the photographic identity page at the end. He frowned.

"Wrong question," he said, raising his eyebrows and turning the passport towards her and holding it open for her to see. She sighed as she saw the picture of a female brunette looking back at her. "Who is he in relation to her?" Tom asked, looking at the photograph. The woman wore her hair to just below her jawline in a bob, her eyes were large and round, her cheekbones high and finely sculpted. She was an attractive young woman. "Sasha Kalnina," he said aloud. Checking her date of birth, he did a quick calculation in his head. "Twenty-seven years old, born in Riga."

He placed the passport in the evidence bag and sealed it before passing it back to Tamara as he went through the dead man's remaining pockets. He found another internal pocket that was zipped and he opened it, withdrawing a roll of notes and a folded piece of colourful paper. The notes were tied with an elastic band. Tom gently removed the rubber band. The notes were in sterling, recent issue, and therefore undamaged due to their being made from thermoplastic polymer. He smiled at Tamara, "They say these things are virtually indestructible." A cursory count revealed it to be roughly a thousand pounds' worth of notes in mixed denominations. He held them up for Tamara to see.

"Well, I don't think he fell from a passing ferry," she said. "Not carrying that amount of cash. What was that in his pocket along with the money?"

Tom unfolded the paper. It was an A4 size flyer, a promotional leaflet advertising a musical variety show. He passed it to her. She read it and her eyes widened as she, too, realised it was a forthcoming performance at Hunstanton's very own Princess Theatre.

"Anyone matching his description reported missing in the last week or so?" he asked.

Tamara shook her head. "No, I thought of that. I had Cassie run a check as soon as I got down here and saw him."

Tom nodded. "We'll have to check back through recent passenger manifests entering the country and see if she's on one of them, ferry, airports," Tom said, disappointed not to find the deceased man's identity on his person. "With a bit of luck, he was travelling with her."

Tamara cast an eye out to sea. "At least we have something to go on. I just hope she's not going to wash up at some point as well."

"Now that would be a thing," he said, agreeing.

"How did you get on with the Finneys?"

Tom frowned again as he stood up, shaking his head. "Pretty much as I expected. Alan Finney was far more interested in some coursing that he says has been going on on his land as opposed to what happened to Billy Moy."

"Any help at all?"

"We'll see. Billy was doing work on the farm last week but I had the idea there was something going unsaid in that house though. But it was more to do with Ginette, Alan's wife."

"How so?"

Tom shook his head. "I don't know. Leave it with me. I got the impression from her that they threw work Billy's way because of some past familial affiliation between Ginette's family and the Moys. I'm hoping to track down Billy's brother today, deliver him the bad news. If it goes back far enough, maybe he'll be able to shed some light on it. Ginette Finney clammed up as soon as her husband arrived."

"Could it be related to his death, do you think?"

Tom bit his bottom lip. "I don't know but I can't see how as yet. It doesn't seem likely at the moment, to be fair. It was just one of those feelings you get."

"A copper's sixth sense?" Tamara said, the hint of a smile crossing her lips.

"Yes," Tom said, grinning at her. "Something like that."

"Great. Well, if it pans out, please could you give me next week-end's lottery numbers while you are at it?"

"I'll do my best," he said, stretching and flexing his shoulders before beckoning the crime scene techs to come over and continue their work. He had got everything he would from the body until it could be transported to the pathologist for them to get to work.

The two of them headed back to the promenade where the man who had discovered the body was still waiting patiently. They introduced themselves and the constable introduced him to them, a man by the name of Marcus Beasley.

"I couldn't believe it," Beasley said, shaking his head as he recounted how he'd found the body. "I didn't think Dave, here," he said, indicating the collie lying at his feet, "was going to start munching on a dead seal carcass but he is more than likely to roll in it." Tom found the notion of calling a dog Dave amusing, but didn't mention it. "He's done it before you know," the man continued. "Rolled in a rotting carcass he found on the beach. I was half a mile away and by the time I got there... well, I'll have you know it nearly brought the contents of my breakfast up the smell was so bad! It took two baths to get the stench off the bloody..." he looked at Tom and then Tamara before looking down at his feet. "Anyway, as I was saying... couldn't believe it." He looked up at Tom again, expressionless. "What happened to him, do you think?"

Tom shook his head. "Too early to say, I'm afraid."

"Terrible business."

"And you are confident you were the first to find him?"

Beasley nodded. "Yes, I believe so. I mean, no one is likely to walk away from that are they?"

Tom wanted to tell him that he'd probably be surprised at how many people would run away rather than get involved.

"And you didn't find anything else lying near the body or did you touch it at all?"

"No, certainly not. I pulled Dave away and called you lot. I left it well alone."

He seemed genuine enough and Tom couldn't see him as one to pick a dead man's pocket for a wallet. He had already given a statement to the uniformed officer and so Tom sent him on his way. He was more than happy to leave the scene.

"So," Tamara said, pursing her lips, "trawling through manifests it is."

"And let's not forget someone gets to go to the theatre," he said, holding aloft the evidence bag containing the flyer. "Maybe he bought tickets or is working on the production. That's a job for Eric when he comes back in tomorrow."

Tamara looked back to where the team were preparing to remove the body from the beach.

"Do you think he looks like the type to go to or work in a *musical variety show*?"

"Takes all sorts," Tom said with a smile as he withdrew his mobile from his pocket. "I just need to call home."

"I'll meet you back at the station," Tamara said, walking away.

Tom nodded and dialled Alice's number. Saffy answered the call.

"Tom, where are you?" she asked, dispensing with a proper greeting.

"I'm at the beach in Hunstanton."

"Without me? *That's so unfair*," Saffy replied indignantly. "Your job is really cool. Can I come down?"

"No, sorry, munchkin," he said, looking over as the body was lifted into a bag. "It's not that kind of trip to the beach."

"Not fair," she repeated and then he heard a scraping sound as the mobile changed hands.

"Tom?" Alice asked.

"Hi, darling," Tom said. "I'm sorry I missed you this morning, but I had to make an early start and didn't want to wake either of you. I'm amazed the dog didn't wake you up when I fed him."

"No, he didn't. I was dead to the world – sorry, unfortunate phrasing – I didn't even hear you come in last night. For a big bloke, you aren't half quiet on the move."

"I glide like a bird," he said, smiling. "How did the rest of the reception go?"

"It was great. Eric and Becca make a lovely couple. I have to speak to you about my mum, though. She collared me when I got home."

"Oh no, sounds ominous. She's not moving in, is she?"

"No, of course not. As if that would ever happen. You know you were so quiet last night, if it hadn't been for the towel on the floor of the bathroom I'd never have known you'd been home."

"Ah, yes. I keep forgetting. Sorry."

Alice laughed. "Will you be home for lunch?"

He looked at his watch and then back at the team. "Unlikely. Hopefully I'll be back to have dinner with you though, I promise. What is it with your mum?"

"Don't worry, it will keep until you're back. It *would* be nice to see you before we go to bed though," Alice said. He didn't sense any irritation or sarcasm in her tone at all.

"I'll do my best."

"I know. You always do. I love you."

"I know."

"*I hate it* when you say that," Alice said and he could tell she was smiling as she spoke.

"I know."

"One of these days, DI Janssen—"

"I love you too," he replied, smiling. "Bye."

He hung up and set off for the car. With a second potential murder case to run alongside the first, he knew this day was going to be a long one.

CHAPTER TEN

"I THINK it should be coming up on the left at the edge of the village," PC Kerry Palmer said to Tom just as he caught sight of the sign advising them they were entering Yaxham, a small village some twenty miles west of Norwich deep in the heart of Norfolk. Tom slowed the car and they both scanned the houses on the village boundary looking for their destination. "There!" Kerry pointed and Tom pulled off the main road, turning into the driveway.

The property was single storey, most likely built in the 1960s, and occupied a large plot bordering extensive fields to one side and the rear by the look of it. It was a nondescript building, grey brick and white plastic windows that seemed out of place in such an old village. The other buildings in sight were more traditional, plain brick or flint-faced, and more in keeping with the area. There were no cars parked on the drive in front of the house but a double garage sat to the edge of the boundary backing onto the fields. It was closed up.

"Do you think anyone's home?" Kerry asked.

"Let's see."

Tom got out of the car and looked at the house. It was late on a

Sunday afternoon and he couldn't hear any traffic noise or sounds carrying on the breeze. He wondered if Yaxham ever appeared busy. He had never been here before and they'd looked up the area on the computer before heading out here, hence why they knew roughly where the house could be found. It was a small village that formed a parish with the neighbouring village of Clint Green. There was no significant draw to the location aside from the potential respite of living amongst people.

Their stones crunched underfoot as they went to the front door, ringing the bell. A shadow soon appeared on the other side of the obscured glass of the door and it opened. A woman warily peered out at them, her eyes narrowing.

"Mrs Moy?" Tom asked. She nodded. "Detective Inspector Tom Janssen, Norfolk Police. This is PC Palmer." Kerry smiled at the introduction. The woman's expression softened but she seemed surprised at their presence.

"Police?" She sounded surprised. "I thought you were religious folks."

Tom looked at her quizzically.

"Sorry," she said, waving a hand absently in front of herself. "We've had Mormons knocking on doors in the village recently. They come out from Norwich I believe."

"Well, we are certainly not looking for conversions, Mrs Moy. We would like to speak to your husband if he is in?"

"Yes, he's inside." She glanced over her shoulder. "I'm Caitlyn, Simon is my husband. Please, come in," she said, opening the door wider and stepping back to allow them to enter.

She closed the door once they were both inside. The hall was lined with a patterned carpet, similar to the ones Tom remembered his grandparents having in their homes back in the seventies. This one looked like it may well have been down just as long. Caitlyn walked past him and led them to the rear of the house and into a large reception room easily six metres long with patio doors over-looking the garden to the rear. Tall conifers lined the boundary, presumably offering the house some protection from the winds that rattled across the open fields beyond.

A man was sitting in a leather armchair, his face buried in a newspaper. At first, he didn't appear to notice them entering. When he did, he took a double-take before lowering the paper and getting to his feet. Before they could be introduced, Tom knew this was Billy Moy's brother, Simon. Apart from having a little more hair on top of his head, Tom felt he could be looking at Billy Moy himself. They were the spit of one another.

"Simon Moy?" Tom asked for clarification. He nodded and Tom introduced themselves again. Simon offered them a seat and they duly sat down on the sofa. Simon sat down again and his wife came to stand alongside him, placing a supportive hand on his shoulder.

"What can we do for the police?"

"I am afraid I have to tell you that your brother, Billy, has passed away."

Simon's lips parted slightly. Caitlyn raised a hand to her mouth and Tom noticed the one on her husband's shoulder tensed slightly.

"Oh... I see," Simon said before drawing a deep breath. He glanced up at his wife who pursed her lips but said nothing. He looked back at Tom. "I–I... how did it happen?"

"I'm sorry to have to tell you that we believe your brother was murdered at his home."

Caitlyn gasped and Simon looked away from them, sinking back into his chair, open mouthed.

"I appreciate this is a bit of a shock," Tom said after allowing them a moment to take in the news, "but we need to ask you a few questions about your brother. Do you feel up to that?" Simon didn't respond. He was staring straight ahead. "Mr Moy?"

"Y–Yes of course," he said, snapping out of it and sitting upright. His wife sat down on the arm of the chair and Simon reached across with his left hand, gently patting her thigh affectionately. "Whatever I can do to help. Murdered, you say? Whoever would do such a thing?"

"Do you know of anyone who may have had a grievance with your brother Billy?"

Simon frowned, meeting Tom's eye. He shook his head. "I'm afraid I'm not the one who would know, Inspector. Billy and I lost touch many years ago."

"When did you last see your brother?" Tom asked, unwilling to let on that he knew the brothers were estranged.

Simon exhaled, his eyes flitting to his wife and away again. "I don't know. It's been years, to be honest."

"That's unusual."

Simon looked at Tom with a quizzical expression.

"To not see a sibling for that long?"

"Well..." Simon said, looking away and slowly shaking his head. Then he shrugged. "How does the old saying go, you can't choose your family?"

"You didn't get on?"

Simon swiped a hand through the air. "It's all a long time ago." He sighed. "Seems daft now, I suppose."

"I understand it may have been around the time of your late mother's funeral. Is that correct?"

Simon sniffed hard before chewing on his lower lip and shaking his head dismissively. "I see the local grapevine is still working well."

Caitlyn placed a hand on his shoulder and he smiled up at her, appreciating the gesture. Tom waited. In the end, Simon relented.

"Hell, it's no secret. Everyone was talking about it at the time. I'm surprised the local gossips haven't already filled you in." He cleared his throat, looking up at his wife. "Maybe you could put the kettle on, love?"

She stared at him for a moment before looking at Tom and Kerry, who was diligently taking notes, and nodded. Slipping her arm away from her husband, she walked into the adjoining kitchen through an arched doorway. Simon watched her go and when the sound of a running tap could be heard, he sat forward in his seat, rubbing his hands together slowly.

"Where was I?" he asked quietly.

"The family falling out," Tom said.

He nodded. "Right, yes. As I said, it was all a long time ago. Back when Dad died."

"When was this?"

Simon thought hard. "Must be... twelve or thirteen years ago at least. Probably more." He laughed momentarily but it was a sound without genuine humour. "It was before Caitlyn and I got together. Anyway, our father passed away and he was a... traditional man."

"In what way?"

"In how he liked to do things. The farm passed to our mother but obviously she looked to Billy and me to keep the place going and... Billy held more sway with her. With both of them in fact. You see, our parents truly valued the old 'heir and a spare' approach to family. Billy was the eldest and so... well, they sort of looked to him as Dad was getting on and his health was failing."

"You didn't like that?"

Simon waved the question away. "It's not that I didn't like it. Billy and I were competitive. Me more so than him, if I'm honest and I thought I knew better. That's not true," he said, smiling at a memory, Tom thought. "I did know better than him. Billy was good with his hands, great on the tools so to speak but a businessman? No, not for me," he said, shaking his head.

"Let me guess, he didn't agree?"

Simon laughed, running a hand across his chin. "No. He thought he knew best. As did Mum and Dad. I knew he'd run the farm into the ground one day... and that was what started to happen pretty soon after Dad died." He shook his head. "Boy, did we have some ding-dongs about it." He splayed his hands wide. "I couldn't stick around and watch it happen, so I moved out and left them to it, Mum, Dad and Billy."

"So, you left prior to your father's passing?"

"I did, yes. But we were still in touch. I mean, I still lived in the area, went round and ran Dad back and forth from the hospital. It was just the farm that I didn't work on any more."

"And what changed?"

"Mum's passing changed it all, I think." Simon's head dropped and he ran both hands down the side of his face and head, meeting at the rear of his neck where his fingers interlocked for a second. He sat up drawing a deep breath. "There's no easy way to say it. Mum left the farm to Billy. It was all his. After that... I couldn't be involved any more."

"That must have been hard for you to take, to be disinherited in that way?"

Caitlyn returned with a teapot on a tray with four cups. She set it down on the coffee table between them all. Simon looked past her at Tom.

"Yes, it was hard. Like I said, our parents were traditional. The eldest was to inherit and," he tilted his head to one side, "although Mum said she wasn't going to follow that path... in the end that's what she did."

"You were hurt?"

Simon nodded. "Gutted, yes."

Caitlyn poured out the tea, passing a cup to her husband and then looking at Kerry.

"Milk and sugar please," Kerry said.

"How much involvement did you have with your brother after that?" Tom asked, accepting a cup and saucer from Caitlyn. Simon stirred his tea before putting the cup down on the table.

"I didn't. I left that day, the day of Mum's funeral and never went back. I've not seen him since."

Caitlyn's eyes flitted to her husband and away again. Tom thought he saw her hesitate before reaching for a plate of biscuits she'd set out and offering them around. Everyone declined.

"Has Billy ever been in touch?"

Simon shook his head. "No. He's not the type."

"Can you tell me about your brother?"

Simon shrugged. "Sure, what would you like to know."

"We understand he was a bit of a loner."

He laughed at that. "Yes, that's an understatement. It wasn't always that way."

"Go on."

"Billy was always a fish out of water around people, Mum and Dad aside, and women in particular. When we were teenagers he fell head over heels in love with one of the girls at school." He looked at Tom with a smile. "I mean full on, you know? It was bordering on obsessive for a while."

"Did she feel the same?"

"Strangely enough, yeah. I mean, probably not quite as intensive as Billy did, but I think she was attracted to his vulnerability. He was a good-looking lad – it runs in the family – and if you could see past his quirks, then Billy was all right. It didn't work out for him though."

"What happened?"

"Ah… parents wouldn't have it. Back then the Moys were doing okay, but some local people have an idea of where they sit in the social hierarchy and Billy didn't tick the right boxes. They put the brakes on it. I remember Billy took it hard, really hard." He bobbed his head. "I suppose we all do when we're that age… but this was different. I think that was when he changed."

"Changed how?" Tom was intrigued.

"Got into all sorts, drinking, gambling… taking drugs and hanging out with the wrong sort of people. Getting into trouble basically." Simon shrugged. "That's why I knew he'd run the farm into the ground. Too much money to play with. The farm was hard work but back in the day it delivered a decent living. With Billy at the helm, though… I could only see it going one way."

"Tell me, I'm curious, what would you have done with the farm if you had inherited?"

Simon raised his eyebrows. "I'd have encouraged Billy to sell. There's no way we would have made a go of it between us. We'd already proved we couldn't work together. It would have been for the best."

"He disagreed?"

"Yes, I suppose he did. Fair play to him for keeping it going as long as he has," Simon said, reaching for his tea again.

"But you have no idea as to who may have held a grudge against your brother?"

Simon shook his head. "I'm sorry, no. If Billy's behaviour continued on in the same way as it was when I left, then I dare say it will be a long list. He squandered our father's legacy turning a name to be proud of into something darker... and nastier. It sounds like his actions have eventually caught up with him."

Tom found his curiosity piqued, but he didn't show it. "As the next living relative, I need to ask if you would be prepared to carry out an identification of your brother's body. I'm sorry, but it is procedure."

"I can do that. When?" Simon asked, sipping at his tea.

"As soon as we can arrange it. Tomorrow morning?"

Simon agreed and they stood up to leave. Walking back into the hall, Tom noticed a small table against the wall. There was a telephone, a notepad and some envelopes lying on it. He casually cast an eye over them but didn't stop on his way to the door. Once outside, Tom thanked them for their time and agreed to meet Simon Moy at the mortuary the following morning. Simon was closing the door when Tom stopped him.

"Do you drive, Mr Moy?"

He nodded. "Yes, of course."

"Car in the garage?" Tom asked, gesturing with his head to the closed garage across the drive. Simon Moy nodded. "What car is it?"

Simon looked at him, puzzled. "A Mazda. Why?"

"Can I see it?"

"Um... yes, if you like."

Simon ducked out of sight before reappearing moments later with a set of keys in hand. He seemed a little perplexed as to why he needed to do so, but he crossed the drive to the garage, unlocked it and lifted the door up. Tom came to stand alongside him, peering into the gloomy interior. Inside the double garage was a Mazda hatchback, seven years old judging from the number plate. Crucially, the car was white.

"Happy?" Simon asked.

Tom smiled. "Yes, thank you very much. We'll see you tomorrow."

He turned and walked to his own car leaving Simon to drop the garage door again without another word. Once sitting inside, Tom started the car and watched as the man re-entered the house, closing the door on them. He glanced across at Kerry. She was watching him intently.

"You wanted to know if his car could have left the paint at the crime scene, right?" she asked.

He nodded.

"What made you think of that?"

Tom put the car in reverse and checked behind them, speaking as he moved off.

"Did you see the letters lying next to the phone in the hall?"

"No, I didn't." She sounded concerned, possibly worried that she had missed something significant and would be admonished for it. Undeterred, she still asked the question. "Why? What did I miss?"

"Several of them were stamped as 'final notice' on the envelopes. Looked like utility bills to me."

"Simon has money problems?"

"So it would seem, yes. How deep those problems are could be interesting."

"And if Billy dies without a wife or dependents..." she said softly.

"Exactly."

"Then why didn't you ask him where he was the night of the murder?"

Tom smiled. "Plenty of time for all of that. At this stage he's just the next of kin and we only have the fact they were estranged to suggest anything. It could just be a policeman's overactive suspicious nature. He pulled out onto the main road and headed back the way they had come. "And did you notice the moment Simon claimed not to have seen his brother since the day of their mother's funeral—"

"That threw Caitlyn, didn't it?" she said. Tom was pleased Kerry had seen it too. "There's more to it, isn't there?"

"I would say so. To be disinherited without your knowledge and not only that but to also find out on the same day you bury your mother must have been infuriating. To lose out financially is one thing but how must it feel at the time?"

"Like a betrayal."

"Yes, by your own family. Your mother, no less. That would foster a lot of resentment in some people."

"Enough to kill?"

He looked at her again, angling his head. "Maybe. I've known people kill for far less."

"He didn't seem too bothered or surprised about his brother's death, did he?"

"No, he was quite pragmatic about it all. But that doesn't necessarily make him a murderer. Come on, let's get back."

He glanced at the clock on the dashboard. If he was going to make it home for dinner, he'd have to get a move on."

CHAPTER ELEVEN

TAMARA GREAVE SIPPED at her morning coffee as the team assembled in the ops room. She'd spent much of the night going through the details they had already gathered regarding both bodies that had been reported to them over the weekend. If ever she needed a reminder of the unpredictability of the job, this weekend had been perfect. They'd all been working up to Eric and Becca's big day and after a period of relative calm in the preceding weeks to suddenly find themselves with two murder cases to solve had caught her off guard.

"Right," she said, getting everyone's attention. "Good morning. Welcome back, Eric," she said and he smiled at her. "I trust the new Mr and Mrs Collet enjoyed their first weekend of marriage?" She held up her hand. "And please do spare us the details."

Eric flushed.

"I expected to be able to offer you some light duties and a couple of extra days annual leave on the quiet but," she turned to the boards behind her where she had been sorting through the information of both cases, "I'm afraid we now find ourselves stretched with these two cases."

"Any word about extra resources coming our way?" Tom asked.

"I'm speaking to the chief super this morning, so we'll have to wait on that. In the meantime, Kerry will be extending her loan spell." Cassie slapped Kerry gently on the shoulder and she grinned, looking sideways at Eric who also smiled. Kerry also blushed. "Let us hope you don't regret it, PC Palmer," Tamara said, smiling. "Okay, so we have two cases. We are further along with the Moy inquiry, so I think Tom will stay on that with Kerry to support." Tom nodded his agreement, perched on the edge of a nearby desk. "Cassie, I want you and Eric to take a look into our mystery man who came ashore yesterday morning. The flyer he had in his pocket suggests he has been in and around Hunstanton recently. I also want you to find the woman he knows or may have been travelling with, Sasha Kalnina. We've no reason to think she went into the water along with him but he had her passport, so it is reasonable to assume they are connected. Find her."

"Did we have any luck with his fingerprints?" Cassie asked, taking notes.

Tamara shook her head. "He isn't known to us. However, the passport he was carrying was Latvian, so if he is from abroad then there is every possibility he is known to police in his home country. Get onto Interpol and see if we can check his prints against known criminals."

Cassie sucked air through her teeth. "I'll start with Latvia then."

"Good," Tamara continued. "You'll need to be phoning around local hotels, bed and breakfasts, even the hospital in search of Kalnina. Other than that, it is getting out and about and knocking on doors."

"Interesting tattoo," Eric said, eyeing the set of photographs pinned to the board. Tamara looked around at them, nodding. "Distinctive. It might be worth asking about the artwork."

"How do you mean?" Tamara asked.

"I'm not an expert on ink, but I understand tattooists are just as identifiable as other artists. They recognise each other's work."

"Is there a local... what do they call it... a parlour?" she asked.

"I don't know what they call it, but there's a place in town, yes. It's close to the theatre, so I'll call in."

Tamara smiled. "Good idea." There was something about Eric this morning. He'd welcomed her greeting with a broad smile but he seemed flat. Perhaps it was having to come back into work a couple of days after the wedding instead of leaving for his honeymoon, an anti-climax of sorts, or perhaps he didn't want to go into such a negative case on the back of his happy event? She didn't know, but he wasn't himself. "Tom, what do you have lined up this morning with the Moy inquiry?"

"The brother, Simon, is coming in to do the formal identification. Afterwards, I hope to catch up with the pathologist before getting an update from the forensics team. Then it's the financials, associates... the usual."

"I have the footage to go through, taken from the supermarket on the night we believe he died," Kerry said.

Tom nodded. "Focus on the argument in the car park. Maybe we'll get a bit of luck with a numberplate on the car belonging to the couple."

"What's the thinking there?" Tamara asked.

"If there was an altercation, Billy is so well known they may have known where he lived or followed him home. Maybe it carried on away from the camera."

"Great," Tamara said. "Anything else?"

No one had anything to add and so Tamara broke up the meeting. Cassie leaned in to Eric.

"Give me a few minutes to file this request with Interpol and I'll come with you to the seaside."

"Yeah?" he said, looking glum.

"Cheer up, Eric. If you're good I might even buy you an ice cream."

ERIC PUT THE FLYER, still in the evidence bag, back inside his coat and retreated from the lobby. He always knew it would be a long shot but the variety show in the flyer wasn't scheduled to begin for another month. The crew, performers and management weren't due in the area for weeks. Cassie was waiting for him outside, hands thrust into her pockets, hair billowing in the breeze, as she looked across the green and past the pier amusements arcade at the sea which was hammering the sea wall with a vengeance this morning. The occasional wave was cresting the wall and flooding the promenade. The storm barriers were fixed in place further along the promenade to stop the car parks from flooding.

She read his expression. "No luck?" He shook his head. "It's not the end of the world, Eric. What's up with you this morning? I know you've just got married but you can't have got into married life that quickly?"

He either missed the humorous edge to her tone or he was too distracted to comment, merely nodding and gesturing with his head to walk up the hill into town.

"The tattoo studio is up there. Are you coming?"

He turned and set off, Cassie falling into step alongside him.

"Are you all right, Eric?"

"Yeah, it's nothing really."

"Looks like something to me. Go on, out with it," she said as they walked. The cold weather was keeping people off the streets this morning. The odd passer-by was moving around them but most people in view were either making deliveries or heading to work. In a month Hunstanton would begin the progressive increase in visitor numbers as the season got underway.

"Oh… it's Becca. She's not happy."

"Why? I thought the wedding went well."

Eric stared at the ground as he walked. "It did. It was a great day, she loved it." He glanced up at her. "We both loved it."

Cassie was confused. "So what happened between then and now? Is it the honeymoon thing?"

Eric shot her a dark look. "What do you know about that?"

She was taken aback. "Only about the mix-up with the dates, otherwise you'd be away by now rather than trying to identify who washed up on the beach."

"Ah, right, of course. Yeah… the dates."

He didn't elaborate further and they arrived at the tattooist's shop. It was a small premises sandwiched between two others with an old wooden door and one display window showcasing various designs available to the purchaser. The sign said it was closed but Cassie could see movement at the rear. She knocked on the frame of the glass door.

A man appeared from a room at the back of the shop. He wore a black T-shirt and jeans with a leather waistcoat. He was bald, or shaven headed, and sported a beard that grew out to a point where it almost met his chest. He was a barrel-chested man and, apart from his face which had multiple piercings, every other inch of skin was decorated with artwork. As he approached them, Cassie had to note the level of detail involved in his ink was impressive. The door was unlocked and he eyed them both. Despite being the senior officer, Cassie was aware this was Eric's assignment and she looked to him to take the lead but Eric was off in a world of his own and so she brandished her warrant card.

"Sorry to trouble you. Detective Sergeant Knight and DC Collet, Norfolk Police, can we pick your brains for a minute?"

He raised his eyebrows, clearly surprised to be visited and nodded. "Callum Nichols. This is my place, come in."

He held the door open and they entered. There was a small counter to their left and Cassie could see the treatment room – if that was the right name for it – in the rear. The walls were adorned with prints and photographs of previous work or what was on offer for prospective buyers: elaborate fantasy designs, animals or Celtic art.

"What can I do to help?" Nichols asked.

Again, Cassie looked to Eric but he said nothing. She held out her hand and Eric realised he was holding the pictures. He passed the folder to her.

"I'm afraid it is quite a grim inquiry, Mr Nichols. Unfortunately a body was found on the beach yesterday—"

"Washed up," he said, frowning. "I heard about it. Some of the guys were talking about it last night."

"Right, yes. Well, we are trying to identify him and he has some distinctive ink. We were hoping you might help us with it?"

He shrugged. "Happy to, if I can."

She opened the folder and took out the enlarged photographs of the deceased man's body art. They'd been careful not to include the head or face so as not to cause upset, although these pictures were in reserve if needed. Cassie slowly passed them over and Nichols looked through them. His brow furrowed and he slowly shook his head.

"Definitely not ours," he said very quickly. He looked up at Cassie. "I would know if we had done these."

"We?"

"There are two of us working here but I'd recognise our stuff. Is he from around here, do you think?"

"Why do you ask?"

"I don't think it's local work," he said, moving the next image to the back of the pack and eyeing the next.

"You're sure?"

He shrugged. "I guess it could be a bespoke commission, but this is a small area, you know? We all know each other and you can spot the signs of each other's work. Much like you can with a painting, if you know what you're looking for. It's almost like a signature. We have guest spots every now and again, though, so I couldn't be one hundred percent sure."

"Guest spots?"

"Oh, travelling artists who are coming to the country or holidaying here might get in touch ahead of time and ask if they can do a day here. It mixes things up, offers something different to our customers, most of whom are repeat business."

"I see. Anything you can tell us about this work might be useful," Cassie said.

"It's not recent," he said, "you can tell from the discolouration. Some of the colours are fading. That could indicate the artist has mixed the ink with something to make it last, lower costs for them. It's not something I would do but maybe this guy wasn't as ethical. Your man here would probably want someone to go over that at some point to bring it back up. It's also not a style I recognise. We get a lot of requests for Celtic artwork, maybe not as much as we did perhaps a decade or so ago when it was all the rage, but there is still a demand. Similarly, oriental stuff, Buddhist life cycles and mythical dragons or the like have an almost perennial appeal."

"But this pattern is not related to those?"

He shook his head. "No. I've not seen its like before. That might help you," he bit his lower lip before passing the pictures back, "in a way. Similarly, the ink could be mixed with different materials to alter the colour or get a different look. You could analyse that maybe."

"Such as?"

"DIY stuff might use pen ink, soot or even blood, believe it or not. Different colours can be made using heavy metals, mercury can give you red or lead and cadmium can offer up a yellow. Cobalt gives you a blue, that sort of thing. That's done at the production stage of the ink manufacturers, though, not on site for obvious reasons. They might blend them with lead or titanium to lighten the colours and also to reduce costs. I don't know if that helps?"

"Yes, maybe. We can bear it in mind." Cassie thought the man seemed to demonstrate a strong constitution. She took out a photo of the deceased's face. "Forgive me, but would you mind looking at him to see if you do recognise him? Maybe he has been in here with someone else or you've seen him knocking around recently?"

He was willing and she gave him the photo. Nichols studied it hard, then shook his head and handed it back.

"Sorry. I've never seen him before and I think I'd recognise him if I had."

"Okay, thank you for your help."

They left the studio and began the short walk back to where the car was parked at the bottom of the hill across from the green. By the time they reached the car, Eric still hadn't said a word.

"Eric?"

He looked across the car at her, key in hand. "What?"

"You're not going to be much use to us this week unless you're able to focus."

He looked glum, pursing his lips and nodding purposefully. "I'm sorry. I am a bit preoccupied."

"That's to be expected. You just got married. But I sense there's more to it."

"Yeah," he said, sounding dejected and leaning on the roof of the car. "I know."

A seagull flew over them, coming to land on the waste bin across the road. It watched them, hoping for them to drop something for it to eat. The birds were well practised in the town.

"So, what's going on?"

Eric took a breath, casting his eyes skyward. "It's the honeymoon... or lack of one."

"Where is it you're going?"

"Originally, we were going to Sardinia. Becca likes hills, walking and exploring, but when George arrived we realised that wasn't going to happen, so we figured we'd stay in the UK and came up with a new plan."

"Yes, you're heading up to Hadrian's Wall country, aren't you?"

"Yep. Becca found this company through her fell-walkers' club. They help with shifting luggage around between locations, so you can walk but not have to carry everything."

"You just have to focus on getting from A to B then, right?" He smiled, nodding. "Sounds great. What's the problem?"

Eric sighed. "Weddings are expensive... more so than I realised. Becca's parents wanted to foot the bill for the whole thing but obviously Mum wasn't happy about that. She's always been keen to ensure she paid her way..."

"And?"

Eric rubbed the end of his nose. He was uncomfortable and she thought maybe she shouldn't have pushed him. Eventually, he took a breath and rallied himself.

"Mum doesn't have a lot of money, but she insisted on paying half. I'm not sure if she had any idea how much the whole thing was going to cost. I know I didn't. In the end it cost a lot more than she had, so…"

"So?"

"So… I made up the difference from savings. I didn't want Mum to feel bad, or to think she'd let me down."

"That's decent of you, Eric. There's nothing wrong with…" Cassie paused as it dawned on her what Eric was saying in his usual roundabout fashion. "You've spent the honeymoon money?"

Eric wouldn't meet her eye. He dipped his gaze to the floor before turning and looking out to sea. Slowly shaking his head, he looked back at Cassie.

"How short are you?" she asked, realising how upset he was.

"Three and a half thousand, if not more."

"Oh, Eric."

"I've no idea how I'm going to tell Becca."

CHAPTER TWELVE

"THAT'S HIM. THAT'S BILLY," Simon Moy said without a flicker of emotion. Tom nodded to the mortician who stepped forward and pulled the sheet up from Billy Moy's chest and recovered the face. Only the neck up had been visible to the dead man's brother, keeping the nature of the wound as well as the signs of the autopsy; the stitches across the abdomen where the pathologist put the body back together, hidden from view. Simon Moy was escorted out of the room and into the corridor where his wife was waiting for him. He turned to Tom. "So, what happens now?"

"We will continue the investigation into his death," Tom said. "Seeing as this is a murder inquiry, we will not be able to release your brother's body until such time as the pathologist deems any further investigation is not required."

"What does that mean?" Simon asked, glancing at his wife.

"In criminal cases there is the possibility that a further investigation may be required. In your brother's case, I understand the cause of death is certain. In that case, I am confident his body will be released to you as soon as possible. You shouldn't have to wait too long to bury him—"

"I'm not dealing with it."

Simon's tone surprised Tom and he was taken aback. Simon held a hand up by way of an apology. "I'm sorry if I sound callous, Inspector, but as far as I'm concerned my brother died years ago. I see no reason to bring him into my life again and certainly not in death."

"That is your choice, Mr Moy."

"Yes, it is."

Simon Moy turned to walk away, his wife hesitated momentarily looking awkwardly at Tom. Then, she inclined her head, smiled weakly and hurried after her husband.

"Mr Moy?" Tom called. Simon stopped at the end of the corridor and looked back. "Where were you on Thursday night last week?"

Simon took a deep breath and made his way back along the corridor coming to stand in front of Tom.

"Why do you ask? Surely, you can't believe I am a suspect here?"

"Do you think you should be?"

He let out an exasperated release of breath, shaking his head. "I was at home with my wife," he said, gesturing to Caitlyn who was now waiting for him by the exit. "Ask her yourself if you want to?"

Tom's eyes flitted to Caitlyn and she held his gaze for a moment before glancing at her husband and away. He returned his attention to Simon, now cutting an indignant pose.

"We will be in touch when the coroner confirms we can release your brother's body," Tom said. "And then you can make your decision as to what you want to do."

Simon Moy offered him a curt nod and walked away without another word. Tom glanced at his watch. He had to get back to the station. Tamara had arranged a briefing and it was due to start in half an hour.

TOM ENTERED THE OPS ROOM. Tamara and Kerry Palmer turned to look at him. He was a little later than intended.

"How did you get on with the brother?" Tamara asked.

"There's a lot to unpick but suffice to say they were not close. I don't think he has any intention of resolving his brother's affairs, let alone arranging a funeral."

"Wow. There's no love lost there."

Tom pulled out a chair and sat down. Tamara turned to Kerry Palmer.

"Have you been through the CCTV from the supermarket yet?"

"Yes. It is pretty much as the staff described. Billy Moy enters through the main doors and does a basket shop. He doesn't interact very much, appears to have a brief exchange with a couple of members of staff but very informal by the look of the body language. I tracked him through the shop and married up what he was selecting with what we found at his home. Nothing unusual at all."

"And outside?" Tom asked. "The set to in the car park?"

"Now that is interesting," Kerry said, turning to her desk and retrieving a folder.

She stood up and crossed to the whiteboard where she proceeded to stick up several stills taken from the security footage. From the angle it was clearly the camera mounted on the pole Tom had noted on the Saturday night.

"The other cameras mounted inside and around the store didn't catch anything as we expected. However, this footage comes from the camera observing the recycling bins. I think it is positioned to catch people raiding the bins but you can see in these stills that they do appear to catch an argument taking place." She pointed to the first two stills. "This is Billy Moy, we can see from his clothing and his distinctive... um... head shape?" She looked around and no one saw fit to challenge her description. She continued, "He appears to be having words with a man who sadly never steps into shot—"

"That's annoying," Cassie said.

"Very," Kerry agreed. She produced two more stills and stuck them up as well. "This first one here catches the rear of a car parked just beyond the recycling bins in the background. Nowhere near enough information to make out a model, let alone a numberplate. However, I watched the footage in its entirety and this vehicle in the background moves off moments after Billy and whoever he was arguing with separated."

"You think it could be the guy?" Tom asked.

"That was my thinking. This last still was taken from a camera a little further down the road. It is mounted on the exterior of a restaurant and takeaway behind the petrol station on the A149. If you look at the time stamp it is moments after the car leaves the supermarket." She put the still on the board. The vehicle was a dark estate car. "This particular car pulls in at the turn just before the entrance to the restaurant and parks up for less than a minute."

The camera wasn't angled at the road, focussing on the premises' car park, and the car had stopped on the far side of a small hedgerow blocking the view of the lower half of the car including the numberplate. Tom stared at the car. There were two occupants. One appeared to have a baseball cap on and the other had long hair hanging to the shoulders. The image was grainy and only recorded in standard definition, the lack of sunlight further hampering observation of any detail. Tom was pretty certain the passenger was a woman.

"I've saved the best until last," Kerry said. "As I said, the car stays put for a minute until several others pass and then pulls out again. Now, on the off chance I called into the petrol station seeing as they have cameras on their forecourts in case of drive-offs. I was able to get a shot with the road in the background and we can clearly see this particular car as it joins back into traffic. Guess which car they were directly behind?"

Tamara cleared her throat. "Please tell us it was Billy Moy's, otherwise it'll be one heck of an anti-climax."

Kerry smiled. "Yes, I believe it was. Were they following him? We can't know for sure but it is a dark car and the timings fit."

"Numberplate?"

Kerry shook her head. "No, the shot only films the car from the side on and the lack of light makes identification of the occupants nigh on impossible."

"Shame. Great work nonetheless, Kerry," Tamara said. "I've been reading through the forensic analysis report that scenes of crime have put together for us. The flakes of paint we found on the tree stump are not particularly insightful. Standard metallic black paint. Sadly nothing exotic enough to help us. However, if we find a vehicle to match it to then they are more than confident they'll be able to do so. They could say it hadn't been there long, so it may or may not be related to the murder. I've emailed you all the report, so please do familiarise yourselves with it."

She turned to the board. "The team did a full sweep of the cabin for prints and produced a number of usable sets for comparison. We have run them and got a hit that I find very interesting."

"Who do they belong to?" Tom asked.

"Danny Tice. Do you know him?"

Tom shook his head. "Should I?"

"Not necessarily. He's been picked up for a string of offences. Mostly petty crimes: shoplifting, pickpocketing and he did six months inside for possession with intent to supply of a Class A drug. That was three years ago."

"Stealing and selling to fund his habit," Tom said. "Anything more recent?"

Tamara shook her head. "No. Until his prints came up here, we've had no dealings with him for well over a year."

"Do we have an address for him now?"

"Not for him directly, but the database has thrown up a list of known associates we should work through."

Tom made a note. "Murder would be quite a step up for him."

"I agree but maybe he didn't go there alone. Definitely one to speak to. Where are we with second-hand shops, pawnbrokers and the like?"

"Nothing reported out of the ordinary," Tom said. "It's only been a few days though. Perhaps they're still sitting on things they stole."

Tamara frowned at him. He knew he was wrong as soon as he

said it. Burglars get rid of what they take as quickly as possible. For starters it holds no value to them sitting in their house and only increases the risk of their being caught with it. If they hadn't offloaded what they took already, then they weren't going to. The question was why?

"Do you think they left town?" Kerry asked. "Because of the aggravated nature of the offence, they went further afield."

"To avoid being fingered for a murder?" Tamara asked. Kerry nodded vigorously. "Good point. It is certainly possible."

"If Tice is still a junkie," Tom said, "he won't be thinking much further than his next fix. Skipping town and running into unfamiliar territory with a load of hot gear... I doubt it somehow, but we should consider it. Kerry, put the feelers out to neighbouring stations. I still think he'd stay in the Norfolk area where he knows his suppliers."

Kerry made a note. Cassie and Eric entered ops saying their hellos while taking their coats off.

"Sorry, didn't mean to interrupt," Cassie said as she and Eric sat down.

Tamara waved the apology away. "One thing that I found odd when going through the report – which I admit I missed at the time – was this." She pointed to a photograph taken at the crime scene. It was a small cardboard box lying on the dining table with the lid alongside it.

"What is it?" Tom asked.

"A shoebox."

Tom's brow furrowed. "The significance of that?"

Tamara shook her head. "No idea. It was on the table, open. Nothing inside. The box is not particularly old, but it has been used as storage but there was nothing inside, no packaging, no odds and ends. Nothing. The box was for a pair of ankle boots, female, size seven. No sign of the boots. I even checked the inventory from the wardrobes. Nothing there either. So, I'm thinking—"

"What's it doing there?" Tom asked.

"Exactly. There's no reason. It may well be insignificant, but it is out of place and I don't like oddities that stand out like that." Tamara stood staring at the board as if she expected an answer to leap out at her but it clearly didn't happen. She sighed and turned back to face the room. "Okay, that's all I have on the Moys. Tom, anything else from you?"

"I'm scheduled to speak to the pathologist," he glanced at his watch, "after lunch to run through the autopsy results. He's already given me the highlights and advised me not to expect anything else earth-shattering. The cause of death was the knife wound to the chest which pierced his heart. Death would have occurred soon after. There were no indications of defensive wounds or trace evidence under the fingernails. Whoever killed him did so without a fight."

"What about the bruising to his face? Was it likely the result of a fall or something?"

"Must have occurred a day or more previous to the death, so that's probably Wednesday afternoon onwards. He had an altercation with someone though because he also had bruising to the left side of his midriff. We know he was working at the Finneys' farm Monday through Wednesday and no one said anything about an accident, so it is worth considering something happened on the Wednesday after he left theirs. Oddly, there was no indication to suggest he had fought back there either. No abrasions on his knuckles or anything. It's like he took a kicking without trying to stop it. Strange."

"I'll say so. Why would someone do that unless the notion of fighting back terrified him more than just taking it?" Tamara drew breath, looking to Cassie and Eric in turn. "Right, you two. Where are we at with the mystery man?"

"We have a name!" Cassie said, eyes focussed on her computer screen.

"We do?" Eric asked, surprised.

She turned her screen to face the room, smiling. "Interpol matched his prints. He's a thirty-eight-year-old Latvian national by the name of Aleksandrs... *Bal–Balodis*. I think that's how you pronounce it anyway. Yes, Balodis. It says here he is originally from *Latgale*, a region in Latvia."

"Where's that?" Eric asked.

Cassie shook her head. "Latvia."

"Yes, I got that part," Eric said curtly.

"No idea. I'll have to Google it," Cassie said. "But we have a name. Looking at what they've sent through, he's not the type of guy you'd want to come across on a dark night. His record is... extensive."

"What for?" Tom asked. "Give us the highlights."

Cassie scanned the document on her screen looking for the most serious offences. "Multiple arrests for violence, fraud, extortion... and there's one here for smuggling."

"Drugs?" Tom asked.

Cassie shook her head, leaning in towards the screen and concentrating as she read. "No. Cars. He was part of a network who stole cars in Sweden, prestige European marques, and shipped them into the Baltic states and Russia, re-registering them and moving them on with new identities. Although, it looks like he was some way down the food chain on that one. He only served two years inside. The operation was worth millions when a combined Swedish, Latvian task force took them down."

"Did you have any luck on the ground in Hunstanton?" Tamara asked.

Eric answered. "The tattooist managed to give us a few pointers, suggesting our guy was foreign," he looked sideways at Cassie, "and it looks like he was right, but he didn't know him or see him personally. Likewise with the theatre. The production depicted in the flyer isn't due into town until next month. I've no idea why he would have it on him. It could be he just picked it up or someone handed it to him in passing."

"Eric, find out if he's been staying locally," Tamara said. "When did he arrive in the UK, Cassie? I want to know. Likewise, if he has been staying here, then what's his business? Who is he visiting? I want some answers. If all else fails today, circulate his photograph and see if anyone bites. Remember he may also have checked in somewhere with the woman, perhaps under her name and not his, and we can presume, for now, that she is still around and about. Let's find her. In the meantime, Tom, Kerry, I feel like getting some fresh air so why don't we take a trip out and see if we can locate Danny Tice."

Someone rapped their knuckles on the door into ops. They turned to see Ken Abbott, a station veteran in uniform, nearly thirty years in and carrying more than a little extra weight in his middle-age spread overhanging his belt, standing at the threshold. He nodded and smiled at Kerry who offered him a little wave in return.

"Sorry to interrupt, Ma'am."

"That's okay," Tamara said, looking around. "We're pretty much done here. What can we do for you?"

"Fly tipping," Abbott said, drawing raised eyebrows from Tamara who exchanged a look with Tom.

"I do hope there's more?" Tamara said.

PC Abbott smiled. "The Moy place was picked clean of electricals and the like, wasn't it?" Tamara nodded. "You asked us to keep an eye out for anything being traded locally... anyway, one of the residents living on Manor Road, on the outskirts of Heacham, you know it?"

Tamara looked at Tom again. She obviously had no idea but Tom did. "The unadopted track opposite the self-storage place on the edge of the village?"

Abbott nodded. "That's the one. One of the residents has complained to us about a load of gear dumped in the woods opposite their house."

"Fly tipping?" Tom said.

"Yeah, one of the lads ducked out to placate them, Sergeant's orders, you know how it is, but he found it's not your usual garbage. They've chucked a television, laptop and a few cameras. That's the sort of thing you're looking for and it's only a couple of minutes' drive from Billy Moy's place, isn't it? Too much of a coincidence."

"Is your man still out there?" Tom asked.

"Yeah. I told him to hold fast until I'd spoken to you."

Tamara smiled. "A little detour on our hunt for Danny Tice then."

CHAPTER THIRTEEN

MANOR ROAD WAS a gravel-lined track located on the outskirts of Heacham before you reached the boundary of Hunstanton. The houses were large and detached, and all positioned on one side of the road. Behind them the land dropped away, with the sea visible in the distance, before the new housing development on the outer edge of Hunstanton sprang up on the opposing slope.

Tom parked the car and he, Tamara and Kerry Palmer got out. The uniformed constable was waiting for them along with a member of the public, a grey-haired lady whom Tom assumed was the person who originally called in the complaint. The constable indicated towards them and the two of them stepped forward to meet the small party. At the edge of the road was a strip of mature woodland occupying the space between the established properties and a small development of newer homes beyond.

PC Wilkins introduced Judith Taylor, confirming she was the complainant. "Ma'am, sir, the items are just over here." He led them a few metres away and the woman called after them.

"Shameless, people dumping what they don't want around here. You should make arrests!"

Tom smiled politely, dipping his head towards Kerry in a silent request for her to try and placate the woman while they examined what she'd found. The collection of electrical goods had been crudely disposed of with very little attempt to conceal them from view. Tom dropped to his haunches and cast an eye over the pile for that is what it was. No care had been made to set them down carefully. It was as if they'd been heaved into the brush without thought. The television screen had smashed, the internal workings visible to see. The lens of a camera had likewise smashed, most likely as it impacted on the items around it. A laptop was beside the pile, seemingly having slid off and the edge was buried in the soil. He didn't hold out much hope for the condition of the screen and the hard drive.

He looked up at Tamara. "We'll have to have all this stuff finger-printed to see if it belonged to Billy Moy." He glanced over his shoulder at Kerry Palmer talking to Judith Taylor. The latter appeared calmer as Kerry had a way of disarming people with her soft speech. The thought occurred that this job was as much about people as it was investigation and she had the ability to diffuse most situations with calm authority. That was one reason he'd taken her on board in the first place. "Let's see if she saw who dumped this lot."

Tamara agreed and they walked back. They did indeed find her a great deal more agreeable, possibly thinking her concerns were finally being listened to.

Kerry spoke first. "Mrs Taylor saw the vehicle that she thinks disposed of the items on Friday evening."

"Friday?" Tom queried and Mrs Taylor nodded.

"Yes, I was just setting out after dinner for my evening walk with the dog," she said, pleased to have all four police officers listening to her. She gestured to a house thirty yards away, set back from the road behind a large hedgerow. "That's our place over there. I say *ours* but my husband passed five years ago and since then it has just been me."

"I'm so sorry," Kerry said.

Mrs Taylor smiled. "Very sweet of you, dear," she said, patting

Kerry's forearm softly with her hand. "It's rather a large house to rattle around in on my own. Well, I say on my own but I have the dog of course—"

"Mrs Taylor?" Tom said gently. "Did you see who left the items?"

"Sort of... no. Well, I saw a man throw something into the brush and I heard a smash, or I thought it was a smash. He glanced up the track and I'm sure he saw me because he hurried around to the driver's door and got in quick smart."

"What did he look like?"

"Young." She frowned. "Mind you, everyone looks young to me these days." Kerry smiled at the comment. "Anyway, he looked straight at me. Nasty piece of work."

"How so?" Tom asked.

"Beady eyes... a black stare on him. Makes me shudder the way he looked at me."

"Can you describe him to us? Was he white? How old would you say?"

"Definitely white... um... age..." She sighed "It was dark and so hard to say. He moved quickly after he saw me. He got in and exchanged words with his passenger—"

"There was a passenger?"

"Oh, yes. Did I not mention that? It was a woman, I'm certain." Her brow furrowed. "Or a man with very long hair. The interior light came on when he opened the door and I saw her. She was white, long hair tied back in a ponytail."

"What happened then?"

She shrugged. "He drove away. Aggressively. Stones were flung up all over the place. He turned left, heading towards Hunstanton."

"And the car, what can you tell us about it?"

She thought hard. "Dark. Old. Battered."

"Anything else? Do you remember the make or model or any part of the numberplate?"

She shook her head. "No. I should have, shouldn't I? The Neighbourhood Watch group always say to make a note of such things, but I have to say, I didn't really think about it."

"And this was when?"

"Friday night. Nine-fifteen on the dot."

"You seem very sure," Tamara said.

"Oh, I am, my dear. Every night, that's when we go out come rain, wind or shine."

"And you're certain it was Friday evening?" Tom asked.

She nodded.

"Okay, thank you, Mrs Taylor."

"Are you going to do something about this?" Mrs Taylor asked.

Tom replied. "We'll make sure this is all removed today."

Kerry smiled warmly at the woman. "You're a credit to the watch group, Mrs Taylor. You should be very proud."

Judith Taylor's expression softened and she beamed back at Kerry before looking at Tamara and Tom in turn before backing away and heading towards her house. Tom frowned.

"That doesn't fit our timeline at all, does it?"

"It's a day late," Tamara said.

"If this is the stuff taken from Billy Moy's house, why would they dump it here twenty-four hours after his murder?"

"Maybe they'd sat on it in their car for a day and realised it would be too hot to hold onto or to sell on, ditching it after dark as soon as they were able to the following day?"

Tom wasn't convinced. If they were looking to dispose of incriminating items having had a day to think about it, he could conceive of far better places than this within easy reach of the area. It didn't make a lot of sense. Unless none of this was Billy's. If not, why would you dump such valuable items in this way? He was fairly confident it would track back to Billy Moy, but how and why it came to be here was puzzling.

"There haven't been any burglaries reported locally from Friday have there?" Kerry asked.

"No." Tamara said. "The address intelligence gave us for Danny Tice, how far is it from here?"

"Less than two miles from here," Tom said. "It's just this side of the town centre."

THE ADDRESS GIVEN to them was a flat at the lower end of the town just off the high street. Tom parked the car a little way up the hill and they scanned the exterior. The building was a four-storey stone-built semi-detached house with a basement flat. The adjoining house was a twin sister to the first and both would once have been very grand, imposing townhouses, but now looked quite shabby and in a poor state of repair. The grounds surrounding both houses, now converted into flats, were unkempt and rarely tended to. Some of the windows had cracked or broken panes and there was no sign of life in either building.

"Which one is it?" Tom asked.

"Ground floor, I think," Tamara said and the three of them got out and crossed the road, making their way down the hill. "Kerry, you go around the back just in case whoever is inside bolts when we knock on the front door."

Kerry hurried down the side of the property between the house and an old van parked off to the left, a vehicle that didn't appear to have moved in years. She rounded the corner and disappeared from view. Tom and Tamara mounted the steps to the front door. Tom pressed the bell but didn't hear it ring. He tried again and then gave up, hammering a fist on the door. They waited but there was no answer. Leaning to his left, Tom peered into the front bay window but the interior was shrouded by thick net curtains draped across the window. They were once white but now discoloured with a brown tinge to them. Tom returned to the door and raised his closed fist again but the latch clicked and the door cracked open, a security chain in place.

"Yeah?"

The tone was hostile, belonging to a narrow-faced man with greasy hair that clung to his forehead and scalp. He sported three earrings in his right lobe and his bloodshot eyes looked sunken with dark patches amplifying the bags beneath them.

"Police," Tom said, showing his warrant card. "We're looking for Danny Tice."

The man smiled to reveal yellow, tobacco-stained teeth and receding gums. "Nah, don't know him."

He made to close the door but Tom braced it with his hand. The man looked up and met his eye. "And you are?"

"None of your business, mate!"

Tom smiled. "Give us a name and maybe we will leave you alone."

He looked up, his eyes narrowing. It was almost as if Tom could see the cogs ticking over in his mind.

"Open the door, Mr Tice," Tom said.

The man sighed, nodding ever so slightly, and Tom released the pressure on the door. The door closed and the sound of the chain being removed began and then stopped. Tom and Tamara exchanged a glance and both of them said in unison, "He's running!"

Tamara turned and hurried down the step to try and get to the rear to support Kerry, whereas Tom eyed the door. It was old, sturdy but the frame was wooden and rotten due to its exposure to the ferocity of the local weather and the corrosive sea air. He took a couple of steps back and launched himself forward raising a booted foot and landing it on where the latch met the frame. The door flexed on the first attempt but on the second the frame splintered and the door flew in snapping the security chain.

Tom ran into a wide hallway. It was dark with only the daylight coming through the door behind to illuminate the way. Proceeding with caution, just in case anyone lay in wait for him, he looked into the front-facing room. Once a grand sitting room, it was now converted into a bedroom. The air in the room was stale with an odour of damp and sweat. It was empty. Moving further into the building, the hallway narrowed, presumably the staircase to the next floor had been boxed in during the conversion. He came to a second room. It was also shrouded in darkness, French doors to the rear were closed with heavy curtains slung across them. He could make out a figure lying on the sofa and he edged in just as a shout went up from the rear.

Tom thought to run to the sound, knowing it was Tamara and Kerry, but he couldn't leave someone behind them. He moved closer but the person didn't acknowledge his presence and when he came to stand over them, he realised it was a woman, perhaps in her early twenties but in this light it was difficult to tell. There was a table lamp next to the sofa and he turned it on. She appeared to be sleeping but as she absently raised a hand in a vain attempt to block out the source of light accompanied by a mumbled complaint, he knew she wasn't sleeping. She was wasted. Passed out would be a more apt description.

She was no danger and he turned, ran from the room and into the next. This was a narrow kitchen, filthy and stinking. The window above the sink was open and the items that had been on the drainer were now in the sink or had crashed to the floor. Broken glass lay at his feet. He peered out to see their charge lying face down on the floor with Kerry kneeling on the small of his back, bracing one arm up his spinal column. He struggled and she tightened her grip bringing forth a tirade of expletives. Tamara was on her haunches in front of him, an expression of bemused satisfaction on her face. It would appear that PC Palmer, despite her stature, had acquitted herself admirably.

"Everything okay out here?" he called to them. Tamara gave him a thumbs-up. He returned to the rear sitting room where he checked over the woman. She was conscious but barely. He crossed the room and drew back the curtains. The sun was on the front of the house and so the change wasn't dramatic but he was able to look around the interior better. There was no protest from the occupant.

As his eyes adjusted to the new light, he scanned the room. He was wrong about the woman, reassessing her as little more than a girl, eighteen or nineteen at most. Tom's opinion on why the girl hadn't been roused by his presence was reinforced by what he saw on the coffee table next to the sofa. A tea light candle had consumed the wick and burned out. Beside this was a plastic straw, a cigarette lighter and a square of tin foil roughly the size of Tom's open hand. This was the telltale paraphernalia of a habitual drug user.

He picked up the foil by the corner and inspected it. Crudely shaped into a shallow bowl, the centre was caked in a dark brown residue, the remnants of the heroin that had been burned off. It was poor quality heroin. Tom had seen enough to know the difference. The process involved heating the powder until it liquified and then inhaling the steam as it subsequently evaporated. The less residue left on the foil after this process denoted the purity of the drug. This was poor, mixed with additives to lower the price or maximise the dealer's profit margin. Tom's money would be on the latter.

He looked at the girl again. She was well and truly high. They wouldn't get anything out of her any time soon. Her brown hair was pulled back from her face and tied in a ponytail. She matched the description Judith Taylor gave of the passenger in the car on Manor Road, but admittedly it was a vague description at best. In the corner of his eye he saw two uniformed officers come into view through the French doors. Danny Tice was handed to them for transport back to the station.

Tom opened the doors to the garden and met Tamara and Kerry coming to join him.

"Good take down," he said.

Kerry smiled. "No problem."

She was being modest. Danny Tice wasn't the most imposing of figures but he still dwarfed the young constable and she'd dealt with him with comparative ease. Tom gestured to the girl on the sofa behind him.

"We'd better call an ambulance for her. There's no way we can leave her here in that state."

Tamara looked past him and shook her head. "How old is she?"

Tom frowned. "Not quite young enough to be his daughter, but not far off it I'd guess."

Tamara blew out her cheeks and entered. They carefully inspected the room but they only found a small amount of powdered heroin in a small zip-lock bag on the mantelpiece above the fire.

"There's a black Ford Focus estate parked around the back," Kerry said.

That piqued Tom's curiosity.

"Any damage to it?" he asked, hearing the hopeful tone in his own voice.

"The front bumper is scuffed and hanging on with gaffer tape," she said, cocking her head to one side and raising her eyebrows.

"Is it now?" Tom said, smiling.

CHAPTER FOURTEEN

TOM ENTERED THE ROOM. Danny Tice looked up at him with a forlorn expression. He was no stranger to an interview room, no stranger to being quizzed by the police. Tom was pretty certain he'd already have his answers prepared. He just couldn't be sure which questions were going to come his way. It was likely that a man such as Danny Tice was well aware that he could be arrested for any number of different reasons. Once he'd been transported back to the station, he'd remained silent, further reinforcing Tom's opinion that the man would hold out as long as possible until he knew how firm his footing was.

Kerry Palmer was already in the room. She had done a marvellous job whilst waiting for Tom to arrive, staring straight at their suspect and unsettling Tice. He was a career criminal, petty offences in the main, and experienced but anybody can be unnerved in the right conditions. Tice was on a comedown from his last hit and his paranoia was already manifesting in his mannerisms, twitching and scratching at different places of his body. He looked almost relieved when Tom entered the room with a cup of coffee in one hand and a folder in the other. He set the cup down on the table in front of Tice, gesturing to it with a nod.

"That's for you if you want it?"

Tice sat forward and inspected the liquid. He picked up the cup and sipped at it, grimacing and putting it back down with disgust.

"I know," Tom said, pulling out a chair and sitting down. "Nothing tastes right when you're on a comedown, does it? You'll completely lose your appetite when the withdrawal symptoms kick in."

Tice sniffed hard, his red-rimmed eyes staring at Tom, but he still didn't speak. He rolled his tongue across his lower lip, which was dry and cracking. Tom sat back in his seat and folded his arms across his chest.

"You were booked in for resisting arrest and attempted assault of a police officer," Tom said. Tice's eyes drifted from him to Kerry and Tom thought he saw a glimmer of a smile form on her face but she swiftly quashed it. "But I expect you're wondering why you're here, aren't you? I can see the thoughts turning over in your head, Danny. *What do they know? How little can I get away with saying and still manage to walk out of here today?* They're all good questions. However," Tom sat forward, resting his elbows on the table before him, "you won't be going anywhere."

"Is that so?"

Tom smiled. He spoke. That was good news. Opening the folder, he took out a photograph of the electrical items that were found on Manor Road. Turning it one hundred and eighty degrees, he slid it across the table in front of Tice.

"You dumped these on Friday evening." Tom held up a hand before Tice announced a denial. "Your fingerprints are all over them. As are," he paused, glancing down at the paperwork in the folder, "Emily Slater's. Is she your girlfriend?"

Tice drew breath but didn't speak.

"No matter." Tom waved the question away. "Emily is rather unwell, suffering a nasty reaction to what the two of you took. It would appear your gear was cut with various other substances," he glanced down and made a point of tracing the following words with his index finger, "traces of cadmium, ethanol and, unsurprisingly, Mannitol. This led to pulmonary congestion and a dangerous reduction in her blood oxygen levels as well as the onset of acidosis. It would appear her kidneys and lungs couldn't compensate for the imbalance in her pH levels… Suffice it to say, she is in a serious condition."

Tom closed the folder and stared at Tice. Silence ensued for nearly a minute which felt far longer. Tice sniffed, touching the end of his nose momentarily with the back of his hand. He met Tom's eye.

"Is she going to be all right?"

The question sounded genuine.

Tom inclined his head. "She is comfortable, but I wouldn't like to be her dealer. Boy, are they in trouble. That gear could have killed her. It still might."

"I ain't a dealer!"

"It wouldn't be the first time, though would it, Danny?"

Tice scoffed, shaking his head in disgust.

"A man with your previous record coming before a judge on charges of dealing and manslaughter," Tom said. "He would be facing a lengthy spell in one of Her Majesty's hotels. Wouldn't you agree, PC Palmer?"

Kerry nodded, glancing sideways. "Not to mention the murder charge."

Tice's head snapped upright and he glared at her, raising a pointed finger. "I never murdered anyone!"

"Touched a nerve, Danny?" Tom asked. Tice glared at him but didn't speak. Tom touched the photo again. "Billy Moy's property."

"What of it?"

"You took it from his house, Danny. I'm not asking, I'm telling you that's what happened. For someone as experienced as you are, you really are short on intelligence leaving your fingerprints in the house and on the property."

Tice dropped his head into his hands, letting out a guttural snarl of frustration. Lifting his head, he sighed, holding his hands up in supplication.

"All right. What is it you want to know?"

"You admit to being in Billy's house?"

Tice nodded slowly.

"And to taking his property?"

He drew a deep breath, turning his face to the ceiling before, once again, nodding.

"Can you answer verbally for the benefit of the recording, please, Mr Tice?" Tom said, pointing to the machine recording every word of the interview.

Tice replied in a resigned, staccato tone. "Yes. I was in the house. Yes, I took the stuff. But," he said emphatically, "I did not kill Billy Moy. Nor was I present when whoever *did* kill Billy Moy, stabbed him. He was already dead when I got there."

"That's convenient."

Tice lurched quickly forward in his seat wagging a pointed finger in Tom's face, startling Kerry, but Tom was unfazed. "Believe me, Inspector Janssen, I find *nothing* about this situation convenient!"

"Okay. I'll give you a few minutes to tell me your version of events and I'll grant you a fair hearing. After that, it'll be down to the CPS to decide what we do with you," Tom said, shaking his head, "but it had better be convincing because as things stand, you're looking good for this—"

"I bloody told you he was dead before we got there."

"We? That would be you and Emily, right?" Tom said.

Tice was angry with himself for the slip. And in that moment Tom knew he was going to hold back as much as he thought he could get away with, unless Tom could keep getting under his skin.

"Yeah. Me and Emily. She was with me for the ride but she had nothing to do with it, the burglary and all that. I'll fess up to that but nothing more. I'm not a killer."

"Go on."

Tice brought his hands up, rubbing furiously at both sides of his face. It made no difference, the colour did not return to his pale complexion.

"I met Billy a while back... when I was labouring on one of the local farms."

"You?" Tom asked, surprised.

"Yeah... well, not many people around available for work these days, is there? They were paying good money, or at least better money."

"Hard work though."

He nodded. "Yeah. Must admit the idea was better than the reality." He looked glum. "Emily and me... we thought we'd get clean, sort our lives out and that." He bobbed his head, pursing his lips as he spoke. "Didn't go to plan."

"Okay, you met Billy on a job."

"Yeah, that's right. Anyway, good guy is Billy, and we got chatting and all that. I told him how hard it was to get off the gear and that, you know. We were still smoking the weed to help take the edge off. I mean, there's not a lot wrong with a bit of weed is there? But your lot," he said, looking between the two of them, "had been pretty good at breaking up the supply around that time. Prices were up and availability down."

Tom nodded. "Yeah, business has been brisk at our end. When are we talking?"

Tice's eyes narrowed as he thought about it. "The end of last summer, going into autumn, maybe?"

Tom thought about it. They had made several high-profile seizures of cannabis shipments in the county the previous year, the end results of a year-long joint investigation with the Met's Drug Squad. They certainly had disrupted the supply of recreational drugs into the region for at least two months until the chains were re-established. Such was the nature of that particular commodity, there was never a shortage of people looking to fund the supply.

"And how does this relate to Billy Moy?"

"He said he knew someone. He said he could sort me out."

"With cannabis?" Tom asked. Billy Moy was a recognised figure in the town but no one had mentioned drugs.

"Well, he came through for us. Good stuff as well, fresh as you like. It kind of went from there."

"What did?"

"Billy..." Tice spoke as if it was an obvious statement he was making, "supplying us."

Tom exchanged a look with Kerry. She appeared to find this as fanciful as he did but, Tom had to admit, Danny Tice was definitely sincere.

"Do you mean to tell us that Billy Moy supplied you with recreational drugs?"

Tice nodded. "Yes... every now and then if I couldn't score elsewhere."

Tom took a moment to think through his next question. This was an unexpected turn of events.

"What was Billy Moy supplying?"

"Weed. Nothing more."

"We've found no evidence that Billy Moy partook of recreational drugs and no evidence that he was in the business of supply—"

"Look! You asked and I told you. Right?"

Tom took a breath. "Okay, take me back to the night you burgled Billy's house. Why did you rip off a friend of yours?"

Tice shook his head. "Me and Emily... needed a score. Everyone was dry, so I called Billy on the off chance. He's always come through."

"And when was this?" Tom asked, taking notes.

Tice looked to the ceiling, rolling his tongue across the inside of his cheek. "Early last week. Monday, I think. He was busy, said he had work on, but he'd be able to see me right as he had a collection coming later in the week. He said he'd be in touch."

"I need more than that, Danny."

"Oh... what do you want to know? I hadn't heard by Wednesday afternoon and by then I was getting a bit panicky. I didn't want to be without anything because, well you know, it gets harder to cope the longer you go without. So, I rang him up and," he looked skyward again, "must have been around five, five-thirty on Wednesday. He told me he had plans and I was to come over the next day after he finished work."

"That would be Thursday, but you said—"

"Yes, Friday was when we went round. As it happens, one of the lads came through with a little smack on Thursday and the day drifted past. On Friday, I figured we would swing by his place and be sorted for the weekend. Take the edge off, you know?"

"I want you to be very clear as to when you went to the property, Danny," Tom said, fixing a stern eye on him.

"Friday, definitely. Not before."

Danny Tice may well be a drug-dependent petty criminal but Tom knew he was also pretty savvy. He was emphatically putting distance between his arrival at the house and when Billy was most likely killed.

"What did you see when you got there?"

"The house was unlocked, the front door open. I called out but didn't get an answer. So, I went inside and Billy was lying on the kitchen floor. He was already a goner."

"How can you be so sure?"

Tice waved the question away, smiling without humour. "Believe me, I've seen enough overdoses in my time to know when someone ain't coming back. Besides, the kitchen knife in his chest and the pool of claret he lay in pretty much made the case, you know. I looked around for the weed—"

"You did what?" Kerry asked, regretting it immediately, glancing sideways apologetically at Tom.

"There was nothing I could do for him."

Tom sat forward, fixing a piercing stare on him. "So, instead of trying to help your friend, your immediate reaction was to look for the drugs you were expecting to buy?"

Tice cocked his head. "Yeah, sounds pretty cold when you put it like that."

"I'll say it does, yes," Tom said.

"Look! He was dead, and I had to—" he let the comment drop, chewing his bottom lip.

"You had to what?" Tom asked. "What did you have to do?"

"No comment."

"All right, let's see if I can fill in the blanks," Tom said, picturing the scene in his mind. "You arrive at Billy's looking to pick up, but you find him dead. Rather than offer assistance, you try to satisfy your own needs first, which is what an addict tends to do most of the time anyway seeing as selfishness goes hand in glove with cravings." Tice glared at Tom but didn't speak. "And when you couldn't find what you came for, you decided to help yourself to everything you could see of value."

Tice exhaled heavily. "Yeah. That's about right."

"I understand," Tom said, nodding slowly. "And who do you think would have been willing to do Billy harm?"

"No idea. Not my concern and definitely none of my business."

"Your concern and sentiment for your friend shines through, Danny."

He inclined his head. "Pleased you can see it, Mr Janssen. Whoever had it in for Billy, it wasn't me. He was dead long before I got there. Check his mobile phone. You'll see the calls, dates and times."

"We'd love to, Danny, but Billy's phone hasn't been recovered. It wasn't with the stuff you took."

"I'd have taken it if I'd seen it. That's me, Inspector. A *druggie* who nicks stuff to feed his habit. I'll hold my hands up to that and take what comes my way, but I'm not a killer."

"Okay, for now let's say we believe your tale of unfortunate coincidences and self-deprecating analysis. Tell me about Billy. You have cast him in a very different light to everyone else we've spoken to."

Tice shrugged. "Do we really know anyone? My parents thought they knew me, bailing me out financially time after time when what they needed to do was close the door on me for good before I bled them dry."

"What's your point?"

"That if parents don't even know their own children, how do outsiders expect to know a weirdo like Billy Moy?"

"That's a curious description for a friend of yours."

"It is what it is," Tice said, sitting back and folding his arms across his chest. "He was weird. *The nutter in the woods*, Emily always called him."

"She didn't like him?"

Tice laughed. "No. She didn't want to come in whenever we went out there. She did the first few times but he always gave her the creeps."

"How so?"

Again, he shrugged. "I don't know. Looking at her weirdly, I guess. It was strange though. I always thought he might prefer men... or boys."

"Why would you say that?" Kerry asked.

"Because..." he hesitated, his brow furrowing, "I never saw him with anyone. Living out there on his own, like that. It's not normal, is it?"

"Are you saying single people aren't normal?" Kerry asked.

"No, it's not like that. You'd have to know him, spend time with him to understand."

"Why clear out his house?" Tom asked.

"Why not?"

Something in the tone of the response piqued Tom's curiosity.

"Why not? Because you are standing in a murder scene. A man like you knows the storm of activity that will come through that house when the body is discovered and yet you strip it of valuables for a quick profit, and at the same time provide us with a cracker of a suspect... in you."

Tice sneered. "Why do you think I dumped the stuff? I made a spur of the moment decision and when we left, I came to my senses. I knew what it would look like, but I was hardly going to put it all back, was I? I did the next best thing and ditched it as soon as I could."

Tom looked at Kerry and then back at Tice.

"You have come up with an interesting story, Danny. I'll give you that. You've managed to put yourself at the scene after the event, despite agreeing to meet up on the night he died – fortunately for you, you were too stoned to attend – explain why your prints are inside and all over the items taken, but you have no idea how Billy came to be stabbed, by whom or any reason as to why it may have happened. I tip my hat to you."

"It is the truth, Inspector Janssen. That's why it's plausible. Ask Emily. She'll confirm everything I said."

"I intend to do just that, Danny. One more question though. You said Billy couldn't see you on the Wednesday night because he had plans?"

"Yeah. So what?"

"What plans did Billy have?"

Tice shrugged. "He didn't say. And no, I didn't ask. Probably staying up late polishing his collection of human heads for all I know."

"All right, that'll do for now, Danny," Tom said, concluding the interview.

Tom stood up, gathering the photographs and his notes together. Danny Tice watched him for a moment, increasingly looking agitated.

"So, what happens now? Are you charging me with the burglary or what?"

Tom looked down at him.

"We will see. First, I'm going to pick over your flat and see if I can find anything of interest. I have to thank you for your honesty today."

"Thanks," Tice said, surprised.

"Of course, aside from the nuggets of truth you offered up, the rest of your story is rubbish but I'll prove that along the way—"

"Hold on a minute—"

"Why?" Tom said turning back as he made to leave. "You're staying here for as long as I can keep you. If Emily's situation worsens I'll do my best to see the CPS charge you with everything

I can think of. And that's if I can't have you charged with murder—"

"I didn't do it!" he said, lurching to his feet. For a moment Tom thought he was about to hurl himself across the table at him but it didn't happen. Tice stood there, facing off against him. The man's expression softened, his resolve waning. "I don't want to go back inside, Inspector Janssen. I'll cop a bit of time for the robbing, I know that, but *murder*... it's not me and you know it."

Tom held his gaze for a moment, then he exhaled. "You have to give me a bit more, Danny. So far, all you've given me is what we can already surmise and I know you're holding back. It's written all over your face."

Tice closed his eyes, his head sagging. "All right." He looked at the recording equipment. "But I can't put it on the tape."

"The machine is off," Tom said. "And my patience is thin, Danny."

"I wasn't just out there to score for myself," Tice said, clearly reticent. "I was scoring for some of the lads as well. You know how it works... when things are running dry, we all try to score and whoever gets a line first buys for everyone. This time, it was me."

"And?"

Tice shook his head. "I had their money, sat on it for a couple of days and when Wednesday came an opportunity came my way."

"So, the money you were going to use to buy from Billy was spent on heroin?"

He nodded. "I knew Billy would see me all right, put a lot of what he'd give me on tick, you know? But when we got out there..."

"No Billy and no weed."

"Yeah," Tice said glumly. "I panicked. I didn't know what to do. I needed to get some money to pay the guys back. If they thought I'd scored gear with their money and not paid it back, they'd do me in."

"That's not enough, Danny," Tom said, shaking his head. "Give me something useful."

"Billy wasn't a dealer... you're right about that, but he was in with some players. It didn't fit well with him and he wasn't suited to it, but he was into them for something and I reckon it was something big."

"Who are we talking about and how did he fall in with people like that?"

Tice rubbed the back of his neck, grimacing.

"Come on, Danny. Don't waste any more of my time."

"I don't know," he said. Then, reacting to Tom's dismissive expression and movement to leave, he reached across the table and grasped Tom's arm stopping him from leaving. "I'm telling you the truth, Inspector. *I don't know.* Take another look around Billy's place. You'll find your answers there, I swear."

Tom looked at his arm and Tice released his hold of him. Tom walked to the door, opening it, before looking back over his shoulder.

"Correct me if I'm wrong, Danny," Tom said, "but you dumped what you stole, so you can't have raised the cash to pay back your friends."

Tice licked the exterior of his lower lip, looking around the room. "Yeah. To be fair, you're doing me a favour. I'm safer locked up in here right now."

CHAPTER FIFTEEN

THE RIDE WAS uncomfortable as the car bounced along the dirt track. The verges to both the left and right were overgrown, the vegetation encroaching on either side of them, but Tom noted the growth was limited much as an overhanging tree is often shaped by the passage of traffic beneath it. This track had been used frequently by several vehicles. He pulled up to a rusting metal, five-bar gate. It was shut but he could see it wasn't locked.

"Is this it?" Kerry asked and Tom pulled the map from the door bin beside him and examined it. The structures were clearly marked and the track petered out just past the gate. He nodded and Kerry climbed out to open it. Tom pulled through and once clear of the tall hedgerow to either side, the barn came into view off to their right.

The track branched off to the old barn, a dilapidated brick building with Dutch gables. Where there would once have been a thatched roof, the building was now lined in corrugated metal sheeting. Several of the panels had slipped out of place or been torn away by storms exposing the rafters to the elements. Tom parked the car and they got out, looking around.

As he had seen from the Ordnance Survey map the largest barn was part of a small complex of outbuildings set out in a horseshoe arrangement, springing from both ends of the main structure. The surrounding pasture lands, too small to farm but good for grazing, were left fallow, looking as if they hadn't been occupied in some time. The boundaries of the Moy land were visible in the distance marked by damaged fencing, distinctive hedgerows or mature trees.

"Last one," Tom said, struggling to fold the map in the stiff breeze and tucking it into his coat pocket.

Following the conclusion of the interview with Danny Tice, they decided to look into Tice's comments and set about determining where the Moys' land began and ended. It quickly became clear that what was once a smallholding of significant note had dwindled over successive years as parts of the family business were packaged up and sold off. The Land Registry confirmed the change of titles and the new owners were often local farmers who purchased land adjoining their own and at the market rates. The reduction in land appeared to accelerate shortly after the death of Maureen Moy, but dramatically reduced four years later.

There hadn't been any sales in the previous three years. However, a quick scan of the business's filed financial accounts in the previous two years showed a reduction in tenanted income from land leased to tenant farmers which had been a constant for the Moys since the death of Arnold, Maureen's husband and father to Billy and Simon. The profit generated however had increased in the same period. Associated costs had also increased whereas the land itself appeared far more profitable than it had done previously, and from a layman's eye it was without good reason.

Something didn't add up.

The cart access to the largest barn was open and they headed for it.

"What are we expecting to find?" Kerry asked.

"Answers," Tom said, entering.

The sky was visible through the roof but the interior was still largely dry. Tom stopped and looked around. The ground at his feet was littered with throwaway pieces of paper, some torn or screwed into a ball but all randomly discarded. At the centre of the barn rectangular hay bales had been stacked two high and arranged in a crude circle. Straw was strewn across the floor within it. Tom dropped to his haunches and picked up the nearest slip of paper as the breeze carrying through the open barn doors threatened to blow it away from him.

Unfurling the paper in his hand, he found a handwritten scrawl that simply read $T - £50 - R4$. He stood up, passing the paper to Kerry. As she read it herself, he walked into the circle, scanning the floor. The straw was disturbed in places, the earth beneath disturbed as if it had been scuffed by dragging feet. At one point, Tom knelt to inspect a discolouration on the ground. The straw was darkening as it decomposed but at this point a darker shade, roughly a hand span in diameter, was clearly visible clinging to both straw and staining the concrete floor beneath.

"What is this?" Kerry asked, holding the paper up as she came alongside him.

Tom glanced up at her before standing, his eyes sweeping the barn. "Are you a betting person, Constable Palmer?"

She shook her head.

"Well, that is a betting slip," he said, indicating it in her hand. "Someone was banking on whoever T is putting someone down in the fourth."

Kerry followed his gaze around the barn. A barn this size could comfortably accommodate upwards of a hundred people, probably more if the organisers so desired.

"Boxing?"

Tom nodded. "Bare-knuckle maybe. I've not heard of dogfighting going on around these parts... and it's a little too open for it," he said, reassessing the bales. "More likely an evening of bouts."

Kerry was visibly disgusted. "Ugh... Blood sports really aren't my thing. Who would set this kind of thing up? Billy Moy doesn't seem capable."

"I doubt Billy would," Tom said, shaking his head. "But he'd have to know about it. It's the perfect location, remote, space for a lot of people to come and go without being seen in the dead of night. Ideal."

"So you think there's merit in what Danny Tice had to say?"

Tom cocked his head. "The problem with addicts, be it drink, drugs or whatever, is you can't trust a word they say. They're selfish, devious, manipulative... and can be incredibly convincing when it suits. Even when they are telling you the truth there is every chance they are also lying. After all, an addict is not only able to lie about what they've done, are doing or plan to do, they are also more than happy to lie to themselves. Bearing that in mind, how easily do you think they'll find it to lie to you?"

"There speaks the voice of experience."

Tom smiled. Kerry seemed worried she'd overstepped the mark, making a move to apologise. He stopped her.

"Yes. I might know a little bit about it."

"Do we trust Tice then? With his suggestion that Billy was in with – how did he put it – players?"

"As I said, there's always a grain of truth in the stories of a man like Danny Tice. He might be a low-life but did you get the impression he was a killer?"

If Kerry thought she was being tested then it didn't bother her. She shook her head. "No. I wouldn't say so. Quite the opposite."

"Me too."

"Not that he wouldn't sell his mother for the price of a wrap if needed," she said, with a half-smile.

Tom grinned. "I'd agree with you there too. Come on, let's have a nose about the other buildings."

They moved through the barn and on into the cobbled yard. The other buildings were in a similar state of repair, all bar one, a single-storey building to their left. The roof of this building had been repaired in places and the ventilation slits in the side walls were blocked from the interior side. Tom gestured towards it and they crossed the yard. The wind rattled across the open ground and they were pleased to reach the barn and step into the lee.

There was only one entrance door, the others having been blocked off. The door was stiff, the wood having swollen within the frame, but with a bit of effort and Tom's strength, it opened inwards. Tom's first thought that this outbuilding was far better maintained than the others was clear as soon as they entered. The interior was shrouded in complete darkness. There was no light slipping through from the outside other than from the open door.

Kerry pointed to several cables laid across the floor, black and roughly three quarters of an inch thick. It was an armoured power cable, the type usually buried in the ground when extending a domestic supply to an outbuilding but one requiring a large degree of load.

"Can you smell that?" Kerry asked. He could. It was sweet, aromatic and very distinctive. Tom looked around and found a light switch. He flicked it and the sound of two fluorescent tubes above them sparking into life carried. Where they stood, Tom could see the cables trailing across the floor and up the interior wall separating the room they were in from the next and disappearing into the rafters. The door to the next room was closed and Tom opened it. Here he found another set of light switches, although these were not mounted to an interior wall and hung precariously free, dangling from the cable dropping down from above.

Reasonably happy that he wasn't likely to be electrocuted by touching them, he flicked the first two on and a series of lights flickered into action, a process repeated for the remaining length of the building, easily thirty metres to the gable end.

"Well, I'll be damned," Kerry said quietly.

The place had been emptied, and recently judging by the detritus that was on the floor. In their haste, they'd harvested as much as they could but remnants still remained. The walls of the building were lined with rigid insulation board, the silver-foil lining reflecting the glare of dozens of UV lamps back at them. Tom looked up where the rafters were infilled with the same material, held in place with makeshift battens. Cables hung unfixed from the rafters. Rigid aluminium ducting was strung throughout the rafter and disappeared through an opening punched through the exterior wall. Tom knew that was to aid ventilation. Portable heaters were positioned throughout the building, many also strung from above in between the lights.

It was an electrical health and safety nightmare. Not that whoever did this was even remotely interested in the safety of those using the facility. Plastic sheeting lined the floor and upon it were set out multiple rows of seed beds. The whole building was set up as an industrial-sized hydroponics bay. Although the crop had been cleared out, and rapidly by the look of it, the smell of cannabis still lingered. It was impossible to shift.

Tom exhaled slowly. "It looks like we found out where Billy got the weed from."

"What's with all the UV lights?"

Tom glanced up at the nearest row of them. "The ultraviolet light increases the levels of THC in the plant, the elements of it that get you stoned."

"Do you think he was running all of this... Billy?" she asked.

Tom dropped to his haunches and picked up a broken stem of a plant at his feet. There were a half-dozen leaves still attached. This was a young plant, yet to flower. He plucked one of the leaves and rolled it between thumb and forefinger. It was still pliable. He shook his head.

"Not unless he found his way back from the dead to harvest his final crop, no. Someone has been through here," he said, pursing his lips. "And they did so in a hurry."

CHAPTER SIXTEEN

CASSIE SLIPPED her arm through her coat and turned as she heard Tom and Kerry enter ops behind her.

"Off somewhere?" he asked her.

"We've had a call from one of the local hoteliers in Hunstanton, a guest matching the description of Balodis has been staying there recently; at the *Admiral Nelson Hotel*. He dropped his key into reception a few days ago and they don't think he's been back. We're just going over there now. How did you get on exploring Moy's farm?"

Tom hung up his coat. "It looks like Danny Tice was telling us the truth, partially at least. There was an established cannabis-growing operation going on in one of the outbuildings along with evidence of larger events in the same location."

"Larger events?" Cassie asked. "Like what?"

Tom caught Eric's attention. "Eric, do you know if Rory still has his finger in illegal gambling?"

Eric joined them. "McInally?" Tom nodded.

"Remind me, who's Rory McInally?" Cassie asked. The name didn't ring a bell and she was confident they'd not crossed paths, although she hadn't been in the area long.

"Rory is an established figure in the community," Tom said.

"The traveller community," Eric said.

"Urgh... pikies," Cassie said, her upper lip curling as she spoke.

"I don't think you can make assumptions about an entire community like that—"

"I beg to differ, Eric, I beg to differ," Cassie said.

Eric ignored her comment. "McInally used to tip his hat to all sorts of endeavours back in the day; off-books gambling, hare coursing... even supplying security to local businesses at one time which was ironic. That type of thing."

"Drugs?" Tom asked.

Eric shook his head. "Not that I recall. He was always a bit old school about that type of thing. At least, that's what he always said. Not his cup of tea."

"Ah," Cassie said. "Why haven't I come across him?"

"He's settled down a bit these days," Eric said to her before looking at Tom. "As far as I know he's still living out on that site between Fring and Sedgeford."

"Thanks, I'll have a word."

Tom didn't have any further questions so Cassie tapped Eric on the arm and gestured for them to make a move. The drive to the hotel didn't take long and it was largely made in silence. Eric was still preoccupied and it was clear to her what was on his mind. They parked directly outside the hotel, pulling the car up onto the pavement. Eric glanced at Cassie.

"There's a car park at the rear," he said, indicating along the road to the next turning. "You take that left and there's an access road—"

"We'll not be long," she said cheerily, gently elbowing his arm and getting out. She heard him sigh as he followed. "Besides, what are they going to do, call the police? We're already here."

Eric shook his head at her. He was such a stickler for the rules. It wasn't the first time he'd pulled her up on this sort of thing. It must be hard living in a world where you're constrained by adhering to every rule and regulation.

"It must be exhausting for you, Eric."

"What is?"

"Being such a nice bloke all the time. Don't you ever want to just throw off the shackles and live a little?"

He looked confused.

"You know, stay out late, drink too much... not pay a bill on time?" She realised belatedly that the last one was a little too on topic, Eric's eyes lowered to the floor. "Sorry, Eric. I didn't think. Have you managed to speak to Becca about it yet?"

He shook his head. "Not quite. She was asking again last night but I ducked the conversation... went to bed early, saying I had a headache."

"Come on, let's go and take a look inside. It'll take your mind off it."

The Admiral Nelson Hotel was part of a terrace of old Victorian townhouses, two of which had been knocked through to form one large premises. There was an outdoor seating area at the front set behind a low wall separating it from the pavement and the road. The building was stylish with bay-fronted ground and first-floor windows. The upper floors would have a great view of the sea beyond the leisure buildings on the other side of the street.

The lady at reception called through to the manager and he ushered them away from the desk in the narrow entrance hall and deeper into the building.

"Mr Balodis checked in ten days ago," the manager, Colin Peters, said, checking past them to ensure no one could hear them. He looked very apprehensive.

"Is something wrong, Mr Peters?" Cassie asked.

"No, no, not at all. Why do you ask?"

Cassie shook her head, dismissing the question. She took out a picture of him provided by Interpol and handed it to the manager. "Is this your guest?"

He nodded emphatically. "Absolutely, yes."

"How long did he book for?" she asked, tucking the picture back inside her pocket.

"A fortnight, this time."

"*This time*? Has he been here before?"

"Oh, yes. Mr Balodis has been a frequent visitor in the past... um..." his face fixed in concentration, "eight months or so. Yes, I think this is his third stay with us. He usually stays for a few days. On this occasion it was much longer."

"Do you know why he was here?"

Peters looked thoughtful. "I remember I asked him once, but he was a little vague. I think he was uncomfortable with the question. I know I was."

Cassie trained her eye on him and he looked awkward. "Why would you say that?"

He shook his head. "I don't know. H–He had a look about him. I thought I shouldn't ask again, so I didn't."

"What type of a guest was he?"

"Perfect, I would say," Peters said, smiling. "He was never any trouble, rarely ate at the hotel other than at breakfast and even then we hardly ever saw him. He was a trouble-free guest."

"You said he was here before. How often?"

"A couple of nights every six weeks or so, maybe a little longer. Bookings like his are a bit tricky in the off season, but as I say, he was an easy guest to have."

"Tricky? In what way?"

"Well, we don't have a lot of business through the winter as you can imagine. We are busy March through September, sometimes a little later if we have an Indian summer. The hotel is rather large and we can't keep it fully staffed for what little trade we see, so it pretty much comes down to my wife and me and a couple of cleaners to keep things ticking over. Winter bookings can be a bit of a pain in that way. And, let's face it, we're not getting any younger."

A lady appeared at the end of the corridor, attracting his attention.

"This is my wife, Audrey," he said, excusing himself and stepping away from them.

"Could we see the room?" Cassie asked.

"Yes, yes, of course." Peters returned and handed her a room key. He indicated the stairs behind them. "First floor. Room seven. I'll join you in a moment."

Cassie followed Eric to the stairs, briefly overhearing the woman speak in a hushed voice as her husband approached. *The agent wants to bring someone around this evening.*

"That'll explain why he's nervous," she said mounting the stairs behind Eric.

"I noticed that too. Why?"

"It looks like this place is up for sale. Having the police crawling all over it because one of the guests was murdered probably wouldn't increase the saleability."

Eric chuckled and took out his mobile phone. A quick search of the internet confirmed Cassie's suspicions. He held the screen up to face her as they came before the door to room seven. "It certainly wouldn't convey quaint Victorian charm, would it?" he said, tilting his head at the phone. Cassie looked at the listing on the property site.

"Wow. Not cheap is it?"

"I'll bet it makes a fortune in peak season."

Cassie had to agree. The forthcoming summer would be only her second since she relocated to Norfolk at Tamara Greave's request and she'd been stunned by how much the population increases once the good weather kicks in. The population of the county seemed to more than double in the summer months. She slipped the key into the lock, noting the *Do Not Disturb* sign hanging from the handle. *A guest who doesn't require housekeeping must be profitable as well,* she thought.

The hotel room reflected the fact that housekeeping hadn't been in for a while. The bed was unmade and clothes were lying across an occasional chair in the corner as well as the small two-seater sofa set out under the bay window overlooking the front. Cassie gestured for Eric to explore the ensuite as she picked her way across the room, careful not to disturb anything, and stood in the bay. The sun was breaking through the clouds and cast a glow across the water. In the distance the sky was less clear with dark clouds gathering, and what she figured was a deluge of rain drifting across the horizon.

Turning her attention back to the room, she cast a critical eye over what she could see. They had no reason to believe this was a crime scene but until they knew where Balodis met his end, this place couldn't be ruled out. However, there was no indication of anything untoward taking place in this room. It was messy but no more so than one might expect. Nothing was damaged or appeared out of place. A quick inspection of the walls and carpets saw no sign of blood or bodily fluids and, wherever Balodis was when he was struck in the head, there would almost certainly be blood. The carpets here were a pale cream colour, good quality, thick and shaggy, the sort of material that would absorb blood in such a way as to be a forensic officer's dream.

Eric returned from the ensuite.

"Anything interesting?" she asked.

"Towels on the floor and they're still a little damp. There are also women's toiletries in the shower. He's not been staying here alone."

"You're sure they're a woman's?"

Eric cocked his head. "Unless he was into painting his nails, I would say so, yeah."

"We'll have to ask about that."

Cassie plucked a tissue from a box on the bedside table, using it to avoid leaving her fingerprints as she eased the drawer of the unit open. It was empty. Moving to the wardrobe, she opened the door. Inside she found several shirts on hangers along with other clothing folded neatly on the shelving next to the rail. A small suitcase was at the base of the wardrobe lying on its back and it was unzipped. She knelt and lifted the lid. It was also empty.

Patting the exterior, she felt something in the zip pocket on the front. She carefully opened it and found a passport belonging to Balodis. There was also a bum bag that she thought at first glance was padded but unzipping it, she found it stuffed with cash. She angled it so Eric could see. There must have been thousands of pounds in a mixture of denominations.

"There you go, Eric," Cassie said, looking up at him, "this is your honeymoon money sorted."

Eric shook his head. He knew she was joking.

"Seriously, though. What are you going to do about your predicament?"

He was about to answer when someone knocked on the door and entered behind them.

"Hello."

It was the hotel manager, Colin Peters. He came to hover around them, seemingly unsure of how he should behave.

"Mr Peters, who checked in with Mr Balodis?"

The man frowned. "No one. It was just him."

Something in his expression irked Cassie but she couldn't pinpoint what it was. He had no reason to withhold information as far as she knew.

"You're certain of that?"

He nodded. Cassie walked into the ensuite, scanning the toiletries to find what Eric described, returning with a small bottle of nail varnish remover. She held it up to him. Peters shifted his weight between his feet.

"Absolutely certain?" she asked again with a knowing look.

Peters looked over his shoulder, why she didn't know because they were alone. He lowered his voice to a conspiratorial whisper. "We do have a policy of only allowing named visitors to stay in our rooms. But my wife..."

"But?"

"Well, I like to be discreet," Peters said, avoiding her gaze.

"I'll remind you that this is a murder investigation, Mr Peters. We don't really have time for your, or your wife's, delicate sensibilities."

"If it was only me, then I tend to turn a blind eye. I mean, Mr Balodis is – was – a valued customer."

"Always the same girl?"

Peters nodded.

"Do you know her name?"

"Not for certain, no," he said, his eyes darting between them. "I think I heard him call her Nina once. I think it was Nina anyway. His accent was very thick."

Cassie took another picture from her pocket, an enlarged copy of Sasha Kalnina's passport photograph, and passed it to him. "Is this her?"

Peters examined the photograph sternly. After a moment, he handed the picture back. "Possibly."

"Possibly?"

He shrugged apologetically. "Yes, it might be her. She looks a bit like that, only that's a brunette and this woman was blonde."

"Naturally blonde or dyed?"

He blew out his cheeks, shaking his head. "I don't know... maybe."

"Okay, what about her. How often did she stay?"

"I don't know." He must have sensed her frustration because he continued before she could respond, speaking at pace. "She was here every time he was, b–but I don't know if she always stayed. Sometimes I saw them meet outside and they left together, sort of."

"Sort of?"

"She was often nervous. I figured she was the anxious sort."

"What might she be nervous of, do you think?"

He shook his head. "I honestly don't know. I thought maybe she was... you know... one of *those* girls."

"One of what girls?"

Peters glanced over his shoulder again before answering. "You know, *a lady of the night*?" He tapped the end of his nose with his forefinger.

"Oh, I see. You think he was seeing a prostitute in your hotel?"

Peters was aghast, his lips parting in horror as he looked to the corridor, fearful someone may have heard. He gestured with both hands to Cassie, silently imploring her to lower her voice. She leaned in towards him fractionally, smiling and nodding. "So, what makes you think she was a sex worker?"

Peters seemed encouraged that Cassie was following his lead. He also leaned in, whispering, "Looked the type, you know? Short skirts and make-up."

Cassie nodded vigorously. "Yes, I know the sort. Was she attractive then?"

"Yes, very," Peters said smiling.

Cassie righted herself, speaking loudly, "Are you in the habit of allowing sex workers in your hotel?"

A guest happened past at that very moment, glancing in at them. Peters put both his hands up in horror but said nothing.

"I shouldn't worry, Mr Peters. You never know, it might make your hotel more appealing on the open market. Tell me, have you seen the woman here recently." He stood staring at her, open mouthed. "Mr Peters? Have you seen her recently?"

"Um... yes. She was here last week, I think." He shook his head. "She didn't stay though. Not here, not in my hotel."

Who he was talking to, Cassie couldn't say.

"What about in the last few days?"

"No, definitely not."

Cassie looked around. "How long did Balodis book the room for?"

"Two weeks. He paid in advance, which he always did."

"Is that normal?"

"No, not at all, but he insisted, every time. I think that was what he was used to. He was due to check out in a couple of days."

"Good, you won't mind leaving his room as it is then."

"But I thought you said he was dead."

"He is, very much so, Mr Peters." She took out a contact card and handed it to him. "I want you to leave the room as it is and continue to act as if your guest is still here."

"What is the point of that?"

She pointed to the card in his hand. "And if you see this woman again, or if anyone asks after him in person or over the telephone, I want you to call me straight away on that number. Day or night. Do you understand?"

"Now look, I'm not a spy or—"

"We're just looking for a bit of cooperation, Mr Peters. The alternative is we brief the press about how our murder victim frequented quality establishments with prostitutes. It will be less helpful to us but I dare say they will—"

"I'll be more than happy to help, Detective Sergeant. Absolutely, you can count on me."

Cassie smiled warmly at him. "Excellent. Now, we just need a minute in private."

Peters smiled nervously and backed out of the room, pulling the door to behind him.

"You were a bit hard on him, don't you think?" Eric asked.

She shrugged. "If you say so. Makes me wonder how he knows what a sex worker looks like?"

"What does a sex worker look like anyway?"

"Short skirt and make-up, apparently," Cassie said.

Eric smiled, looking around. "Are we really going to leave everything as it is?"

"I think so. At least for a couple of days. The hotel owners can't really complain as Peters already has his money and we haven't put the victim's name out in the press yet, so—"

"You really think she might come back here?"

"If she doesn't know he's dead, yeah, why not? He had her passport, so if she wants to leave the country she'll have to come back looking for it."

"Good point. We've got no record of her registered in the UK, though," Eric said. "So, if Peters is right, and she isn't staying with him, and therefore unlikely to be travelling with him... what's he doing holding her passport?"

Cassie tilted her head to one side, striking a thoughtful pose. "You've got me there, Eric. I'd love to ask her. Do you have an evidence bag?"

"In the car, why?"

"I'm happy to leave everything as it is but there's no way I'm leaving the cash here with nosey-parker downstairs."

Eric grinned.

He turned to leave and she called him back. "Eric, your honeymoon money—"

"Oh, can you leave it alone please—"

She held her hand up to silence him. "I'll lend it to you."

"What?"

"The money." She shrugged. "I've got it sitting in the bank doing nothing... so, I'll lend it to you."

Eric's lips parted and she could see the relief in his expression before it faded. "But... the plan is gone. I missed the deadline for payment and they kept the deposit."

"Blimey, Eric. Airbnb, last minute bookings... whatever. You'll find something suitable. It'll be okay."

For a moment she thought he looked about ready to cry.

"But I think you need to speak to your wife... get it all out there. Getting your marriage off and running on the back of a lie isn't a good start."

He nodded. "Yeah, you're right."

"I'll even look after little George for you if you want to take Becca out for the evening, do the surprise right?"

"You? A baby?"

She laughed, waving away his concern. "I am an aunt, you know? I do have some experience around children and I am considered to be their favourite aunt."

"Yes, I forgot your sister had kids. How many aunts are you competing with?"

Cassie frowned. "True, I am the only one, so I win by default, but it still counts, right?"

"Yes, I guess it does." She turned away to pick up the bum bag. "Cass?"

She looked up at him.

"Thanks."

"Aye, no problem," she said. He smiled. "But you owe me... and more than just a few grand," she said with a wink. He laughed, nodded, and left with a spring in his step. Now all she had to do was think of a way to explain to Lauren that their new bathroom would have to wait a few more months.

CHAPTER SEVENTEEN

TOM JANSSEN DIALLED Alice's mobile whilst sipping at a cup of tea and reading through the notes of the forensic report compiled from Billy Moy's home. As expected, it left him with more questions than answers. Alice picked up.

"Hey, it's me," he said, putting the report down on his desk and focussing on her. "I just thought I'd see how your day was going."

"Not quite as planned," she said. "Mum called first thing."

He heard an element of frustration in her tone but there was something else as well. Was it concern?

"Oh, yes, you said she'd spoken to you about something. We never got around to talking about it."

"Yes, and there's more—" he heard a door open in the background and Russell, Saffy's dog, bark. It was an odd sound, as if he was distressed. Then Saffy herself called.

"Mum! He's been sick again."

Alice sighed.

"What's up with the dog?" Tom asked.

"He's been puking today. This will be the third time," she said, before angling the receiver away from her mouth. Her voice was muffled. "It's okay, darling. Just leave it and I'll take care of it in a minute." She came back to Tom. "I don't know what's wrong with him. He barely touched his food this morning. Do you think he might have a bug?"

"More likely he's been eating random plants in the garden again," he said. "You remember that weird berry bush he kept stripping back. It's a wonder he didn't die back then."

"Oh, don't say that."

Tom felt bad. "I'm sure it'll turn out to be an upset stomach, like you said. Is he drinking?"

"A little."

"That's good. If he isn't better later then we can take him to the vet's tomorrow. If he gets any worse, maybe we'll have to give the out-of-hours vet a call." Hearing Saffy in the background reminded him of something. "I thought Saffy was going to your mum's today?"

"That's why she called. She's not well, had to cry off."

"Again?"

"That's just it, Tom." Alice fell silent and he could tell she was on the move, closing the door to the kitchen. That worried him.

"What's going on?"

"Mum... Mum said she's not just feeling bad. She's really ill, Tom. They are sending her for tests."

He could hear the fear in her voice.

"What kind of tests?"

"She's going in for an ERCP so they can take a look at her small intestine."

"What's that for?" He didn't know but it didn't sound good. Alice stopped talking and Tom waited, the silence hanging thick on the line.

"It's where they put a camera down your throat..." she took a deep breath and he could visualise her steadying herself, he knew she was close to tears, "... and look for narrowing or blockages. In Mum's case, they are trying to see signs of... they'll take a biopsy at the same time—"

"What is it they think she has?"

"Seemingly, she's been showing signs for a while but... she didn't want to worry us. Apparently, they've already found the markers and..." her voice momentarily cracked "the X-rays show a tumour, so they're... um..."

"I'm so sorry," Tom said, Alice choking back tears. He wasn't sure whether to ask but felt he had to, "What's the prognosis, do we know?"

"No, not yet."

Tom exhaled deeply. "I guess that's why she's been rowing back on the childcare recently. Why didn't she say?"

"That's Mum," Alice said with no hint of anger in her voice. Tom looked up to see Kerry Palmer standing at the entrance to his office, waiting expectantly. She silently mouthed, "Shall I come back?" Tom held up his hand, asking her to wait. He wanted to go home, to be with Alice but he knew he couldn't. Not yet at least.

"Alice, I have to—"

"I know, don't worry," she said. "I'll be all right. It's just a bit of a shock, you know. I haven't got any more details, Mum was pretty vague when she called earlier."

"Do you want to go round to hers?"

"No... well, yes, but she's asked me not to. She's having a bad day and I think she's worried about the procedure tomorrow."

"Okay. Listen," he glanced at his watch, "I'll be home as soon as I can get away. All right?" She didn't say anything but he knew she was nodding and biting her lip. "I love you," he said, seeing Kerry avert her gaze from him in the corner of his eye, looking awkward.

"I love you too," Alice said, hanging up.

He put the mobile down on his desk, annoyed with himself for his inability to say something more useful. He looked up at Kerry, realising he had no idea how long she'd been standing there. If she heard anything, she acted as if she hadn't.

"What have you got, Kerry?"

"Sir, I've been looking into Simon Moy a bit further, you know, seeing as you noticed his arrears while we were there?" He nodded. She stepped into his office. "Well, I did the usual, financial checks, that sort of thing, and looked into any court documentation with Simon Moy attached. Two months ago, a judge issued a *suspended possession order* against his home."

"What is that?"

"It is where the mortgage lender initiates the repossession protocols but rather than issuing the sanction of repossession, the judge has given them time to sell the property. It usually only happens where the proceeds of the sale will wipe out the monies owing inclusive of any arrears or interest."

Tom sat back in his chair. "Simon Moy is in more trouble than I thought. No 'for sale' board outside the house, though."

Kerry shrugged. "Maybe they want to keep it away from the neighbours? Some people are funny about that sort of thing."

"True. I sense you have more?"

She smiled. "I do, yes. You remember looking at Simon's car in the garage?"

"Yes, of course."

"Well, he didn't tell us he had a second car in the household, did he? A Toyota Avensis estate car." Tom met her eye, intrigued. "Black... and conspicuously absent the day we called around." Tom went to speak but she held up her hand. "And who do you think accepted a caution for affray this time last year following an altercation in Dereham high street? None other than Simon Moy." She stepped forward and placed a printed sheet of paper in front of him.

"Now that is interesting. Who was he scrapping with?" Tom asked, scanning the document.

"A man called Charlie Barnes."

The name meant nothing to Tom. He looked up at her quizzically.

"A local man, he has a history with us. Petty things, a few arrests for possession, two convictions for assault and one acquittal in a case of fraud three years ago."

"Do we know where he is now?"

Kerry checked her notes, shaking her head. "No, nothing current."

"Why would Simon Moy be fighting with someone like that?"

"The arresting officers and nearby witnesses stated that Barnes was the initial aggressor but, following a stern exchange of words, it was Simon who threw the first punch. Barnes refused to offer comment when questioned and both men were cautioned and released later that day."

"I think we need to speak to Simon Moy again, don't you?" Kerry nodded. "Give him a call and ask him if he wouldn't mind dropping in for a chat first thing tomorrow morning. I imagine an interview room might spook him enough to open up a bit."

"What if he doesn't want to come?"

"Then tell him we'll issue a warrant for his arrest, but that we'd rather he came in voluntarily. Otherwise the press will have a field day with it. Should do the trick."

"Why tomorrow and not today?"

"Can you get me the contact details of the lad at the supermarket?" Tom said, not answering the question. "The one who saw the altercation in the car park between Billy Moy and the couple."

"Yes, of course." Kerry looked thoughtful. "May I ask why? Do you think it could have been Simon Moy and his wife after all?"

"A couple, a man of similar size and build to Billy, driving a black car. A black, Japanese car at that. Yes, I think it's possible. The lad that was working at the time may not have paid as much attention as we'd have liked, but he's had a bit of time to think about it since we last spoke to him. Maybe he'll remember a few more details, something that could be useful to us."

Tom noticed Tamara Greave enter the ops room and make a beeline for his office. He gestured for Kerry to crack on. As she reached the door he called to her and she turned. "Well done, Kerry. Very good work today."

She smiled, flushing slightly. "I hope it all works out," she said. He cocked his head slightly. She suddenly looked concerned, as if she'd said something wrong. "Sorry. It's just I overheard. Your call, before. I hope your friend is okay."

"Alice's mum," Tom said. Kerry smiled again, bobbing her head. "And thank you. I hope so too."

Tamara and Kerry passed each other at the threshold, Kerry stepping aside and acknowledging the DCI as she passed. "Ma'am."

Tamara smiled at her and closed the door, turning to Tom. "Right, where are we? The chief superintendent is on my back something chronic over these two cases. He knows we are a strong team, but we're not superhuman!"

Tom laughed, the humour dissipating quickly. She looked at him with a look of consternation. "That's not a positive face," she said. "I want positives, Thomas... I need positives," she said, sinking into the chair opposite him.

"Nothing to worry about," he said. "I just spoke to Alice. Her mum isn't well, that's all."

"Ah, serious?"

"Could be, yes."

"Sorry to hear that. How's Alice doing?"

He looked glum. "Pretty well I think. Although, the dog puking isn't making her day any easier."

"Well, Alice's mum aside, I'll happily swap your vomiting dog for my mum and dad."

Tom's brow creased. "What have they done this time?"

She shook her head. "I don't know... nothing, yet, but something's brewing and I fear I will be the last to know as usual."

Tom shot a half-smile her way. "Never a dull moment with Francesca, is there?"

"So, where are we?" she asked, sitting upright and changing the subject.

"Kerry is going to bring Simon Moy in for a more formal chat," he said. "His financial arrears are worse than we originally thought. He also has another car, a black estate that he neglected to mention when we dropped by his place."

Tamara thought about it for a moment. "You think he might be desperate enough to go to his brother for money? They haven't been in touch for years."

Tom shrugged. "So he says, but desperate times call for desperate measures. He was in the process of losing his home. I don't know about you, but I'd willingly sacrifice a little pride and dignity if the alternative was losing everything I had."

"Fair enough... but murder?"

"Cautioned for affray last year, apparently."

Tamara pursed her lips. "Okay, sounds good. Give him a squeeze and see what comes out. Anything else?"

"I've had the forensics report back and I've been going through what they found burning in the yard."

"And?"

"Photographs. Within the remnants were pictures of people but nowhere near enough to be identifiable. All of which explains why we didn't find images in the dark room or anywhere else in the property, aside from some old family albums tucked away in a bookcase in one of the bedrooms. They were family shots though, the boys when they were little, both parents present. I wonder if it was also Arnold Moy's hobby – photography – as the forensics team reckon a lot of the liquids, pegs and so on were decades old."

"So it might not have been Billy at all? Taking pictures, I mean?"

"If that's the case, why burn them now?" Tom said. Tamara shrugged to signify she didn't have an answer. "However, all the kit that Danny Tice admits to lifting from Billy's house has been catalogued and examined. There were several cameras, both vintage – i.e. film – and a digital camera. The latter they say is reasonably new, perhaps three or four years old, which infers it is Billy's, seeing as his father was dead long before that."

"So, they could be Billy's snaps," Tamara said. Tom agreed. "The incineration could be coincidence."

"Can't rule it out." Tom picked up the report in front of him, refreshing the details in his mind. "The laptop that was recovered was too badly damaged to start up but technical services are confident they'll be able to retrieve much of the data stored on the hard drive. Hopefully, Billy spent a bit of time using it."

"I thought he was supposed to be a recluse? Doesn't that mean spending time online would be unusual for him?"

Tom shrugged. "Or the complete opposite. Maybe he preferred the digital world to the real world. After all, you can be whoever you like sitting behind a keyboard and one thing is for certain, what people thought Billy Moy was all about appears to be very different to what we've seen so far."

"What about the Balodis murder?" Tamara asked. "Are Cassie and Eric on top of it?"

Through the window of the door, Tom saw Cassie and Eric enter the ops room, Cassie with a face like thunder. "They've got a lead on where he was staying in Hunstanton." He nodded towards them. "Let's ask them."

They both left Tom's office just in time to hear Cassie greet Kerry's hello with a grunt. Tom caught Eric's eye, indicating Cassie. "What's up?"

Eric grinned. "Don't mind her, she's just grumpy because she got a parking ticket."

Cassie spun in her seat, glaring at Tom and Tamara. "Twenty minutes! That's how long we were there, twenty bloody minutes. You'd think they had nothing better to do."

"Oh dear," Tamara said with mock sincerity, trying hard not to smile.

"Seriously. Twenty, maybe thirty minutes. I swear traffic wardens are just irritated because they failed the entrance exam for the police." Cassie looked around, checking if she had an audience. She did. "They're like dentists, couldn't handle a full medical degree and just took the chapters of the book dealing with teeth and dropped out early!"

Eric placed a reassuring hand on her shoulder. "If you pay within thirty days they'll halve the fine—"

She snatched her shoulder away from him. "Yes, thank you very much, Eric. I am well aware that the extortion is limited if I roll over."

"You were bang to rights, though," Eric said, still smiling.

"Something that does not make it any easier for me," she said, raising her eyebrows.

Tamara cleared her throat. "Okay, aside from minor parking infringements, how did you get on?"

"Well, I think." Cassie looked at Eric and he nodded his agreement. "We found several thousand pounds in used notes and there were signs that a woman has been staying there with him." Eric made an unnatural sound, drawing her eyes to him. "Although, as Eric is right to point out, the hotel owner claims he was staying there alone. Under a bit of pressure, he did acknowledge that, perhaps, Mr Balodis was partaking of time with a sex worker. He strenuously denied she ever stayed at the hotel."

"Could that woman have been Sasha Kalnina?" Tamara asked.

Cassie raised her eyebrows, glancing sideways at Eric before answering. "Hair colour was different to the passport but she could have changed it since it was issued, but the hotelier couldn't confirm it."

"Start canvassing the known local sex workers, then," Tamara said.

"We've only the hotel owner's opinion to go on," Cassie said. "I'd put money on it being Sasha."

"Well, if she's not staying with him all the time, she is staying somewhere. Find her."

Cassie and Eric turned away and set about their task. Tom thought he saw Kerry slyly studying Eric as he went over to his desk but when she saw him looking at her, she quickly turned away. Tom noticed Cassie also picked up on it before he saw her open the plastic wallet containing her parking fine, screwing the sleeve into a ball and tossing it into the bin beside her desk in disgust.

Tamara leaned in to Tom. "So when are you speaking to Simon Moy again?"

"Tomorrow," he said. "I want to speak to someone else first and I also have a feeling it will go on a bit, the conversation with Simon Moy, and I need to be home tonight."

Tamara put a reassuring hand on his forearm, smiling. "Moy can wait until tomorrow."

CHAPTER EIGHTEEN

TOM OPENED the door to the interview room. Simon Moy immediately lurched to his feet, striking an indignant pose. He glanced at his watch, shaking his head.

"Honestly, I agreed to come here at your request first thing this morning and I've been sitting here for over an hour—"

Tom held up his hand in supplication. He held a folder in his other hand. He smiled apologetically.

"And your patience is very much appreciated, Mr Moy," he said. Gesturing to the seat he'd leapt up from, Tom smiled again, warmly. "Please, do sit down."

Simon Moy exhaled in frustration, turned and straightened his chair before sitting down again with a deep sigh. "Whatever it is, please can we just get on with it? I have things to do today, Inspector."

The response was curt, bordering on aggressive. Tom pulled out his own chair, sitting down and placing the folder in front of himself. He looked over his shoulder at the uniformed constable who was standing with his back to the wall. Tom faced Simon Moy.

"Has someone offered you a cup of tea, Mr Moy?"

"I'd rather you just told me why I was here, asked whatever you wanted and let me get on."

"As you wish," Tom said, opening the folder. He took out a number of sheets of paper and began looking through them, careful to angle them away from the interviewee who appeared more interested as time passed without anything being said.

"So?" Simon Moy asked. "Why am I here?"

The door to the interview room opened and Kerry Palmer entered. The uniformed constable left and Kerry took a seat beside Tom. They exchanged a look and she nodded almost imperceptibly, but to Tom it was more than enough.

"Right, where were we?" Tom asked. "That's it, yes." He took the documents in his hand and he set them out side by side in front of Moy whose eyes darted from one to the next and back again.

"Now, hold on a minute! You've got no right—"

"Court order," Tom said, setting the relevant document down on the table in front of him. "We have every right."

Moy's expression changed from frustrated indignation to resignation within moments.

"There's your life laid out in front of you, Mr Moy," Tom said. "Financially speaking, at any rate. Do you need me to run through them for you, so you know what they are? That's confirmation of your mortgage arrears, the confirmation documents of the arrears loaded onto prepayment meters, both electric and gas, forcibly installed at your home address following court proceedings for non-payment—"

"Yes!" Moy snapped. "I bloody well know what I owe—"

"Non-payment of council tax for eleven months," Tom said, placing another document on top of the others.

"Do you think I wouldn't pay them if I had any bloody money!"

"And yet," Tom said, pulling out another piece of paper, a copy of a receipt from a local bodywork repair centre, "you have been able to find money for this." He set the receipt down on the desk. Moy looked down at it, his lips parting slightly. The anger subsided to be replaced by resignation. He slowly closed his eyes and took a slow intake of breath. "We found this in the glove box of your car, Mr Moy. The car that you picked up from the garage yesterday. Oh," he said, putting a warrant down on the table, "we served this warrant at your home this morning. Shortly after you left to come here. Your wife was kind enough to let my colleagues in."

Tom sat back and folded his arms across his chest.

"What?" Moy asked.

"Whenever you're ready," Tom said. Moy shook his head as if he didn't understand. "Tell me why the rear of your car needed a respray? Why was it so urgent when you have," he cast a hand slowly across the paperwork in between them, "so many more pressing bills to pay?"

Moy took a deep breath. "My wife had a... minor collision with a concrete post when parking the car. If you don't deal with these things once the outer seal is breached, then it can lead to further problems down the road."

Tom nodded. "Of course, that's true. However, your wife said it was *you* who was driving when someone scraped the car while it was parked up in a public car park. Were there two incidents?"

Moy's eyes narrowed, then his expression lightened and he smiled, holding up a hand he wagged his finger at Tom pointedly. "You know, I think my wife is right. My memory is a bit off these days, what with the stress of all this," he said, waving his fingers at the paperwork. "Yes, come to think of it, I recall it now. My wife is right."

"Which car park?"

"Sorry?"

"Which car park were you in?"

Moy shook his head. "I'm afraid that's not something I recall."

"Shame," Tom said. "Of course, your memory being what it is, you'll remember bigger events, those with emotional connotations... that sort of thing?"

"Yes, I'm sure. You have something in mind?"

"Well, for instance when you last spoke to your brother?"

Moy sighed. "Now, I know we've been over this and I hadn't seen Billy in years—"

"So you weren't arguing with him last Wednesday night in a supermarket car park?"

Moy met Tom's gaze and the two men stared at one another, Tom wondering if the man was calculating what they may or may not know. He decided to move things along.

"Because we have an eye witness who not only places you at the scene, but also saw the two of you going at it. Your wife had to call you away. Now, you left that out when accounting for your movements."

Moy tried to swallow, finding his mouth dry and struggled.

"Water?" Tom asked.

He declined, staring down at the paperwork in front of him. He was breathing heavily and Tom could see his neck flushing red. Was it embarrassment, anger, or just the end result of being caught in a lie?

"I saw my brother that night," he said quietly. Looking up, he met Tom's gaze and then glanced at Kerry. "And we argued, that's true."

"About what?"

Moy scoffed, shaking his head. "The same thing as always, money."

"You asked him to give you money?"

"Lend! I asked him to lend me money... lend us money, me and Caitlyn." He put his hands together, interlocking his fingers, as he looked to the ceiling. "We are about to lose our home... one way or another." He slammed his hands down on the table, palms flat and glared at Tom. "Do you think I would have gone to him if I had *any other choice*?"

"That's quite a temper you have, Simon. Does it run in the family?"

"I didn't kill my brother," Moy said, sitting back and folding his arms defiantly across his chest.

"So, what did happen, because when you got in the car that wasn't the end of it, was it?"

"We drove away... and I parked up down the road," Moy said, raising his eyebrows and concentrating hard. "Billy came past in that beat-up old car of his."

"What car?"

"That battered old thing he drives sometimes," Moy said, his brow furrowing. "A Mazda... or a Datsun or something. Really, really old car anyway. I'm amazed he still had it running, but Billy was always good with motors."

Tom thought about it. There was no such car at Billy's cabin or in the outbuildings. They'd found an old Land Rover Defender parked in one of the cart lodges but nothing matching that description.

"And what happened next?"

"Nothing."

"Come on."

"No, honestly," Moy said, splaying his hands wide. "I swear. Look, I'll level with you, Billy wouldn't help. He told me I was old enough to deal with my own mess. He flat out refused to help us. I was angry, *okay?*"

"Very angry?"

"Bloody furious! I begged him to help me... I gave up my last shred of pride and dignity... and he laughed at me."

"So, you followed him—"

"No! I didn't."

"Go on, you wanted to. You wanted to teach him a lesson, take out your frustration on someone," Tom said, "anyone. And it was your brother in the firing line. All that resentment, all that anger at being denied your share of your birth right, the injustice of it all finally boiled over and you lashed out—"

"No!" he shouted, jumping to his feet. Tom felt Kerry flinch beside him, but he didn't move himself, merely kept his eye on Simon Moy who glared at him, breathing hard. "I wanted to. I'm not going to lie, but Caitlyn talked me down, and..." Moy retook his seat, his shoulders sagging as he sat down "... we went home. The thing is, when I got up the next day, I knew Billy was right." He sucked air through his teeth. "My brother was right. I got myself into this mess and I had to face it, rather than running from it and trying to have others bail me out. It was time to face my demons."

"Meaning?"

"I called a couple of estate agents and put our house on the market, instructed them to get as good a deal as they could in the shortest possible time." Moy placed his hands on the table in front of him, trying to control his breathing. "And I enrolled in Gamblers Anonymous." He took a breath, shaking his head. "Maybe it's too little, too late to save our house, but... maybe it will save my marriage."

Tom thought on it. Everything he said was plausible.

"And the car, why have it fixed?"

Simon chuckled. "I don't know what else you want me to say, Inspector. I've told you already."

"Show me your hands."

"Excuse me."

"Your hands," Tom said. "Hold them out."

Simon Moy did as requested, holding them out palms up and then flipped them over. Tom examined the knuckles. They were clean, undamaged.

"What are you looking for?"

"Thank you," Tom said. Moy put his hands back in his lap. "How did you get into so much trouble financially?"

He blew out his cheeks. "I've never met a man without a weakness, Inspector Janssen. For some it's drink or drugs. For others it's women or a combination of all of them."

"And yours?"

"The thrill of a flutter," Moy said, running a hand across his bald head from forehead to crown where he scratched absently. "Do you know, it got so bad that I was banned from every betting shop from

Dereham to Cromer, and I can't even open an online account anymore. They say the industry likes an addict, I mean what business doesn't want repeat custom, but even they turned their back on me."

"In my experience an addict always finds a way."

"You're right about that, Inspector. I used my wife's details, friends, colleagues, anyone I could to try and carry on, recoup my losses so to speak."

"How did that work out for you?"

Moy smiled but didn't answer.

"Thought so. What about the illegal bookies. They wouldn't shun you."

Moy shook his head. "Nah, I don't know anything about that." He averted his eyes from Tom's scrutiny and it was clear that although they'd found, for a brief moment at least, clarity and truth, the veil of deceit quickly came down once more.

"Tell me about your relationship with Charlie Barnes."

Moy's eyes narrowed, his expression shuttered. "Who?"

"Charlie Barnes. You were arrested last year after a public altercation with him. You remember?"

"Oh, that. Yeah," he said, turning the corners of his mouth down, "that was nothing."

"It was enough to have the two of you arrested and cautioned." Tom sat forward, placing his elbows on the table and bringing his fingers together to form a tent. "Now, I have the impression you are trying to be truthful with me, so let's not waste each other's time, right?"

Moy exhaled heavily, biting his lower lip. He looked away as he spoke, "I owed money. Charlie Barnes was encouraging me to pay it."

"He works for someone or you owed him money?"

"Someone else. A bookie. He was reminding me of my responsibilities."

"So, why did you go after him? That must have been risky."

Moy chuckled. "Yes, not very smart of me. It's a good job your lot turned up or I might have got a proper good hiding. Anyway, I got the message."

"And did you pay?"

Simon Moy sniffed hard, rubbing at the end of his nose with the back of his hand. He then offered his hands up in surrender. "You always end up paying, Inspector. Everybody does."

Tom concluded the interview and stepped out of the room. Tamara came to meet him from the adjoining room where she'd been watching a live feed from a camera mounted in the corner of the room.

"What do you think?" she asked.

"I think he's on the level, for the most part at least."

"Why did you ask him to show you his hands?"

"Because of the bruising to Billy's face. Both the FME and the pathologist are in agreement that the bruising happened at least a day before he died."

"Indicative of a fight?"

"Maybe so, yes. I wanted to see if he was showing any signs of having landed a punch. Faces are hard, bony. They leave damage on those wielding their hands just as much as on the recipient."

"And?"

"No sign. But it was days ago and it wasn't a full-on beating, I was just curious."

Tamara looked back at the interview room as the door opened and Simon Moy was led away to the custody suite. Tom intended to hold him as long as they could while they investigated his story.

"Do you think he could have killed his brother?"

Tom watched the back of the man as he walked away from them down the corridor.

"Well, he's lied to us, kept things from us and only told the truth when it became obvious we could catch him out in another lie... and he has a temper on him. Anyone capable of an explosive reaction like that at the flick of a switch..." he angled his head to one side. "All it takes is one second and everything changes."

"Have forensics take a sample of paint from his car and try to match it to the sample we found at Billy's. Until then, we don't have enough to take it further," Tamara said. "Did we find his prints inside the cabin?"

"No, we didn't, and you're right, we don't have enough. Not yet."

CHAPTER NINETEEN

CASSIE KNIGHT CAME to stand alongside Tamara who was deep in thought as she read over the information boards detailing what they knew about Aleksandrs Balodis. The information was scant. Besides the man's criminal record obtained through their links with Interpol, they knew very little about him. He had never appeared on the radar of any UK constabulary before now.

"Penny for them?" Cassie asked.

Tamara shook her head. "Why was he here?"

"Balodis? The Border Force have documented him making half a dozen trips to the UK in the last eighteen months. He flew into Heathrow on the last three occasions. Manchester and Glasgow twelve months before that. Neither Greater Manchester or Police Scotland have any knowledge of what he was up to. Maybe he was just topping up his frequent flyer miles," she said, smiling.

"Or he used a different name when he was here."

"Or that, yes."

"But you're missing my point."

Cassie frowned. "Sorry, what is your point?"

"Why did he come here? To Hunstanton, I mean. I know we

have our fair share of crime but we're not exactly a draw for foreign gangsters are we?"

"Can Balodis be considered a gangster?" Cassie said. "It's pretty low-level stuff—"

"That he's been caught for, yes. Maybe he's earned his respect and stepped up a level."

"Doesn't answer your question, though," Cassie said, distracted by the phone on her desk ringing. "Excuse me."

She hurried over to answer it, at the same time clocking Eric was on the *Trip Advisor* website. She picked up the receiver, realising Tamara was coming over to them. Eric had his back to her and Cassie deftly put her knee into the back of his chair.

"Hey!" he protested, spinning on her and immediately seeing the DCI approaching. He swivelled back and managed to hide the browser as Tamara came to stand beside Cassie.

"DS Knight," she said calmly, winking at Eric who looked both mightily relieved and horrified in the same moment.

"DS Knight," a nervous voice said. "It's Colin, Colin Peters. We met this afternoon at my hotel."

"Yes, of course, Mr Peters. What can I do for you?"

"The woman – the one you were asking after – who you think may have known Mr Balodis."

"Yes, what about her?"

"I think she was here today, at the hotel. About half an hour ago. She just wandered into the reception by herself."

"Are you sure?"

"I–I think so, yes. It looked like her."

"Did you speak to her?"

"Yes, I asked her if she was all right. She seemed... odd."

"Odd?"

"Yes, out of sorts might be a better description," Peters said. "I have to admit I didn't recognise her at first but when I spoke to her, she appeared rather rattled."

"What did she say?"

"Nothing at all. She backed away from me and then I realised who she was and I reached out for her and she turned tail and fled."

"Fled? Were you rough with her?" Cassie asked. Tamara and Eric were waiting on tenterhooks beside her. "I asked you to call me Mr Peters, not detain her."

"I–I know. I'm terribly sorry, but I panicked and didn't quite know what I should do."

"Did you see where she went after leaving your hotel?"

"No, no, I'm afraid I didn't. She was in a bit of a state, though. Upset, dishevelled."

"I didn't notice whether you had CCTV at your hotel, Mr P—"

"What use would I have for any such thing in Hunstanton, dear me?"

In case one of your guests is murdered and the police are trying to catch the killer, off the top of my head, Cassie thought but didn't say it. "Okay, well, if she comes back please call us straight away, Mr Peters."

"Of course, Detective Sergeant, of course."

Cassie put the phone down, looking between Tamara and Eric.

"She came back."

"The money?" Tamara asked. "Or maybe her passport?"

"Or looking for Balodis," Eric said. It was a good point. They had withheld the name from the media up until now. There was every chance she hadn't heard.

"Or both?" Cassie said, thinking aloud. "If it is the money she's after, then she can't think Balodis is dead—"

"Or she knows he is but doesn't think we have him," Tamara countered. "Either way, if she's come back it stands to reason she's after something." She met Cassie's eye. "So, she'll come back again. The hotel manager may have scared her off this time, but if she's come back once, then she'll likely do so again."

Cassie sighed. "I know what that means."

Tamara grinned. "Try not to get a parking ticket this time."

"Twenty minutes!" Cassie said, holding up two fingers. "That's all we were. Ridiculous."

Eric looked pained.

"What's up, Eric?"

"Ah... I was going to speak to Becca tonight, about..." he nodded his head in a knowing way, "you know?"

Tamara looked at Cassie. "Do you know what he's talking about because I don't."

That would explain the *Trip Advisor* site, Cassie thought. "Yeah, I think I can keep an eye out for Sasha on my own this evening. Eric has something to do with the family, don't you Eric?"

Eric looked momentarily confused and then realisation dawned and he nodded.

"Well, you can't watch the hotel on your own," Tamara said.

Cassie snorted. "Of course I can. It's one woman who runs away from Colin Peters of all people. I think I can manage."

Tamara stared hard at her, then looked at Eric. "I'll remind the pair of you that this is a murder inquiry."

"I can always call for support if she shows up, it'll be fine. I can handle it."

"Eric, is everything all right? It's not George is it?"

"No, no, he's grand, honest. It's... I know it's daft but it's honeymoon related. I've had a problem and," he looked at Cassie, "I've only just been able to get it sorted and what with the case and all—"

Tamara placed a hand on his shoulder. "It's okay, Eric. Maybe I'll go with Cassie tonight instead."

"Girls' night out, it is then!" Cassie said triumphantly. "It'll be like old times."

Tamara shook her head. "Not exactly like old times, Cassandra."

"Full-naming me already... it's been a while since you've done that."

Tamara fixed her with a stern glance.

"What have I done?" Cassie asked.

"Get your coat," Tamara said, crossing the room to pick up her mobile and bag, "and this time I'm bringing the food and drink."

"Oh no," Cassie whispered. "That means cardboard vegan wraps and industrial strength black coffee."

"I heard that, Cass."

Cassie silently cursed and Eric grinned at her.

"Did you find something suitable?" Cassie whispered in Eric's ear as she stood up.

"Yes, I think so. Becca's going to love it!"

"Good," Cassie said, touching him gently on the shoulder. She thought she saw Kerry Palmer shoot a dark look at her from across the room but, when their eyes met, Kerry smiled warmly. Cassie picked up her mobile phone, slipping it into her pocket. Kerry's back was turned to her now and she indicated to Tamara that she'd be a minute and the DCI said she'd meet her downstairs at the car. Cassie leaned in to Eric, lowering her voice. "I thought you and Kerry went way back?"

Eric glanced at the seconded constable briefly, nodding. "Yes, we were in the same intake, went through basic training together. Why do you ask?"

"How come she didn't come to the wedding?"

Eric looked perplexed. "She was invited, but she had to work. You know, stepping into CID was a big offer for her."

Cassie patted him on the shoulder, standing up. "Yes, of course. Good luck with the wife."

"Thanks."

She left ops, hurrying down the corridor to find Tamara.

THEY QUICKLY REALISED that where they needed to park the car in order to observe the hotel wasn't possible. There were several hotels and guest houses on Westgate and none of them had parking at the front, the road was too narrow and parking was prohibited as Cassie found to her cost that morning. On the corner of Southend Road, however, was a bed and breakfast tucked away and surrounded by mature trees. It wasn't open for business yet, the owner being an elderly couple who were semi-retired and chose only to trade in the peak months of the year. A polite request saw them offered the use of an upstairs guest room overlooking both Westgate and Southend Road, giving them the best possible view as well as discretion.

There was a knock on the door and it cracked open. Muriel, their host, peered in on them.

"Would you care for a cup of tea?" she asked.

"No, we're fine, thank you," Tamara said.

"How about some cake? I made it fresh this morning."

"Cake sounds lovely," Cassie said before Tamara could decline. The thought of an evening eating Tamara's bean wraps and vegetable crisps fresh in her mind.

Muriel smiled approvingly and retreated from the room.

"What a sweet lady," Cassie said. Tamara agreed, standing as she was at her vantage point watching the road. "I really could have done this alone, you know?"

"I know," Tamara said over her shoulder.

"How are things with you?"

"In what way?"

"Well, home, job... got a boyfriend?"

Tamara shot her a withering look.

"All right, I only asked... geez."

Footsteps outside sounded Muriel's arrival and Cassie opened the door for her. The woman passed through with a tray in her hands, two side plates with large slices of what looked like some kind of fruitcake and two glasses of fruit juice. She was a consummate host.

"This is all very exciting," Muriel said, looking between them as she passed a plate to Cassie who accepted it gratefully. She'd missed lunch and dinner wasn't looking promising either. "It's like being in an episode of *Columbo*."

Cassie nodded, smiling politely. Muriel made to pass a plate to Tamara who declined, much to their host's disappointment. It was evident that she wasn't going to leave until someone had eaten something. Cassie lifted the slab of cake, which she found heavy, and took a bite. It was a fruitcake or, at least, a close approximation of one. However, it was burnt and cakes that were burnt carried the taste throughout. Not that Cassie could indicate that, what with Muriel steadfastly watching her eat.

"Delicious," Cassie said, trying desperately to swallow the dry, charred husk.

"I'm so pleased. My husband, Derek, is watching his weight and so he's abstaining for a while, so there is plenty more where that came from!"

"Wonderful!"

Muriel left the room, a big grin on her face. Cassie coughed what was left of the mouthful into her hand, searching for a bin. She couldn't find one.

"It's no good. This will have to go down the toilet."

Tamara wasn't listening, she was distracted by something. Cassie noticed and came alongside as Tamara raised a set of pocket binoculars and looked down the street to their right.

"Is it her?"

Tamara shook her head. "No, I just recognised someone. Caught my eye as he drove past. Probably nothing."

For *probably nothing*, it seemed to occupy her for several minutes before she eventually set the binoculars down on a small table underneath the window.

"What do you think of Kerry?" Cassie asked.

Tamara glanced at her. "I've been impressed. Her attitude is spot on."

"Yeah, true. Willing to miss her friend's wedding for work shows dedication, I guess."

"Sorry?"

"Missing Eric's wedding because she was asked to work. That's—"

"She volunteered," Tamara said, turning her eye back to the street below. "I think we had someone else scheduled for that weekend. Lucky for her, I guess."

Cassie thought hard. "Yeah, lucky."

"Why do you ask?"

She shrugged. "Doesn't matter. Just had a thought. Don't you think it's a bit odd how she—"

"That's her!" Tamara said, excitedly beckoning Cassie to the window. "I'm right, aren't I?"

Cassie looked and immediately saw who Tamara was pointing to. A woman was leaning against a car parked in the bays just up the hill, the only area of on-street parking before the road disappeared around the bend. She was trying to look casual but failing miserably.

"Yes, that's her."

"Come on, before she does another runner," Tamara said, making for the door. "You should thank her. She's just saved you from having to flush those two pieces of cake."

"Clog the toilet more like."

Once out on the landing, they found Muriel hovering outside the bathroom. She moved aside and they hurried past her and down the stairs. They slowed their pace as they left the building, confident that Sasha wouldn't recognise them. The last thing they wanted was to spook her into running before they had a chance to even address her.

"How do you want to play it?" Cassie asked as they crossed Westgate and started up the hill, walking side by side and trying to look like two friends on an evening walk.

"Keep it casual," Tamara said, her hands thrust into her pockets. It was cold now, the sun setting across the water behind them. They walked up the incline, Sasha was visible lingering at the rear of a beaten-up silver hatchback. It wasn't clear if it was hers. She had half an eye on the hotel entrance less than forty yards away, but she was agitated, unable to remain still.

Cassie tried to initiate small talk as they walked, Tamara picking up the conversation as well. Sasha was paying no attention to them, her eyes fixed on the hotel. As they got closer, Cassie could see what Colin Peters had referred to. She looked dreadful. Her hair was unkempt, hanging free to the shoulder but she looked as if she'd been dragged through a hedge backwards. She was very slight, waif-like, and roughly five-three tall. The breeze coming in off the sea must be cutting through her, dressed as she was in jeans, a thin jumper and with only a sleeveless body warmer to keep out the cold.

They were within ten feet now and Sasha retreated from the path, moving to the rear of the car. *Was she moving away from them deliberately?* Cassie didn't think so. They'd never met. Why would they be a threat? She laughed as if Tamara had said something amusing. The DCI did likewise. Sasha was watching them now, barely a step away. They came alongside and Tamara moved ahead of Cassie and took one step past her before turning back.

"Sasha Kalnina?"

Cassie moved to her left just as Tamara spoke, stepping from the pavement and into the road to Sasha's left. The woman didn't hesitate. She threw herself at Cassie, lashing out. It was all Cassie could do to avoid the blow. The hand flew harmlessly past her face, but Cassie was suddenly off balance and the action also caught Tamara off guard. Sasha bolted, running out into the road, Tamara ordering her to stop. The sickening sound of metal colliding with a person followed, a screech of tyres and a short series of bangs as Sasha rolled up the bonnet of the car, struck the windscreen and was hurled back into the road where she landed in a heap with a dull thud.

"Call an ambulance!" Tamara shouted, running to where Sasha lay six feet in front of the car. The driver got out, hurrying over to kneel at Tamara's side.

"I didn't see her... she just ran out!"

He was panicking but Tamara ignored him, trying to assess the extent of the injuries. Cassie edged closer, mobile pressed against her ear giving information to the call handler. She hung up.

"They're on their way. How is she?"

"Alive," Tamara said.

Sasha groaned. She was semi-conscious and Cassie cast an eye over her. None of her limbs were at awkward angles, so that was a good sign. Similarly, she couldn't see a head wound. The car must have been slowing down for the bend at the bottom of the hill, travelling at slow speed. Fortunate.

"I didn't see her," the driver repeated to anyone who might be listening.

"We know," Cassie said, perhaps more aggressively than she'd intended. He put his hands to the sides of his face. She looked at him, initiating eye contact. "We know."

Sirens in the distance could be heard. The ambulance station was part of the town's police station and less than a mile away. Cassie stood up just as Sasha mumbled something in her native tongue, her eyes remaining closed. Tamara made soothing sounds, carefully moving the hair away from her face and gently stroking her cheek. Cassie moved to the rear of the car which had hit her to guide the ambulance crew to their location. A handful of passers-by were gathering to watch the scene unfold but none was encroaching or at risk of getting in the way.

The ambulance stopped and the first paramedic climbed out as Cassie saw a liveried police car coming down Westgate to join them. Tamara moved aside to allow the medics room to work, explaining quickly what had happened. They set about assessing the injuries. Sasha was speaking again, only this time it was clearer and her eyes were open. Cassie saw a brightness in them, wide and cat-like. She was an attractive young woman with beautifully sculpted cheekbones, as young Eastern Bloc women often had. *How do such pretty girls end up with men like Balodis?*

Tamara directed one of the uniformed officers to move the driver of the car away and take his statement, the other was tasked with keeping the onlookers under control. These numbers were growing with all the lights and sirens drawing people out to investigate the commotion.

"Cass?"

She broke her gaze away from Sasha, looking at Tamara.

"You go with the ambulance when they're ready to move her and I'll meet you there."

CHAPTER TWENTY

THE WARD SISTER APPROACHED THEM. Cassie smiled and introduced Tamara. "This is my DCI, Tamara Greave."

The sister acknowledged Tamara, speaking directly to her.

"She has just come back up from the fracture clinic. It wasn't a particularly bad break, and she is young, so she should recover quickly. You can go through and see her now, if you'd like?"

"Yes, we would. Has she said anything?"

"Not a word, no. She's like a startled rabbit, the poor thing. A result of the shock, I suppose."

"Yes, probably," Tamara said, glancing sideways at Cassie who raised her eyebrows in reply. They walked along the corridor past several ward rooms, all of which had patients in their beds, many of whom were surrounded by family or visitors. Sasha was in a room by herself, a luxury not often afforded to all but the most seriously ill.

"Do you know where her family are?" the sister asked. "Only, we haven't been able to notify anyone that she's here. Not that she's asked us to."

Tamara shook her head. "As far as we know she doesn't have any family in the UK." That was true, although they really didn't know much about Sasha at all. "How long will you keep her in here for?"

"I'm not sure. The doctors are doing their ward rounds at the moment, but I know they were concerned about the bang to the head she took. The results of the CT scan were positive, so I should imagine she will be discharged this evening but, as I say, you'll have to wait for confirmation of that."

They reached a closed door where a uniformed constable was waiting outside. He acknowledged both Tamara and Cassie. The sister stopped at the door, turning back to them and barring their way momentarily. She must have something on her mind.

"Is something wrong?"

The ward sister hesitated. "I–I don't know if it is my place to say."

"Go on."

She glanced over her shoulder at the closed door as if she could see through it to the bed beyond.

"She was in a bit of a state. I think she may have been living rough, if that information is of any use to you. I'm hoping she is still here when the evening meal comes around."

"Thank you, we'll bear it in mind. Is she allowed to eat anything now?"

"Yes, there's no reason why not."

Tamara looked at Cassie and she nodded. "I'll head down to the cafeteria and see what I can find."

Tamara knocked on the door and entered. Sasha was sitting up in bed, several pillows behind her. Her right arm was in a cast from her hand to just below her elbow. The left side of her face was scratched around the cheek and eye, and steriliser strips sealed a gash on her forehead, level with her temple. The skin around the eyelid was swollen and darkening. Tamara had the briefest glimpse in her mind's eye that Sasha may have already had the black eye before they attempted to speak to her. The discolouration did look several days in the making.

"How are you, Sasha?"

She eyed Tamara warily as she walked to her bedside, her lips eventually forming the briefest of smiles but it faded rapidly.

"Do you speak English?"

She nodded slowly.

"I'm from the police," Tamara said, showing her warrant card. Sasha paid it no attention, turning her face away. "The nurse tells me you are going to be all right. Luckily the car wasn't going fast, hey?"

Sasha sniffed but didn't respond.

"It is important for you to understand that you're not in any trouble with us." She still didn't look up, absently toying with her fingers in her lap. "Sasha," Tamara said, pulling up a chair and sitting alongside the bed trying not to be a threatening presence. Some people were intimidated by the police. "I need to ask you about Aleksandrs Balodis." At the mention of the name, she looked up at her, holding Tamara's eye. "You know Aleksandrs, right?"

She nodded, her lips pursed.

"Do you know where he is?"

She shook her head.

"I need you to tell me when you last saw him. Can you remember when that was?"

Sasha looked away, closing her eyes and putting her head back on the supporting pillows.

"My... head hurts," she all but whispered.

"You took quite a blow to it when you bounced off the car, I understand. It is to be expected."

Sasha looked at her again, her eyes were haunted, sunken. Tamara looked her up and down, seeing the dirt and grime ingrained in her skin, especially noticeable under her fingernails. They were painted red, although the colour was flaking and the ends of the nails were pitted and chipped. Tamara chose a different approach.

"What brought you here to England, Sasha?"

"I came here to work," she said, her mouth clearly so dry she was struggling to speak. Tamara poured her a cup of water from a jug set beside the table and passed it to her. Her lips were cracked. She sipped at the liquid, smiling her thanks as Tamara took the cup and placed it on the cabinet beside the bed.

"What work do you do?"

"I clean," she said, dipping her head as she spoke.

"Who for?"

She shrugged.

"I mean, do you clean for a hotel, a shop or someone's home?"

"Business. Shops…"

Tamara smiled. The door opened and Cassie entered. She smiled at them in turn and passed Tamara a packaged roll. It was a brown roll with a tuna mayonnaise filling.

"Are you hungry?" Tamara asked, holding it aloft. She knew the answer because Sasha's eyes all but lit up at the sight of it. Tamara opened the packaging and passed it to her. Sasha tentatively accepted but once it was in her hands she set about it with gusto. Tamara exchanged a look with Cassie, who hovered on the other side of the bed trying hard not to crowd the woman.

They let her finish eating, handing her another cup of water, before starting further conversation. She looked more relaxed now.

"Sasha, we need to know about your relationship with Aleksandrs. Do you feel like you can tell us now?"

Sasha took a deep breath and nodded. "Where is he?"

Tamara caught Cassie looking at her but kept her eyes on Sasha. "When did you last see him?"

She was thoughtful, concentrating hard. Perhaps she was trying to find the right words because, so far, English words didn't appear to come quickly or easily. It was possible she was translating in her head before speaking. "The last week. Monday… maybe Tuesday. I cannot remember exact."

"Okay. And what is he to you?"

Her eyes narrowed and she glanced at Cassie and then shook her head. "I don't understand."

"You and Aleksandrs… you are lovers?"

She shook her head slowly, her expression pensive. "We… are

friends. Where is he? Where is Aleksandrs?"

"I'm afraid I have..." Tamara wasn't sure if she would understand. "I am sorry. Aleksandrs is dead."

Her mouth fell open and she stared at Tamara, then glanced at Cassie, her eyes seeking confirmation. Cassie nodded.

"Yes, it is true. His body was found on Sunday."

"His body was found on the beach," Tamara said. "I am sorry."

It was hard to tell, what with the emotion and trauma of the day, but Sasha's eyes glistened as if she was about to cry. She blinked away the tears.

"Is that why you were at the hotel? You were looking for Aleksandrs?"

She nodded, suddenly looking fearful. "Am I... in trouble?"

"Why would you be in trouble?"

She looked furtively around the room. "Because I work... here in the UK."

Tamara thought about it. Depending on when she arrived in the UK, she may need to apply for a work visa, but those waters were muddied with EU nationals at this time and Tamara couldn't be certain of her status. A situation which was probably quite common at the moment.

"You don't need to worry about that right now," Tamara said, ensuring they had eye contact when she said it. Sasha didn't appear convinced but there was little Tamara could do to assuage those particular fears. Perhaps she had been working illegally or not declaring her earnings rather than being here illegally. It wasn't really her concern. Unless the friendship she had with Balodis was one of coercion and control. This was a growing problem in recent years with migrants seeking a new life in a foreign country and unscrupulous criminals promising one thing and delivering something altogether very different. "Is that what Aleksandrs did for you? Help you to find work?"

She held Tamara's eye, nodding slowly. She was scared and therefore very unlikely to offer any more information than the bare minimum. She needed to trust them in order to open up. The fact she was talking to two female detectives didn't appear to be helping.

"You will probably be discharged from here this evening, Sasha." Her eyes widened and Tamara reached out, placing her palm on the back of her left hand now lying beside her on the bed. "Do you have anywhere to stay?"

She shook her head.

"Where have you been staying these past few nights?"

Sasha sniffed hard. Then she shrugged. Tamara looked over at Cassie.

"Maybe we could give Mary a call?"

Cassie smiled. "Yes, I can do that."

Mary Bloom ran a local charity with a presence all along the north-west coast of Norfolk helping homeless people or those seeking refuge from domestic violence. Tamara smiled, Sasha returned it.

"We'll make sure you have somewhere safe to stay—"

"My... things... my belongings?" Sasha said.

Tamara looked around, pointing to the far side of the room where her clothes, as well as a small backpack she had with her in Hunstanton, were in a plastic bag on the floor beneath a plastic visitor's chair.

"They are over there, don't worry." Sasha strained to see but the bed was at such an angle she couldn't. Cassie crossed the room and picked them up, bringing them to the bed. She held them out and Sasha slowly reached out and once her fingers curled around the back, she snatched it and brought it close to her chest, holding on as if they were the most precious things to her in the world. Cassie held up her hands in surrender, apologetically. Sasha held Cassie's gaze for a moment before her expression softened but she still held the bag tightly to her chest.

"You don't have to worry, Sasha. Mary is a lovely lady. She will take good care of you."

Sasha nodded but said nothing, holding her bag closer still.

"You are safe here," Tamara said. "I promise."

The two detectives stepped out of the room. The constable smiled as they passed and neither Tamara or Cassie spoke until they were a few metres away from the room and wouldn't be overheard.

"What do you make of her?" Cassie asked.

Tamara cocked her head. "Frightened."

"Yes, I thought so too. What of? Us?"

"Or who might be the better question? It could be us... or someone else."

"If it's Balodis, she has nothing to fear—"

"Unless he doesn't work alone," Tamara said.

Cassie stopped and turned to face her. They were alone at the entrance to the ward.

"Do you buy it that she is working as a cleaner?"

Tamara didn't believe that, not at all. "No. Maybe Colin Peters had a point."

"Sex work?"

"It might explain her reluctance to talk. And the bruising, if she's being forced."

"Yeah, I saw that too." Cassie sighed. "She wouldn't be the first young woman to be lured to the UK on the pretence of becoming a cleaner or an au pair."

"If that's the case though, why would she come back to her abuser?"

Cassie shrugged. "He had her passport for starters. And if she's been properly groomed... or if she thinks she had nowhere else to go or anyone else to turn to, then she might come back to the man she's most familiar with. Maybe Balodis is low in the hierarchy and she thought she could get around him somehow?"

"Perhaps. The passport is the first thing they take off these girls so they can't leave."

"Hey, wild thought," Cassie said, "what if Balodis was looking to get her out of it?"

Tamara smiled. "Star-crossed lovers meet in extreme circumstances... that sort of thing?"

Cassie snorted. "Well, if you put it like that it does sound a bit Hollywood. It would explain a lot though, to be fair. It's more likely she met him to try and get her passport back and was willing to kill him to do so. Accident or by design, I couldn't say. Ah, ignore me, I'm just thinking out loud."

Tamara had to accept both theories were plausible scenarios. "If we can get her settled into Mary's, maybe she'll open up a bit more tomorrow."

"Are you sure you want to go the touchy-feely way? We could sit her down in an interview room and apply a little pressure. It might garner faster results."

Tamara shook her head. She disagreed. "That girl in there, and let's face it that's pretty much what she is, a girl, is traumatised. By what, I don't know but she's scared of us, of whatever she's into and who knows what else? We've no reason at this point to believe she's done anything wrong, so what do we threaten her with? Take it slowly, earn her trust and she'll more than likely open up. Okay?"

"You're the boss, Boss," Cassie said with a wink. "It was just a thought. Of course, if she killed him then she's more than likely to do a runner at the first opportunity. You know that, right?"

"If she does, she won't get far. We'll keep a uniform beside her here until she's discharged and then keep a car outside the refuge. Changing the subject, what's going on with you and Eric?" Tamara asked as she tapped the exit button to unlock the doors to the ward and allow them out.

"What do you mean?"

"I've got eyes. Don't think I haven't noticed the two of you have been as thick as thieves recently."

Cassie waved the question away. "Don't go there, I beg of you. Besides, it's more interesting to ask what's going on between our fledgling detective constable and Eric."

"Kerry? Whatever do you mean?"

Cassie raised her eyebrows. They reached the lift and she pressed the call button alongside the doors, turning to face Tamara.

"Better get those eyes checked, Boss."

CHAPTER TWENTY-ONE

TOM TURNED the key in the lock, easing the door open in the hope of not drawing the dog's attention. Saffy would be asleep by now, at least she should be, and the excited barking of her Jack Russell always woke her. Unless it was three o'clock in the morning and the dog wanted to be let out, then it was always him who woke. As it happened, he needn't have worried, poking his head into the living room from the hall he saw Russell lying in front of the wood burner, a gentle flame licking the ends of a freshly placed log within it, on his back, feet in the air, tongue hanging out of his mouth to one side. Alice looked up from where she sat on the sofa snuggled underneath a tartan throw, feet up, watching the television with a steaming cup of hot chocolate in her hand. She barely acknowledged his arrival.

"Evening," he said, raising his eyebrows.

"Ssshhh…" she said, waving a hand in the air and pointing at the television screen. Then she beckoned him to join her. "Come on, you'll miss the good bit."

"I'll just look in on Saffy first."

The dog moved ever so slightly, keeping a watchful eye on him to see if he would head towards the kitchen. If so, he was likely to spring into action. He didn't. Tom took off his coat and hung it up. Climbing the stairs, he took off his tie, throwing it into their bedroom as he passed, heading for Saffy's room and avoiding the creaky floorboards en route. Carefully opening the door to her room, the interior bathed in the soft blue of her night light.

Saffy lay horizontally in her bed, her head all but hanging off the edge of the bed. How she slept in that position he didn't know. He crept over to her, cupping the back of her head with one hand he took the weight and slipping his other hand under her body he gently rotated her into a better position. She stirred, mumbled and then her eyes opened, focussing on him. He stroked her cheek and whispered that he loved her and her eyes closed. She'd never fully woken. Santa Paws, her favourite teddy bear this week, lay on the floor beside her bed and he tucked the cuddly toy under her left arm. Drawing the duvet up over her, he kissed her forehead and backed out of the room.

His mobile rang while he crossed the landing and he hurried down the stairs as he answered the call. It was Kerry Palmer.

"Hi, sir—"

"Tom," he said, correcting her.

"Right, yes, of course. Tom."

"What's up, Kerry, I thought you were done for the day?"

Kerry Palmer left ops at six o'clock. He didn't mind. They were still waiting on technical services coming back with their review of Moy's laptop.

Frustration was growing at their lack of leads. Billy's world bordered significant criminality but he wasn't a player. Everything they knew about him pointed to an awkward, slightly odd man who existed on the periphery of society. His links to criminality seemed to follow the same path. The bank accounts, both personal and business, showed various inexplicable cash injections, but none of them were for the amounts one might expect to be the result of selling a large cannabis crop. A back-of-the-fag-packet calculation of how much could be garnered from the set up on Billy's property ranged from anywhere between one hundred and two hundred thousand pounds worth. The amounts Billy was depositing were low four-figure sums.

Tom spent the previous couple of hours before he, too, went home reviewing the pathology and forensic reports on Billy Moy and his residence once again. The killer appeared to have left no trace evidence on Billy himself or the murder weapon. There were numerous sets of fingerprints found within the house but very few were considered fresh. Those relating to Danny Tice and his girl-friend were found exactly where Danny said they would be, nowhere near to the body. Tice could have wiped them clean but, if he had, why wouldn't he do the rest of the areas he touched as well. His prints in particular were found in multiple locations, so it wasn't a case of his missing one or two. Besides, Tice was many things but Tom had a feeling that he wasn't the killer. He had no motive. Billy Moy could consistently provide for him, and to an addict that provision was almost priceless.

"Yes, I'm sorry to call so late," Kerry said. Tom checked his watch, it had just gone half eight.

"That's okay, what's on your mind?"

"I've had a nudge from the guy in tech services who's been helping us with Billy's laptop. I wanted him to call me as soon as he had something."

"And?" Tom asked, poking his head around the door at the bottom of the stairs and gesturing to the mobile. Alice smiled and carried on with the film she was engrossed in.

"Good and bad. He says they've been able to recover some of the files from the hard drive. A selection of images, but the history is unrecoverable which is a bummer. He's sending them across on an encrypted zip file for me—"

"Kerry, that can wait until the morning. We've been at it non-stop since Saturday, you even longer. Take a break. You'll be no good to anyone if you're half asleep tomorrow."

"Yes, I suppose so."

"Spend some time with your other half."

"Yes, I will," Kerry said, sounding distracted. "Come to mention it," she took the mouthpiece away from her, her speech muffled, "Yes, I'll be right there. Just hang on a second, darling." She returned to Tom. "Sorry about that, he's looking for something in the kitchen."

"Have some downtime, PC Palmer," Tom said. "You've earned it."

"Right, s–Tom. I will. Goodnight."

"Goodnight."

Tom entered the living room, putting his mobile on the coffee table. Alice lifted the throw to allow him space to sit under it beside her and he slid onto the sofa. She lowered the throw and shifted herself to lean into him and he slipped his arm around her shoulder.

"Everything all right?" she asked absently, placing her head against his chest.

"Yes, two dead men, no suspects and a mystery I've yet to unravel."

"Sounds good. You'll get there."

"I know." Tom took in the scene on the television. He had seen this several times before, and every time with Alice. "Is this…"

"Yes."

"Ah, first or second?"

"First, of course. Now quieten down," she said, patting his stomach. "Elle's just about to blow the case wide open."

Tom smiled. "Yes, I wouldn't want you to miss the big reveal."

Alice nestled further into the crook of his arm, ignoring the gentle sarcasm.

"I spoke to Mum today."

"How did it go for her?"

"Hard to say. You know what Mum's like. She never wants to make a fuss and always plays things down. I think that's why she hasn't said anything up until now."

"She's tough, your mum."

"I know. I wish I took after her…"

Tom moved himself forward so that he could angle his head and look at her, raising one eyebrow quizzically.

She laughed. "I don't wish I was completely like her, don't worry."

"I'm pleased to hear it," he said, sinking back into the sofa and allowing her to settle into him again.

"I think she's dealing with it better than I am. From what Mum said, I reckon Dad is struggling with it. He's not someone who cares for feeling useless."

"No, he's always looking for a solution, needing to fix things."

"Yeah," she said, sighing, "and he can't do anything to fix this. I'm sorry I'm exposing you to this film again... I just wanted something... familiar to take my mind off it."

"I know."

Tom kissed the top of her head, using his free hand to stroke her hair as they watched the remainder of the film. He found himself wishing a ditzy blonde, romantic comedy character would pop up to make sense of the case he was working on. This was Alice's favourite film and Tom quite enjoyed it too, even for the umpteenth time of watching. Not that he would openly admit it. He was telling Kerry the truth on their call, everyone needed to disconnect at times. Working a murder case was akin to standing by a river and trying to save someone else from drowning. You always have to keep one foot rooted on the riverbank or risk being washed away by the same torrent threatening to drown them.

Billy Moy was a man who kept much of his life secret and Tom was certain that one aspect of that life got him killed. They would get there. He was sure of it.

KERRY PALMER HUNG UP, squeezing the mobile in her hand. The sound of her neighbour's music, a mix of 90's techno classics – so he told her the last time she complained – offered up repetitive thuds of muffled bass through the wall. That would go on for another hour or so before peace and quiet would follow when he left for his night shift. It happened like that most evenings unless he wasn't working a shift. Then it would go on longer. One of these days she planned to knock on his door fully clothed in uniform. That would give him a fright, especially if she timed it for when his friends were over for a gaming night and the aromatic smell of cannabis filtered through the partition walls.

Hauling herself up and off the sofa, a clatter came from the kitchen.

"All right, all right, I'm coming already. Just wait for me, would you?"

Muttering about impatience under her breath, she walked into the kitchenette of the one-bedroomed flat she'd moved into last year having saved the deposit up for the previous three.

"Typical! You couldn't just wait for a minute, could you?"

The cat looked at her quizzically. It stepped forward and put another paw in the leftovers of her dinner on the plate set beside the sink, the knife and fork were on the floor along with a splattering of cauliflower dahl. Slipping her hand under the cat's midriff, she scooped him up in her arms. The cat started purring almost immediately and Kerry hugged him close, kissing his head and then putting him down on the floor. The cat stopped to sit down, momentarily licking one of its paws clean – of food no doubt – and then resumed its course weaving in between her, legs, tail erect, rubbing his cheeks against her.

She retrieved a packet of cat food from the cupboard, careful not to tread on the creature who was oblivious to his getting in the way, and tore off the top of the packet and emptied it into the bowl. He set about his meal, immediately disowning her.

"You're welcome."

Kerry flicked the kettle on and folded her arms across her chest, eyeing her reflection in the kitchen window. She looked tired. She *was* tired, but at the same time this had been the best week of her life. At least since she'd joined the police. The thought of going back to marshalling drunks on a Friday and Saturday night in the town didn't appeal. But then there was Eric. She pushed him from her mind. He barely spoke to her these days. It was too late to say anything now anyway.

Walking back into the living room, she almost tripped over the cat who ran past her, leaping up onto the window sill and turning to look at her. She undid the latch and opened the window allowing the cat to slip out. He wouldn't be back until six o'clock tomorrow morning where he would appear at her bedroom window, howling to be let in.

"Goodnight, Miaow. I'll see you at my bedroom window in the morning. Same time, same place."

She drew the curtains and sat down on the sofa, staring at the television. It was off. She glanced at the remote control but she wasn't interested in watching anything. Sitting forward, she lifted the lid on her laptop and tapped the touch pad, bringing it out of hibernation. She cracked her fingers as the fan spun into action and the machine fired up.

"Right, let's see what you were up to with your cameras, Mr Moy."

CHAPTER TWENTY-TWO

TOM FELT CONSTRICTED. He wasn't comfortable, his body tense and his position seemed precarious. The wind struck the window near him, buffeting it with firm regular gusts, and despite the strength of the hinges the casement blew shut, startling him. He opened his eyes, hearing the gulls cawing overhead. They were inland. There must be quite a storm front over the North Sea.

He was lying on his side, perched on the side of the bed with a portable heater leaning against him under the duvet. Small, compact and immovable, Saffy was snuggled into him, sleeping soundly. When she'd come through, he didn't know. He must have been dead to the world. Reaching to the bedside table, he picked up his watch and squinted to read the time. It was approaching six in the morning.

He slipped out of bed, careful that his massive frame didn't bounce the little girl awake, stretching as he stood up. He gently reached past the curtain, closing the window properly so it wouldn't slam again. Saffy could sleep for another hour or so before she would need to be readying herself for school. For a time, after the death of her father, the little girl would come through to their room every night at some point, but this had lessened. Now, she didn't appear to need the reassurance but enjoyed the sense of closeness she got in doing so. Usually, whoever was the first to wake upon her arrival would end up sleeping in a spare bedroom, or Saffy's, depending on how they felt.

Tom didn't fit in Saffy's cabin bed.

As quietly as he could, he gathered fresh clothes from the chest of drawers and his wardrobe and walked out onto the landing pulling the door to, but not closed, behind him. Peeking into Saffy's room and then the guest room, which was always made up, he didn't see Alice. He got dressed on the landing and made his way downstairs. Russell appeared in the hall, greeting him with his usual deference before leading the way into the kitchen.

Alice was seated at the breakfast bar, still in her pyjamas, cloaked in a heavy dressing gown which swallowed her up. It was Tom's but he never wore it. She smiled as he entered and he crossed to her, bending down and giving her a warm kiss on the lips.

"Good morning, gorgeous," he said, smiling.

She smiled. "Thank you, but I look dreadful and you know it."

"Not to me," he said, checking the kettle had water before flicking the switch on. Alice didn't appear to have slept much; dark rings hung beneath her usually bright eyes. She looked sad. He plucked the cafetiere from the shelf above and scooped two healthy measures of freshly-ground coffee into it. "Couldn't sleep?"

"Is it that obvious?" She shook her head, lifting her tea. "Thinking about mum." She sighed. "And our little diva came through around three, so it was an interrupted night."

"Ah... yeah, I didn't hear her."

"That's because you were snoring. I'm surprised you didn't wake the dead last night."

He laughed. The kettle gently rocked as the water boiled.

"Plans for the day?"

She frowned. "After I've dropped Saffy at school, I'll drop into work for a couple of hours and then go over to see Mum, I think."

"I thought you were rostered off for the next couple of days?"

She nodded. "I am, but I've got paperwork to catch up on and I'd rather not face it when I have a shift to run."

"Admin day." Tom stirred the brewing coffee with two deft swirls of the dessert spoon, appreciating the aroma, and put the lid on. "If you want to call in at the station and tackle my pile as well—"

"Don't give me that, Inspector," she said with a sideways smile. "If there's anyone I know who is on top of his paperwork, let's face it, it's going to be you! You are so annoyingly good at all that stuff."

He cocked his head. "I'd say you're exaggerating, but I know it's true."

She laughed. A muffled call came from upstairs. Someone was awake. Alice made to get up but Tom put a hand on the back of hers.

"I'll go and get her ready. You stay there, finish your tea."

She smiled her thanks and he headed upstairs to help Saffy get dressed. Not that she needed the help, not really. She just enjoyed the positive interaction.

ENTERING OPS, Tom was surprised to find the room bathed in light. Only one computer was on, the one at Kerry Palmer's temporary desk but the constable was nowhere to be seen. He hung up his coat and wandered over to her desk. He found himself admiring the background image on the monitor but then realised it was a picture file. The shot was taken from an elevated position facing down into a wooded valley. Mist swirled through the trees so the photographer must have been at quite a high elevation to have such a panoramic view.

"Morning!"

Tom turned to see Kerry enter, smiling at him, a takeaway cup of coffee in her hand.

"Good morning." He gestured to the screen. "Did you make an early start?"

"Yes, I was impatient." She hesitated as she approached. "That's okay, isn't it?"

"Yes, of course. What have you found? Anything interesting?"

"I think so," she said. Tom moved aside and she slid into her chair and turned to the screen. Minimising the picture, she pointed to the icons on the screen. "Tech services were able to recover some of the data but the majority was lost. Something about damage when it was transported and dumped, exposure to the elements, proximity to magnetic devices... blah, blah, blah... it's enough to say the hard drive was knackered. However, it seems Billy Moy not only liked to practise with photographic films, but he also appreciated digital cameras." She looked up at Tom. "It seems he wasn't afraid to embrace modernity, too. I think the appeal of digital cameras, aside from simple uploading, is they are so less cumbersome when it comes to carting them around great distances—"

"Like climbing mountainous regions?" Tom asked, referring to the image he had walked in to.

"Yes, absolutely. I looked up the model of digital camera Billy Moy was using. Would you believe that costs upwards of three grand new?"

"Expensive hobby," Tom said, perching himself on the edge of the nearest desk and folding his arms.

"Takes quality photographs though," Kerry replied, "and doesn't weigh even a third of the film equivalent."

"Right, Billy was keen. What else?"

"The computer geeks told us they couldn't salvage much from the hard drive, aside from these photographs. For instance, the browser history was completely unrecoverable, which is a shame because I'm a firm believer that someone's internet history is like a window to their soul."

"I thought that was the eyes?"

Kerry grinned. "Old school. Now we're in the twenty-first century and it's all iPads and Chrome."

"Let's not have a look at Cassie's then," he said, raising his eyebrows. "What did they find?"

"Photographs, some taken by Moy himself, we believe, along with others he downloaded. Here's a sample of the type of thing he had."

Kerry clicked on a folder and the icons changed to tiles, mini-images of the photographs themselves. Tom leaned in and she helped him by clicking on the first. It was a dark image, obviously taken at night. The focus of the shot was a window. The lights were on and the photographer must have been standing outside. From the angle it appeared to be an upstairs window and although the detail was very good, it must have been taken from distance. Kerry clicked through to the next and it was clear they were images taken in sequence. Something seemed to be across the lens but after studying several pictures, Tom realised it was a branch with some foliage protruding from it. The photographer was concealed within trees.

A woman stepped into view, the camera taking a burst of images, and had Kerry clicked through at speed they would have made a video. The woman looked familiar but Tom couldn't place her. She began undressing and the images continued until she stepped out of sight.

"Is this Billy Moy's camera or has this been downloaded?"

"This is Billy's own footage. Tech services are certain. He took these and uploaded them." She angled her head and looked up at him. "And there are a lot more."

"Same woman?" Tom asked.

"Funny you should ask," Kerry said, closing this sequence and opening another folder.

This burst of images looked very similar but at the same time different. Tom thought it might be the same room, perhaps another aspect of the property. The style of the window frame was certainly identical. Then he realised it was a ground-floor window, it was the angle the camera was at that was different. The woman stepped into view. This time she was dressed only in her underwear, moving around the room differently as well. She seemed less poised, more carefree. It dawned on him that something wasn't right. He looked down at Kerry, a knowing expression on her face.

"At first, I thought it was the same woman as well."

"It isn't?" he asked.

She shook her head. "They look the same, similar height, build, hair colour and length—"

"But?"

Kerry double clicked and brought the first set of images up. She found the picture she was looking for and enlarged it.

"There."

Tom was looking at a semi-naked woman in her underwear, in the process of undoing her bra strap. He didn't know what he was supposed to be seeing. "Help me out here, Constable?"

With a pen in her hand, she pointed to the waistline just above the top edge of her knickers. Tom stared hard, then glanced at Kerry.

"That's a telltale scar. Caesarean Section. Without doubt."

Kerry put an image from the second set alongside the first, tapping the screen with the end of the pen.

"No scar."

"That's right," Kerry said. "It's a good job Billy Moy took his pervy hobby so seriously, otherwise we'd never have this level of detail. You just wouldn't get the detail in this resolution from a hundred quid's worth of camera."

"Other women?" Tom asked.

She shook her head. "Nope. Just this one... or two. But I'm pretty sure they're taken at the same property. Look here," she said, opening up another series. "These must have been taken in the summertime when the evenings are lighter. Look at the ambient light on the exterior. This wasn't a one-off or even a two-off – if there is such a thing – because he's been back here repeatedly. And there's more."

She opened another folder containing media files. Picking one at random, she opened it. These were video files recording two women on this occasion. One was lying on a sun lounger in a bathing suit alongside a swimming pool. The other came into view and the operator zoomed in on her as she dived into the water.

"Any other videos of anyone else other than these two?"

"A few, yes. But they are downloads from websites focussing on voyeuristic fetishes, not filmed by Billy himself. Although, I'm presuming it was Billy doing the filming but he doesn't appear in shot. It would be good to know if he was a heavy breather. He certainly gets excited while… well, you get what I mean?"

Tom frowned. "I thought tech services couldn't retrieve the browser history?"

"Didn't need to with these other ones," she said. "The sites usually overlay their website address across the footage. This type of thing is disseminated across public message boards, chatrooms and uploaded to multiple sites and then shared via social media. It goes on and on. It's all free advertising that will bring more users to the parent site. However, the downloads were time and date stamped. The time is useless because it will either be in the camera's default setting or simply the time zone of the person recording, but the ones starring his two favourites have been recorded on and off over the last couple of years. And when I say *on and off*, I mean he has literally dozens of photos and video of these two."

"A bit of an obsession."

"Downright creepy is what it is. If it was me, and I found out he was doing this, I'd bloody well kill him!"

She looked at Tom, suddenly fearful.

"I mean, not literally, obviously. I'd report him to the proper authori—"

"Don't worry, I get it. I'd feel the same if he was filming Alice or Saffy."

"Do you think…?" She looked at the still frames again, comparing them. "Yeah… maybe. Sisters?"

"I'm thinking not, no."

"I wish I knew who they were," she said, staring at the screen.

"Well, it's a good job you have me then, Kerry," Tom said, tapping her shoulder with his forefinger. She looked at him expectantly. "And I know just where to find them." He pointed at the screen. "Can you print some of those off to take with us?"

"Sure. Where are we going?"

CHAPTER TWENTY-THREE

Tom slowed the car as they made their way up the gravel-lined driveway. Glancing at the clock, it had just passed eight o'clock and he was worried they might have taken too long getting here. The morning rush hour was something different in coastal Norfolk. One day your journey would be uninterrupted only to run the exact same route the following day to find it take almost a third longer. If you were unlucky enough to pick up a tractor or a tourist, who didn't quite know where they were heading, you could find yourself in a significant tailback.

Driving into the courtyard, Tom saw a Range Rover parked outside the entrance to the property. Voices carried from indoors as they got out of the car. Approaching the vehicle from the rear, Tom spotted damage to the offside rear corner. Range Rovers, despite their luxury finish, were still incredibly hardy and weighing more than two tonnes, they could both cause damage as well as take it.

Tom dropped to his haunches, examining the scuffs and scrapes along that corner. The vehicle had impacted on something ragged, and subsequently pulled away from it leaving another set of almost identical markings. Kerry stood at his shoulder. He looked up at her and she nodded.

"Santorini Black," she said, pointing at the car. "It's distinctive, premium paint."

"Should be easy to match in that case."

The voices grew louder and two people came out of the house, startled by their presence. Ginette Finney was surprised.

"Inspector Janssen. W–What are you doing here?"

Her daughter stepped out from behind her, dressed in her school uniform, nervously looking at Tom and Kerry in turn.

"We wanted a quick word, if that's okay?"

She glanced at her watch, then her daughter. "My husband is inside—"

"I would like to speak to you first, if you don't mind?"

"I'm afraid this is a rather bad time, Inspector." She put a hand on her daughter's shoulder. "You see, we're just leaving for school."

"I appreciate that, Mrs Finney, but it is rather important."

She met Tom's eye and held his gaze, unwavering. She wasn't smiling anymore.

"Of course. If you think it important?"

"I do."

Ginette swallowed hard, as if her mouth was suddenly dry. She looked at her daughter, smiling weakly. "You go and wait in the car, Kimmy."

Kim didn't need to be asked twice and she slipped out from under her mother's grasp and clambered up into the front passenger seat, closing the door and nervously tucking her hair behind her left ear, but staring straight ahead.

"What's this about, Inspector? You do look very serious."

Tom looked at Kerry who stepped forward with a folder in hand. She opened it and passed the first of the downloaded screen-shots to Ginette. At first, the woman's eyes lingered on the image and she appeared reluctant to accept it, but after an awkward moment, she did so.

Holding the image in her left hand, she brought her right up to loosely cover her mouth, stuttering intakes of breath followed but she didn't take her eyes off it. Ginette didn't utter a word.

"That's you, Mrs Finney," Tom said.

Her eyes darted up at him and away again, back to the image, her expression fixed but clearly agitated.

"And something tells me you're not altogether surprised to see them," he said, watching her intently. "Feel free to correct me if you believe I am mistaken."

Almost imperceptibly, she shook her head. Tom nodded to Kerry and she passed Ginette the next image. She looked up at Kim, still staring straight ahead as if they weren't there.

"Kim?" Tom asked.

She lowered her head, answering almost inaudibly, "Yes."

"I think Kim might be late for school today, Mrs Finney."

"You don't understand," she said, suddenly thrusting the pictures back into Kerry's hands.

"Explain it to me then."

Ginette tried to push past him and walk to the car. Tom didn't try to restrain her.

"You can't run away from these questions, Ginette. You can talk to us here or at the station if you'd prefer."

She spun on her heel to face him, anger flashing. Kim looked up, an expression of anguish on her face. She'd been paying attention all along. "Damn you! Damn all of you."

"What the hell is going on here?"

Tom turned to see Alan Finney standing in the doorway, hands on his hips.

"That's just what we would like to know, Mr Finney. Where were you last Thursday night?"

The farmer was momentarily taken aback, his face changing as he sought an answer to the question. Realisation dawned and his expression took on a scowl. "Now, you just hold on a damn minute—"

Tom snatched the pictures out of Kerry's hand, his patience wearing thin, stepping forward and holding them up in front of Finney's face. The scowl faded and he averted his eyes from the images.

"I think the two of you have some questions to answer," Tom said, "and I've had enough of you giving me the runaround."

Finney held up his hands in supplication, his tone conciliatory. "Now look, I can see where you're going with this, but it's not what it looks like—"

"Is it not?"

Tom turned the images so that he could see them himself, tapping the topmost one with his forefinger. "Your wife!" He put the first to the back and held the second aloft, lowering his voice and ensuring the image wasn't visible to Kim, still sitting in the car. "Your daughter!" Tom hissed. He forcibly placed the pictures in Alan Finney's hand and took a couple of steps to the rear of the Range Rover, pointing to the damage. "And you smacked your car when leaving Billy Moy's place. In something of a hurry, were you?"

Finney firmly shook his head. "It's not what you think, it just isn't!"

Tom marched across, squaring up to him. "Then you'd better start talking because right now, I'm thinking about dragging you back to the station in chains—"

"I *didn't* kill him!" Finney barked. His eyes shot to his daughter, watching them from her vantage point. "I didn't, and that's the truth." He chuckled but without any genuine humour. "And wanting the truth to be anything other than that is a waste of your time, because it just isn't so."

"You went to Billy's house that night," Tom took the images and held them up to him. "And you confronted him about these, didn't you?"

Finney refused to look at the pictures, shaking his head.

"And then you lost your temper and you killed him—"

"No! That's not what happened at all." His head bowed and he ran both hands through his hair. "You're not listening. I went there, yes, that's true. We had words…"

"Words?"

"Yes, words," Finney snapped. "And... all right, I was tempted to put one on him."

"You struck him?"

"No... yes, sort of." He shook his head, grimacing. "Wouldn't you want to lay into him? Put yourself in my place, Inspector Janssen... and you catch this... this *vermin* touching—"

"Alan, please!" Ginette barked at him. Her husband fell silent. Tom looked at her. Behind Ginette, he could see Kim had started to cry.

"Maybe we should go inside," Tom said, adopting a conciliatory tone.

Alan Finney bobbed his head in agreement and gestured with an open hand for them to enter the house.

GINETTE FINNEY USHERED Kim upstairs to her bedroom, whilst Alan led the detectives into a large open-plan kitchen, dining room, offering them seats at a table beside an expansive wall of glass. It overlooked the pasture adjoining their house. Alan sat down opposite Tom, his hands nervously clasped together. They waited until Ginette entered the room, coming to stand behind her husband where she placed her hands reassuringly on his shoulders. It was an affectionate and supportive gesture. Alan reached up with his right hand, resting it on top of Ginette's left.

Tom knew he should be separating the two of them and arranging transport to the station where they could be interviewed. However, Tom had an inkling that he might get more out of them this way rather than being heavy-handed.

"I think you ought to start from the beginning, don't you?" Tom said, gesturing to Kerry to make notes. Alan Finney made to speak but it was Ginette who spoke over him. Surprisingly to Tom, he appeared happy for her to do so.

"I'm afraid it begins with me, Inspector." Her hands drifted away from Alan's shoulders and he reluctantly released his hold on her left hand, lowering his head as she took a seat beside him. "I told you before how my family have been living in these parts for a long time."

"Yes, I do recall you said the same about the Moys. And also that your mother and Billy's – Maureen – were somehow entwined."

"Yes, that's right. You don't need all the details, but my mother had a difficult time of it for a number of years and it was Maureen who helped steer her through it all, in one way or another."

"And you felt beholden to her, to look out for her son, Billy?"

"Sort of, yes. I wasn't entirely... candid with you, Inspector." Tom leaned in to the table, resting his elbows on the surface and interlocking his fingers before him. "You see, Billy and I are the same age. We went right through school together, from juniors up to high school and... our mothers being so close, it was inevitable that we would spend a lot of time together."

Tom saw Alan bristle slightly, covering his mouth and chin with one hand and slowly rubbing his fingers as his wife spoke. He looked ready to talk but refrained, allowing her to continue.

"Billy... Billy was a *special type* of boy; do you understand what I mean by that?"

Tom inclined his head, indicating he needed more clarification.

"I guess these days someone would say he has some kind of social disorder or dyslexia, or something I don't know, and maybe he'd be treated differently, but when we were growing up he was just considered thick, pushed to the back of the class and pretty much left to his own devices. But he was a sweet boy... arguably a little disturbed at times, but a sweet boy nonetheless."

"Can you define disturbed?"

"Prone to intense emotional outbursts, often if things didn't go his way. He would overreact to the slightest setback. That sort of thing. He could fixate on things, still does – did – anyway."

"That's why he is so good with machinery," Alan said, lifting his head to interject. "Stays focussed until the job is done. The man would skip lunch if he had a job to do." He shook his head. "Not many are built like that these days, to be fair. I don't have many working for me as dedicated to their tasks. More's the pity."

"You were saying, Mrs Finney?"

"Right, yes. Billy didn't have many friends at school. He found it hard to socialise. I suppose many do in their teens, all those hormones floating around, I guess. I did and he found it awkward, trying to stay latched on to me while I was growing, moving away from him."

"He had feelings for you?" Tom asked.

"Infatuated is the word—"

"Alan, please. Let me explain."

Alan Finney held up a hand by way of an apology and made a signal of locking his lips shut with an invisible key.

"Billy had feelings for me. Eventually, it all came to a head and I had to tell him that it wasn't going to happen. Not then, not ever. He took it hard. Very hard... but that was all years ago and after his mother died, I knew he was struggling with the farm... with life." She glanced at her husband. "I was still his friend. A good friend. So, I spoke to Alan—"

"And talked me into throwing work his way from time to time," Alan said, begrudgingly. "He was good, that much is true, but if I'd known how bloody weird he was then I would never have entertained the idea."

Tom took a breath, allowing Kerry to catch up with her note taking.

"This weirdness you speak of," Tom said, "does that relate to the pictures?"

Alan scoffed. "We didn't know about that until last week. One of the stable hands saw him at the back of the house, loitering somewhere he had no business being."

Tom waited patiently, fixing his gaze on Alan. After a few moments, he splayed his hands wide.

"Yeah, it turns out he was perving... but he ran off when challenged."

"When was this?"

"Last week, while he was supposed to be working in the barn. Kimmy," he coughed, evidently uncomfortable. "Kimmy had been at an after-school sports club. She got home early evening and... had been for a shower. I realised what he must have been looking at. It turns out..."

He couldn't say the words. He grew more increasingly agitated. Ginette took a deep breath and picked up the narrative.

"It turns out... Billy hadn't moved past his... attraction to me. I don't know what reignited his interest, but it would appear he also saw me in our daughter."

"And when we asked Kim if she'd had any problems with Billy, she told us how he'd..."

"How he'd what, Mr Finney?"

"*Touched her*, Inspector," Alan said through gritted teeth.

"Not abused, Inspector," Ginette said. "We should be clear, but Kimmy said he'd helped her into the saddle," she took another breath, again stuttering the intake, and then speaking very quickly as if she needed to get it out as fast as possible, "placing his hand where it shouldn't be... and leaving it there, stroking."

Alan slammed a flat palm against the table making Ginette jump.

"Now do you see why I went over to his place? Why I roughed him up a bit? The pervy sod bloody deserved it!"

"And this was when exactly?"

"Wednesday night – evening. Wednesday evening."

"The night before his death, Mr Finney," Tom said, "and let us be clear, you're admitting to going over to Billy Moy's home and attacking him."

"I know! And I'm guilty of throwing him around, certainly, but I swear on my daughter's life that it was on the Wednesday, not Thursday, and he was very much alive when I left him."

"The photographs?"

Alan shook his head. "I made him burn them. As I said, we didn't know he was taking pictures... it makes me sick to think of him standing out there, watching... my family. Kimmy is only

216 J M DALGLIESH

fifteen, Inspector Janssen. You think about that for a second. *Fifteen!*" Alan sat back, looking to the ceiling and back to Tom again. "Anyway, he fessed up, told me what he'd been up to. He even showed me the pictures, the dirty little bastard. He promised to stop. He said he'd tried everything he could to do things differently, and that he knew it was wrong, but it wasn't working."

"What wasn't working?"

"I'm sorry, what do you mean?"

"You said that Billy told you *it wasn't working.* So, what wasn't working?"

CHAPTER TWENTY-FOUR

ALAN LOOKED PERPLEXED. He glanced sideways at his wife, open mouthed, but her expression was vacant. He turned back to Tom.

"I'm sorry. I–I don't know what he meant by it. Is it important, do you think?"

"Perhaps. Tell me what happened after you confronted him and he showed you his collection."

Alan shrugged. "Like I said, I threw him around a bit. I'm not proud of that, but don't ask me to feel sympathy for him. He offered to destroy the photographs. We took them out into the yard and burned them... in an old makeshift brazier that he used for garden waste and stuff, I guess. I thought that was it. I suppose," he flicked a hand towards the folder on the table next to Tom, "he had more. I knew I couldn't trust him."

"This fight you had—"

"It wasn't a fight, as such," Alan said. "I was furious. I confronted him and I lost my temper. That's it. It wasn't a fight."

"How many times did you strike him?"

Alan's eyes looked skyward, sucking air through his teeth. "I'm not sure I did." Tom looked at him with scepticism. "I swear it. I pushed him around, squared up to him... Billy started whimpering

and then crying like some little child... telling me he deserved it."
Finney tensed, his fists clenched. "I wanted to kill him, to beat him
to a pulp, but he just lay there, in a ball at my feet... crying. It was
the most pathetic thing I'd ever seen."

"It would be very easy in the heat of the moment to reach out
for the closest thing at hand and strike him with it—"

"I did not beat him nor did I stab the man to death. As God is
my witness, Billy was alive and kicking when I left."

Tom stared at him, reading the expression on his face. He was
willing Tom to believe him. "Tell me about the house."

"Which one?"

"Billy's. How did you find it?"

Alan shook his head. "Like any other. I'd never been in there
before, so I don't know what you're looking for me to say."

"How was it? Tidy, messy, anything out of place, unusual?"

Alan laughed. "Inspector Janssen, this was Billy Moy we're
talking about. The man's odd at the best of times." Tom stared at
him and eventually, Alan relented. "It was... nothing to write
home about. Bland, ordinary. Like how most people live.
Ghastly."

"What happened to your car, Mr Finney?"

"Oh, as I left," he waved his hands in a circle in front of his face,
"I reversed into something outside the house. I heard it but I
wanted to get away from there. Get home to my family. I'd done
what I set out to do. My mind wasn't right, that's all." He shook his
head. "I was angry, confused... shaking. Probably unfit to drive, to
be honest. I only saw the damage the next day. I haven't got around
to fixing it."

"If you thought Billy Moy was interfering with your daughter,
perving on your family, why didn't you call us?"

Alan Finney took a deep breath, glancing sideways at his wife.
Ginette made to speak, struggling to find the words.

"That was my fault, Inspector. Norfolk is very close-knit, I'm
sure you know... and if your business becomes public, then everybody, and I mean everybody gets to hear about it."

"You were concerned for your reputations?" Tom asked, trying hard not to show his incredulity at that thought.

Ginette shook her head. "No, of course not. Well, maybe a little, but it was Kimmy I was thinking of." She sat forward, imploring Tom with her eyes. "She's at that age, you know? Something like this, the comments, the finger pointing... it would follow her around for the rest of her life. We couldn't put her through that—"

"And what about the potential for Billy Moy to interfere with other children?" Kerry Palmer said, speaking for the first time, clearly annoyed. "Perhaps their parents would like to know if he was a danger to them—"

"I'm sorry," Ginette said, looking directly at Kerry. "But I will always put my family first, before all else. That's what parents do."

Alan held up his hand as if he was presenting in a business meeting. "You may not agree with how I – we – handled this situation, but we did what we thought was for the best."

"For whom, Mr Finney? Best for whom?" Tom asked.

Alan didn't reply, averting his eyes from Tom's gaze. Tom felt the response was genuine, Alan Finney showing his true colours belittling those less well off than himself, the very characteristic that seemed to make most people dislike the man intensely. His wife, Ginette, clearly felt comfortable hiding behind her image of a protective mother. There was every chance that this was the truth or, at least, their perception of it.

"Are you telling me, Mr Finney," Tom said, "that you didn't inflict any physical harm upon Billy Moy? Furthermore, he was alive and well when you left the house that night, and I want you to be crystal clear with me, that this was last Wednesday?"

He nodded. "Yes, Inspector. That's the truth. I went there, Wednesday evening, and confronted him. He admitted what he'd done and I oversaw his burning of the images he'd taken... at least, I thought I had. And then I left and returned to my family."

A few moments of silence followed until Alan spoke again, and Tom heard something he had never heard before in the man's tone, humility... and fear.

"W–What is going to happen now?"

Tom drew himself upright. He looked between the couple.

"I want you to call someone you know who can either come and sit with Kim or take her to theirs for a while." Ginette nodded. "Then I'm going to arrange transport for the two of you back to the station and all of this is going on record, formally."

"I would like our solicitor present," Alan said quietly.

"Which is your right. And then I'm going to have a doctor scrape every orifice of yours for DNA samples to compare with our crime scene." He stared hard at him. "I'm also impounding your Range Rover and I'll take it apart piece by piece looking for traces of Billy Moy inside it. Once all of that is processed and comes back, I'll look at it and if there is any suggestion that what you've told me isn't the complete truth, I fully intend to charge you with murder."

Ginette gasped whereas Alan held Tom's gaze. "And if not?"

"If not?" Tom said. "I hope for your sakes you are telling me the truth. Otherwise I'll do everything I can to ensure you spend the best part of the next twenty years as a resident guest at one of Her Majesty's finest hostelries."

Alan glanced at Ginette who appeared terrified. Her husband smiled at her weakly. Turning to Tom with a stern expression, he slowly nodded at him. "Then I put my faith in you to do your job properly, Inspector."

"Do you believe them?" Kerry asked as the second patrol car moved off. Alan Finney shot them a nervous look from the rear passenger seat.

"Does he strike you as the kind of man who would allow someone to effectively get away with touching up his teenage daughter?"

"No," Kerry said, shaking her head. "Quite the opposite. He strikes me as the entitled sort who thinks he's above everyone else because of everything that he has, his standing in the community, and the fact that when he speaks everyone listens. The notion that a – how did he describe him? – *pathetic* little bloke like Billy Moy could take pictures of his wife and daughter getting undressed, videos as well... and even putting his hands on Kim, and think he'd get away with doing so without punishment? I can't see it." She looked at Tom, the two police cars transporting the Finneys away left the courtyard and disappeared from sight. "Even if he is telling the truth, and all of that happened as he described it, I wouldn't put it past him to have stewed on it for another day before going back on the Thursday and killing Billy. What about you?"

Tom hadn't responded to her thought process. He couldn't necessarily argue with her logic, but it wasn't the only view to take. Kerry noticed.

"Do you believe him?"

"Curiously, your very argument could be used to give weight to his story being the truth."

Kerry's eyebrows met in concentration. "How do you mean?"

"Think about it. The Finneys are socially elevated. Any hint of a scandal, a sex abuse scandal no less, could be very damaging to them."

"But it wouldn't be their fault—"

"No, not at all," Tom said, "but people like the Finneys like to control how they are seen. The image they project is just as important as the material items they possess. Tongues wagging, fingers pointing. *How did they not know? How could a man allow an abuser to have access to their daughter? Can we trust our children around them?"* Tom splayed his hands wide. "These are common questions that are often raised in these scenarios. They are completely unfounded, obviously. But then again, I'm sure there will be those who would love to knock Alan Finney down a peg or two, even if they don't believe it themselves."

"So their reputations would be worth defending at any cost?"

"Not only theirs, but in their mind, their daughter's as well."

"But Billy Moy had a shiner... someone fought with him the day of or the day prior to his death," Kerry argued. "The pathologist said so. If not Alan Finney, then..."

Tom nodded, pursing his lips. "Indeed. And that's why we'll try and find a trace of Billy's DNA inside Finney's car or some sign of him having been in a fight, which will be hard more than a week after the event, but we'll try. And after he's been poked and prodded, we'll go back over all of this with him time and time again until he's so sick of telling his story that he's ready to crack, looking for inconsistencies. If he's telling the truth, then his story won't change. After all, you only have trouble remembering a lie, the truth should be plain sailing."

"What about Billy Moy being a potential abuser? That could open up a whole new line of suspects if he has access to anyone else's children."

"Yes, get onto social services and see if he's ever shown up with them. It's a pity his browser history was fried, otherwise it might have made for interesting, if not disturbing, watching. Of course, we only have the Finney's word on that, so let's ensure we keep it between the team. If it gets out that we're looking at this angle, all hell is going to break loose and I'd rather know ahead of time if that's likely to happen."

CHAPTER TWENTY-FIVE

TAMARA SLIPPED her mobile back into her pocket, intimating to Cassie she was ready to go inside with a tilt of the head towards the refuge. Cassie thanked the uniformed officer, standing beside his patrol car, and crossed the road to join her.

"Anything to report from overnight?" Tamara asked, looking past Cassie to the policeman.

"All was as quiet as can be. No one visited the refuge overnight, nothing to report."

"Good. Hopefully, Sasha is well rested and a bit more talkative today."

They walked up to the door and pressed the bell. The refuge was a secure facility, but only by way of restricting the access of individuals for obvious reasons. Their location wasn't a secret and it wasn't uncommon for the perpetrators of domestic violence to seek out their spouses here. Although, with a direct line to the local police no one had ever breached the security to make it inside. They didn't have to wait long. Mary Bloom unlocked the door, opening it as wide as her welcoming smile.

"Good morning, Tamara," she said, nodding to Cassie as well. "Come in, come in."

"How's our girl?"

Mary closed the door behind them, the sound echoing on the tiled floor of the entrance hall. Her smile faded and she rocked her head from side to side. "Sasha's been... subdued. She hasn't said very much at all."

"What do you make of her?"

"Hard to say, really. You brought her in to me late last night and I offered her something to eat, the poor thing looked half-starved, and then got her settled in her bedroom. She went off almost straight away."

"Did she say anything to you at all?"

"Only that she's been practically living rough this past week, bless her, eating out of bins and sleeping wherever she found somewhere safe and dry. And let's face it, there hasn't been much of that lately. The street is no place for anyone, let alone a little thing like her."

Cassie shrugged. "She strikes me as quite a tough cookie."

Mary looked at her inquisitively. "Appearances can be deceptive, DS Knight."

"Yeah, maybe," Cassie said, casting an eye around the lobby. "In my experience, people usually turn out just as you see them."

"Well, it's a good job I'm here to temper your preconceptions then, isn't it?"

Cassie smiled. Tamara thought this was where she should step in.

"Can we see her?"

"Yes, of course. Come with me. Sasha is having tea with me in the kitchen."

Mary led the way along a narrow corridor towards the back of the building. Pushing open a fire door into the kitchen, Tamara saw Sasha sitting at a table in a conservatory accessed through the kitchen and overlooking the garden with the sea in the distance. The refuge was located on the edge of Hunstanton, a residential home that was added to and extended over the years, now offering temporary accommodation for up to six women should it be required. Mary Bloom had been awarded an OBE for her efforts in establishing the facility almost single-handed.

Sasha was lost in thought, staring out at the sea and didn't notice their arrival. She wasn't startled when Tamara stepped into view, instead offering her the inkling of a warm smile. Tamara returned it.

"How are you feeling today?" Tamara asked.

Sasha's smile broadened slightly and she raised her right arm, wrapped in a cast. "Sore. But I am better. Thank you."

Her eyes were far brighter than they'd been the previous day and her complexion was also vastly improved with colour returning to her cheeks.

"What a difference a good night's sleep can do for you," Tamara said, gesturing to the chair next to Sasha's. She nodded and Tamara sat down. Cassie lingered in the background. Mary Bloom came over to the table.

"Shall I make us all some more tea? Or coffee perhaps?"

"Coffee for me, please," Tamara said.

Cassie held up her hand, declining. Mary picked up Sasha's now empty cup and busied herself in the kitchen. Tamara took out her notebook and a pen, opening it to a fresh page.

"Sasha, do you remember us talking last night?"

She nodded.

"Good. You told us that you are working as a cleaner, but you couldn't tell us where."

Again, she nodded.

"Can you remember today?"

"I–I work where... tell me to work."

"Who by?" Tamara asked. She looked away. "Who tells you where to work, Sasha?"

She shrugged.

"How did you come to be here in Norfolk, Sasha?" Tamara hoped to put her at ease, get the conversation going and then maybe draw out more information.

"At home, I look after my grandmother." Sasha looked up at

Tamara. "She is old, very old. She needs... how do you say... to be caring for?"

"To be cared for? She is in a nursing home?"

Sasha smiled, nodding. "Yes, she has people to look after her." She leaned in towards Tamara. "It is very expensive in Latvia."

"It is very expensive here, too," Tamara said, smiling.

"So, I came here to England to work. I can send money back to my home."

"And what about your parents. Do they look after your grandmother as well?"

"No. My father left when I was very young... and my mother was ill, very ill. She is not here anymore."

"I'm sorry."

Sasha smiled weakly. "I came here to help my family, my grandmother. Now, all I want is to go home to see her. I should not have left."

"Aleksandrs Balodis has your passport. You knew that?"

Her expression became wary, watching Tamara as she answered, accompanied by a curt nod. "He was to give it to me. That is why I went to hotel to try and find it. Then I can go home."

"Mary tells me you have been sleeping rough these past few days."

Sasha looked at her, uncomprehending.

"You have nowhere to sleep. To live."

She nodded. "Yes, that is true."

"How would you pay for your ticket home?"

Sasha exhaled, wringing her hands. "I do not know. I–I hoped Aleksandrs would help me... somehow."

"Aleksandrs," Tamara chose her words carefully, "was killed last week, Sasha. Do you know where this may have happened or why?"

She shook her head, averting her eyes from Tamara once again.

"You told us yesterday that the two of you were friends. Can you tell me of any other friends that he spent time with or places he went to?"

Mary arrived at the table with a tray holding three steaming cups. She set it down. Sasha glanced at her and then Tamara, moving a hand to her stomach.

"May I please go to the bathroom?"

"Yes, of course," Tamara said.

Sasha smiled gratefully, moving her chair out as Mary set a mug of tea in front of her before passing a cup of coffee to Tamara. As Sasha left the room, Cassie sighed.

"You're not wrong about her being subdued," she said to Mary. "I've met chattier corpses." Tamara shot her a dark look and Cassie apologised, holding up a hand. "I'm sorry. But she doesn't say a lot."

"That young woman has been through a great deal," Mary said, offering Cassie a disapproving glance. "You mark my words. I dread to think what she's been put through."

"You believe she may have been trafficked here?" Tamara asked.

"She shows all the hallmarks, yes. I'm surprised she's willing to talk at all."

"She is scared," Tamara said. "She bolted from us yesterday before we were able to identify ourselves as police officers—"

"I expect she would have run even if you had," Mary said. "The police aren't usually very compassionate when it comes to dealing with sex workers press-ganged into service." Tamara was about to object, but didn't get the chance. "Present company excepted, obviously. I just mean in general, sex workers are not regarded highly by the police the world over, as if their lives are worth less because of what they do. And the fact that so many of these poor souls have been forced into it doesn't seem to cut much ice either."

"That attitude will not be found in my office. Will it, DS Knight?"

Cassie shook her head. "Absolutely not, no."

Mary's gaze lingered on Cassie, judging the validity of the comment but she said nothing. Cassie folded her arms across her chest, then walked to the conservatory window to get a better look of the view. A figure ran past on the street outside.

228 J M DALGLIESH

"Bloody hell!" Cassie barked, turning back to the room. "Do you have a gate from the garden to the street, Mary?"

"Erm... no. For security, we closed—"

"She's only gone and bloody legged it," Cassie said, running for the front door as Tamara's chair scraped the floor tiles as she stood, before taking off after her detective sergeant.

The front door was swinging closed as Tamara reached it, forcing it back open. Cassie was already in the street, looking at the constable who was leaning against the front wing of his patrol car chatting to two women passing with their dogs on leads. He seemed momentarily oblivious to their presence until Cassie shouted at him.

"Oi!"

The constable leapt away from the car, startling those talking to him, and spun to face them.

"Fat lot of use you are, PC Plod!"

Cassie shot him a withering look and ran off in the direction Sasha had taken. Tamara also glared at the constable who raised both his arms wide in protest, bewildered and oblivious to the cause of the verbal assault.

"What?"

The refuge was on a bend and rounding the corner the pavement narrowed. The roar of a diesel engine sounded from behind them and an orange Transit van approached, cutting the corner so much that the rear wheels mounted the kerb forcing both women to check their runs. Cassie hit out at the side panel with the flat of her hand, shouting at the driver. "Moron!"

The van didn't stop, accelerating away from them. Sasha was at least a hundred yards away from them now, running downhill. The two detectives resumed their run, pushing hard. Ahead of them they saw the brake lights of the van come on as it came alongside Sasha. She seemed to notice their presence, her run faltering as she looked to her right. The side door to the van slid open and two sets of arms reached out, grasping her and hauling her into the van. Her legs flailed as she struggled but the van accelerated away and Sasha disappeared from view.

"Hey!" Tamara yelled. It made no difference. Even if they could have heard her, the van drove away at speed. Both women pulled up. Cassie bent over, resting her hands on her knees as she drew breath in huge gulps, grimacing. Tamara already had her mobile in her hand, dialling the control room.

"Did you get the index?" Cassie asked between breaths.

Tamara shook her head. "Partial. L34 J something. You?"

"No, sorry. Too busy trying not to get run over."

"Damn it!"

The beleaguered constable arrived behind them. Cassie shook her head at him.

"What?" he asked for the second time.

Cassie pointed down the road. The van was nowhere to be seen. "Orange Transit. They just grabbed her."

He turned, breaking into a run back toward his patrol car. "I'll get after it."

"Just in the nick of time," Cassie muttered under her breath. She looked at Tamara, who thanked the call handler and hung up.

"The word is out. Hopefully they won't get far."

"That's just it though, isn't it? Maybe they won't go far and they'll be off the road before any of our units get to see them—"

"Yes, I'm well aware of that, but at the moment it's all we've got."

Tamara had a gnawing moment of self-doubt. Maybe Cassie was right the day before and they should have put Sasha in an interview room after all. At least they would still have her.

"Well, safe to say she was lying to us," Cassie said, watching the patrol car speed past them with blue lights flashing.

"How do you mean?"

"Someone was looking out for her or watching us to see what we were doing. Either that, or we've just witnessed the most brazen random abduction this country has ever seen. That girl isn't a cleaner."

"Why, though? They must be worried about something."

"Or she has something they want?" Cassie theorised.

"Damn it," Tamara repeated, but without as much venom this time.

CHAPTER TWENTY-SIX

"GIVE ME SOMETHING ON THE VAN." Tamara threw her coat across the nearest desk as she entered the ops room. Eric had a telephone clamped to his ear and Kerry Palmer was furiously poring over listings on a computer screen. Tom Janssen came over to meet her.

"Eric is on the phone to the DVLA and Kerry is running through the Police National Computer trying to find a match."

"There can't be too many beaten-up old orange Transit vans knocking around Norfolk, surely?"

"Are you sure about the registration?" Tom asked. "An L plate puts it around ninety-four—"

Cassie interrupted. "It was rusty as hell and driven by a lunatic, so I think it fits."

"Got it!" Kerry shouted excitedly and all eyes turned to her. "This has to be the one. It was registered to a local address until three years ago."

Tamara came to stand behind her, looking over her shoulder. "Where is it registered now?"

Kerry looked up, frowning. "It was recorded as going for scrap."

"Well, it didn't make it," Tamara said.

"Could someone have taken the plates and used them on another vehicle?"

Tamara shook her head. "I can't see that. Use the same plates on another orange Transit. No. There will be another reason. Who was the last keeper of the vehicle?"

Kerry looked back at her screen. "Hang on a second." She said the name quietly, "Charles Barnes."

"Cassie," Tamara said, "find out everything we know about—"

"It's Charlie Barnes," Kerry said.

Tom joined them. "That can't be a coincidence, can it?" Kerry shook her head.

Tamara felt her frustration growing. "Who the hell is Charlie Barnes?"

"Simon Moy was arrested and cautioned a while back following an altercation with another man, Charlie Barnes."

"Billy's brother, Simon?" Tamara said, confused. "What was the ruckus about? How did they relate to one another?"

"We don't know. Neither man was willing to speak about it after the arrest. Seeing as they were the only ones involved, they were cautioned and warned as to their future behaviour and released. It came up when we were looking into Simon Moy."

"This Barnes guy," Cassie said. "Where was he living at that time?"

"No fixed abode," Tom said. "He stated he was living at a local homeless shelter run by the church, but the arresting officer doubted it. I don't know why, it was just mentioned in the notes."

"Then I want Simon Moy back in here immediately, and he needs to tell us what he knows about Charlie Barnes."

"I DON'T KNOW THE MAN!" Simon Moy said, holding his hands up apologetically. "It was six of one and half a dozen of the other—"

"Mr Moy," Tom said, leaning in to the table and bringing his palms together to form a point. "I don't think you fully appreciate the situation."

They had collected Simon Moy from his home, under protest, an hour earlier and he was now sitting in an interview room repeatedly claiming ignorance.

"I'm sorry to hear that you are having this trouble, but, as I've told you repeatedly, I don't know the man. If I could help you then I would."

Moy smiled. It was a smile Tom had seen many times on multiple faces over the years. It was artificial, forced, and didn't cut any ice with him.

"Mr Moy, I know from the arrest report that you were just as much of an aggressor as Charlie Barnes. I'll level with you, I'm not interested in what you were getting up to back then. All I'm interested in is finding Charlie Barnes."

Moy fixed his eye on Tom. It felt like he was taking his measure, assessing what he needed to say in order to get out of the interview room. There was a brief flicker of acknowledgment in the man's expression before he folded his arms across his chest, sighed and sank back in his chair.

"Mr Moy?" Tom said. "We really don't have all day. May I remind you that we are dealing with an abduction here. The longer it takes for us to get the information we need, the more chance that it could escalate further."

"Escalate?"

"Yes. We don't know why they took this woman but we believe there is a strong possibility that her wellbeing is at risk." He stared hard at him, forcing him to make eye contact. "I believe that you are a very flawed individual, Mr Moy."

Moy snorted. "Well, thank you very much for saying so."

"Should anything happen to her, would you like to have that on your conscience for the rest of your life?"

Simon Moy sniffed hard. He was uncomfortable. Tom pressed.

"If we find her soon, there's every chance she'll be okay. If not, I fear we'll be finding another dead body. And believe me, if that's the case, then sitting in this interview room will be the least of your problems." He glanced sideways at Kerry Palmer. "Is that journalist we always talk to still at reception?"

"I believe so, sir, yes. She's itching to speak to us for an update."

"Perhaps we can let her know of a local man who is unwilling to help us, leading to the death of an innocent young—"

"All right!" Moy said, exhaling and sitting forward. He waved a hand to indicate the two of them. "There's no need for the threats and the intimation of what people will think of me. I get it. Okay? I get it. I don't see how any of this is related, but I get it."

"Let us figure that out. Charlie Barnes?"

Moy took a deep breath, scratching the top of his head. "Right, Charlie. You remember I told you I was banned from all the bookies in Norfolk? Well, I might be exaggerating but certainly all of the local chains closed their doors to me and I ran out of new names and borrowed IDs for the online accounts. But," he said, splaying his hands wide, "addicts can be resourceful people, you know?"

"Back street bookies?" Tom asked.

Moy nodded. "And back street events."

"Such as?"

"Unlicensed boxing... cock fighting, hare coursing... you name it. There are a lot of people who can't use regular channels. Plus, it's a damn sight more exciting if you're in on the action."

"Where does Charlie Barnes fit in to all this?"

"Charlie... is a go-to guy when people like me are evasive."

"He's a debt collector?"

Moy inclined his head, screwing up his nose. "I'd go with low-life... enforcer. Not a very good one. I mean," he chuckled, "I slapped him and got away with it."

"How much did you owe?"

"I don't recall... two to three grand. It's hard to keep track with the interest they stick on it."

"Where can we find him?"

"Charlie?" He shook his head emphatically, reading Tom's expression. "I don't know. I really don't know. If I did, I'd tell you.

That's the truth. I told you," he said, imploring Tom with his eyes, "I don't know how I can help."

"Who does Charlie work for?"

The question struck a chord. Moy sat back but suddenly looked concerned.

"I–I don't know who that might—"

"Enough of the evasive crap, Simon. Tell me who Charlie works for."

Moy ran his hands down across his face, sniffing hard.

"I'm waiting."

He closed his eyes, one hand across his mouth and holding his chin. "McInally. Rory McInally."

"Thank you," Tom said, standing up and making for the door.

Kerry Palmer got Moy's attention. "How did you manage to stop them coming after you for the money you owed?"

Moy smiled. "Fortunately for me, my mother-in-law croaked... and my wife got a few grand."

"How lucky."

"Yes, it was for me, not so much for the mum-in-law, but then they say *God works in mysterious ways*, don't they?"

"And your argument with your brother," Kerry said, "you still needed money." The smile faded from his expression. "Is that all people are worth to you, the value of how much money you can get out of them?"

He wagged a pointed finger at her. "Don't think to judge me, young lady. Only one person ultimately passes judgement on me, and I don't plan on meeting my maker any time soon."

"Come on, PC Palmer," Tom said, standing in the open doorway, making room for a uniformed officer to step in and chaperone Simon Moy. "We have somewhere better to be." He looked at Moy. "You're free to go." Moy made to stand up. "Just as soon as I say so."

Moy frowned and Tom left the room.

"How long are you going to leave him there?" Kerry asked, falling into step alongside him.

"As long as possible."

"Good," she said, smiling.

"Not only to inconvenience him, but I wouldn't put it past him to curry favour with Rory McInally by tipping him off to our approach."

"He wouldn't do that, would he?"

"I trust him just as much as you do. If it meant he could open up a new line of credit, then I expect he would, yes."

Tamara Greave stepped out of the adjoining room where she'd been watching their exchange via the camera feed from the interview room.

"Do you know where we can find McInally?" she asked.

"Yes. A few years back he made an effort to go legit with his interests," Tom said, hesitating for a moment. "At least, that's the impression he tried to give off. He's one who has always been on the periphery of police investigations, somehow always managing to slip out of reach any time we got close to him. As a prominent member of the traveller community, a patriarch of sorts, some say, he's moved around between regions on and off for years."

"Has he any involvement in trafficking or the sex trade?"

Tom shook his head. "If he has, then that's a new one on me. I reckon Simon Moy was on the level when he told us what he knew; the illegal gambling, payday loans outside the scope of the FCA – or any other official body – and bare-knuckle fist fighting are the areas Rory has traditionally dipped in and out of. He was implicated in a race-fixing scandal in and around the Jockey Club a few years back and he's rumoured to have dipped a toe into recreational drugs. I think the race-fixing probe put the frighteners on him for a while, pushing him towards legitimising his interests."

"Into what?"

"Property," Tom said, the two of them heading back to ops. "I refreshed my memory after speaking to Eric. Rory McInally bought a patch of agricultural land spanning a large area that bordered two settlement boundaries with a view to developing it."

"Is that the campsite you talked with Eric about the other day?"

"Yeah, that's the one, although it's much more than a campsite these days. Rory obtained planning permission to open a holiday camp there, restricted occupancy rules, limited scope for building and so on. The councillor sitting on the planning committee who helped push it through was eventually pulled up for some misdemeanour and forced to resign. The details of what went on haven't ever been properly made public but, as I understand it, the suggestion was that some agreement was made to greenlight the project."

Tamara sighed. "I do love a bit of political corruption, don't you?"

Tom laughed. "Yeah, looks that way. In any event, Rory's been dividing up parcels of land and selling them off to the highest bidders. Some of them changing hands for ten to fifteen thousand pounds, other plots for four or five times that. Seemingly, the place is a real mish-mash of developments. There are caravans being occupied all year round, log cabins and anything in between. It's become a bit of a planner's nightmare. Some people are living out there all year round whereas others are restricted to seven months. There are backdated planning applications underway, environmental health orders, evictions notices... you name it, then it's going on."

The two of them entered ops. Tamara caught Eric's attention. "Briefing in less than half an hour, Eric. I'm going to speak with the chief superintendent and round up as many bodies as we can."

Eric nodded. He looked at Tom. "The custody sergeant is looking for you. Simon Moy's solicitor is here and wants an update on what we are planning to do with his client."

"He can wait." Tom looked at Tamara and she agreed.

"Kidnapping, trafficking women... sounds like quite a step up for him."

"Yes, I'm surprised but, then again, he's never been shy when it comes to making money."

"This campsite... holiday park, what can we expect from the residents?"

Tom thought about it. "Many, if not the majority, will have little or nothing to do with McInally. It has become something of a hillbilly site masquerading as an upmarket holiday camp. Think about it, if you're priced out of owning property in one of the nearby towns or villages, you can buy one of these plots, with a questionable planning decision, and stick a caravan on it. You've got your own home in the countryside for the cost of a new mid-range car. At those prices, it's worth a punt. Some of the cases underway have been running for several years already and no one has been forcefully evicted just yet. The council have got themselves in a right mess over it."

"Minimal resistance then?" Tamara asked. Tom was confident there shouldn't be too much push back. "In which case, would McInally risk taking her back there, if that's his legitimate enterprise?"

"Right now, it's all we have. How do you want to play it?"

"I'll run it by the chief super, but I think we need to go in there hard and fast."

"Search warrant?" Tom asked, already confident of the answer.

"No. Even if we don't find her, then I'm damn sure we'll find something to give us leverage. We will have to."

CHAPTER TWENTY-SEVEN

THE POLICE OPERATION was underway late afternoon. Ideally, Tamara would rather carry out such a raid at the crack of dawn, thereby catching their targets off guard and often still tucked up in their beds. Today, they didn't have the luxury. The convoy of police units, as many uniformed officers as they could gather on such short notice, assisted by colleagues from the King's Lynn station, moved onto the site at speed spreading out to close off the entrance and prevent any vehicles from leaving.

As expected, they didn't face any resistance. Their presence, far from covert, brought people out of their properties to watch the deployment with a mixture of curiosity, surprise and bewilderment. Tamara was out of the car quickly, issuing orders, the officers fanning out in search of the orange Transit van. They brought with them their own canine units; the handlers deemed sufficient to quell any potential protest but there wasn't any to speak of.

The group advanced through the site, knocking on doors and searching every residence, outbuilding or caravan present. Tom spotted a familiar figure step out onto the veranda of a two-storey log cabin occupying a large plot overlooking a small lake on the eastern edge of the site. He was tall, once powerfully built but now showing signs of an ageing frame and sagging skin. Curiously, he was only wearing boxer shorts, slippers and a thick dressing gown, topped off with a Russian fur hat with ear coverings hanging down at the sides. He caught sight of Tom whilst taking a steep draw on a cigarette and exhaling the smoke towards him, accompanied by a disdainful look.

Tom called Tamara over and gestured towards the odd-looking man and they crossed the short distance to his property. Rory McInally leant on the railing lining his veranda, watching their approach and casually glancing around at the police sweeping across the site.

"Does he look in the least bit concerned to you?" Tom said under his breath.

"Not at all."

They came to stand before Rory McInally, looking up at him on his raised veranda. He smiled but the expression was far from genuine.

"Long time, no see, Inspector Janssen. What brings you here..." he looked at two officers beginning a search of the land around his own cabin, "in such a subtle manner?"

"I see you're dressed for the weather, Rory."

McInally glanced down at his front, the smile broadening. "I was enjoying an afternoon in the hot tub around the back, until I heard you lot disturbing the peace."

The man didn't pull his dressing gown around him, seemingly oblivious to the cold snap in the air of early spring.

"We're looking for a van belonging to Charlie Barnes," Tamara said.

McInally exhaled another cloud of cigarette smoke, then picked something from his left ear with his forefinger, casually inspecting it before wiping his hand on his dressing gown.

"Never heard of him."

"Really?" Tamara glanced at Tom. "So we won't find him or his orange Transit van parked around here then?"

"Ah... an orange van rings a bell but I can't say I've seen it around here for some time." He looked at the officers scouring the neighbouring properties. He gestured towards several with a flick of the hand. "I don't think you're likely to find an orange van in the log store over there, do you? I know the entrance requirements for the police force are dropping every year, but even the dumbest policeman should know that."

"Okay, enough of this," Tom said, mounting the steps and coming before McInally, who tossed his butt aside, sniffing hard and wiping his nose with the back of his hand.

"Yeah, cut the crap, Janssen. Let's not be wasting any more of our time. Things to do and all that."

"Water's getting cold, I should imagine. We're looking for a young woman—"

"There are apps for that these days—"

"I thought we were cutting the crap, Rory?"

McInally turned, leaning on the railings and folding his arms across his chest.

"Who are you looking for?"

"Sasha Kalnina."

He scrunched up his face, glancing first at Tamara and then towards the sky. "Can't say I know the name. What is she to me... or Charlie for that matter?"

"She was abducted off the street this morning."

He shrugged.

"And she is the witness in a murder case," Tom said.

"Murder? Now, why didn't you say so. That *is* serious."

"Where is she?"

He shrugged again. "Never heard the name before," he shook his head dismissively. "And murder really isn't my game, Inspector. You know that."

"How about trafficking women?" Tamara asked. "Enticing naive young women to the country and forcing them into prostitution will be a new avenue for you as well."

The casual demeanour shifted ever so slightly, McInally bringing himself upright. He slowly pointed an accusatory finger at her. "Now look, don't be trying to tie me to any of that. I'm a lot of things – have been a lot of things – but I don't deal in people, never have."

"Maybe you should discuss that with Aleksandrs Balodis," Tom said.

Rory McInally paused, eyeing Tom warily. Something appeared to pass unsaid between them for a brief moment, McInally fixing Tom with a shuttered expression.

"Say who again?"

"Aleksandrs Balodis," Tom repeated.

"Can't say I know that name either. Doesn't sound like a local."

"Well, his body washed up locally."

McInally sniffed, breaking the eye contact. "That's very sad. Condolences to the family."

"I'll be sure to pass that on. I'm sure his relatives will appreciate the sentiment. So, what business do you deal in these days, Rory?" Tom asked, looking around. "This is a nice place. Maybe HMRC should come over, take a look at your finances and see just what you can and cannot afford."

He scoffed at the threat. "Do your worst, Inspector. I have nothing to hide."

"Oh, I doubt that very much, Rory."

The radio in Tamara's hand crackled into life and she stepped away from them. McInally kept half an eye on her. Tom noticed.

"Worried about something, Rory?"

McInally smiled. It was artificial and somewhat forced. "Not at all, Inspector. In fact, I'm quite amused. You must be amassing quite an overtime bill with all of this lot."

"We're working on commission these days, Rory."

He laughed. "In that case, I hope you can go without eating for a while. I knew cutbacks were harsh, good for business, but harsh on your lot. They say crime doesn't pay... and I don't think it pays for you, does it?"

Tom smiled. "I'm paid well enough."

"Oh, good. I have a lovely plot of land just over the other side of the lake there." He waved to their right and winked. "I'll do you a good deal."

"Nah, I'm picky about my neighbours."

McInally put a hand across his heart and feigned offence. "You do me damage, Inspector. It cuts deep."

Tamara returned, accompanied by two uniformed constables, a serious expression on her face. "You'd better put some clothes on, Mr McInally."

This time Rory did appear genuinely annoyed. "Whatever it is you think you've found, it's got nothing to do with me."

"We can discuss it at the station."

The two constables guided him inside to get dressed. Tom was curious.

"Have we found her?"

She shook her head. "No, nothing so far."

"Then what?"

"Dogs."

He frowned. "I beg your pardon."

"There's an outbuilding at the furthest point of the site. We found a number of dogs in there, sixty-odd, although it's hard to be sure as they're all in there together. A mixture of breeds. Cassie reckons they're all pedigree."

"Stolen?"

"Likely, yes. We'll need to get a vet down with a scanner. Some breeds retail at two to three thousand a pop. Most of them will be microchipped, for sure. Then we'll know. But there's no sign of Sasha or the van. What did you make of his reaction when you mentioned Balodis?"

Tom thought about it. "He was uncertain, guarded."

"I thought so too. But is that an indication of something more?"

"Guilt, you mean?"

Tamara nodded. "Or concern that we found the body."

Tom sighed. "Or for once, he really didn't know who I was talking about and was contemplating whether one of his lieutenants has cocked up?"

Tom's mobile rang. He answered as Rory McInally came out of his home, now fully dressed, escorted by the two officers and sporting a set of handcuffs. Tamara smiled at him as he passed. He glared at her.

"My solicitor will have a field day with you lot. By this time tomorrow, the two of you will be issuing parking tickets!"

Tamara didn't reply, merely broadening her smile as he descended the steps and was led away. Tom hung up, putting his hand on her upper arm, he encouraged her to come with him.

"Come on, we've found the van."

"Where is it?"

"Dumped on the Sandringham Estate."

They hurried back to the car, coming across Eric on the way. Tom called out to him as they passed.

"Stay here with Cassie and make sure every inch of this place is turned over. We're looking for anything that we can use to apply pressure to Rory McInally."

"Will do, but where are you off to?"

"Uniform have found the van not far from here."

"Any sign of Sasha?"

Tom shook his head and got into the car.

THE DRIVE to Sandringham took less than fifteen minutes with the blue lights and sirens on. Their location was close to the estate's visitor centre and popular children's play area on one of the approach roads off the A149. The road took them through the woods and before reaching the designated car parks there were small areas amongst the trees often used by locals to park their cars while walking their dogs through the country park.

A uniformed officer flagged them down as they approached, guiding them to park on the left between the trees. The van was off the road and had been driven into some brush. It was still clearly visible and looked abandoned rather than parked in an attempt to hide it from view.

Tom dropped the window, the constable leaning in to them, acknowledging both in turn.

"A passer-by called it in three quarters of an hour ago, thought it looked odd. Obviously it was flagged and flashed up immediately."

"Have you been inside?" Tom asked.

He shook his head. "It's all locked up. Had a walk around it but can't see or hear anyone."

"Let's have a look."

He went to the rear of his car, opening the boot and bringing a claw hammer from a box he had inside. Falling into step alongside Tamara, the three of them approached.

"It's definitely the one they used to snatch Sasha," Tamara said.

They found the van just as the officer described. The doors to the cabin were locked and there was nothing of note on view. Tamara tried the side door but it didn't give either. Returning to the back end, Tom forced the claws of the hammer into the gap between the rear doors and, using his immense strength, popped the lock with apparent ease. He exchanged a glance with Tamara. Both of them held their breath as he swung the door open.

The constable angled a torch beam into the interior. It was empty, the side panels and floor just as battered as the exterior. In the corner at the front of the van, a figure was curled up in a ball. Her arms were bound with cable ties at the wrists, as were her ankles. The smell of the interior was an odd mix of oil, grime and human sweat.

"Sasha," Tom said quietly.

Tamara climbed into the back of the van, inching her way carefully towards the woman. Her face wasn't visible, hidden as it was between her bound hands.

"Sasha?" she asked. It was hard to tell in the dim light, but Tamara thought she saw a flicker of movement. "Sasha, it's me, Tamara from the police."

Slowly and very purposefully, Sasha's hands moved slightly to reveal a fearful, wide-eyed expression. She stared through her bound hands, her breath coming in short ragged intakes.

"You're safe now, Sasha."

Tamara came closer to her, gently reaching out and touching her hands. Sasha blinked, flinching at Tamara's touch despite her taking great care. Her eyes were red-rimmed and her cheeks were streaked as tears passed through dirt and grime. Her left eye was swollen, her lower lip split in several places. It too was enlarged and looked sore. Her injuries present that morning had now multiplied. Tamara looked over her shoulder as she helped the woman to sit up and place her back against the side of the van.

"Call for an ambulance!" She turned back to Sasha, trying to reassure her with a smile. "It's over, Sasha. You're safe now."

Sasha's expression remained the same, her eyes watching Tamara warily.

"No one is going to hurt you anymore."

Tom got into the van, Sasha panicking and trying to move further into the corner. Tamara did her best to calm her. Tom checked his approach, passing a pocket knife to Tamara who used it to cut the ties binding Sasha's hands and feet. Tom retreated from the space, realising his mere presence was intimidating her. He could see that she had taken something of a beating, so much so that she'd dared not make a sound when the police first approached the van.

THE PARAMEDIC TREATING Sasha deemed her physical injuries to be largely superficial and once she was safely in the back of the ambulance, accompanied by a police officer, Tamara came to stand alongside Tom who was inspecting the van.

"How is she?" he asked.

"Messed up. Physically, she'll be sore for a while and they'll check her over at the hospital to make certain, but I think she'll be okay. Mentally? That's something altogether different."

"Has she said anything about her abductors or what they wanted from her?"

Tamara shook her head. "Not a word. She's scared to death, I'll give her that—"

"But there's more?"

"I get the feeling she's just as scared of us as she is of them."

"I spoke to Cassie. There's no sign of Charlie Barnes at the site. I'm having a forensics team come down to pick this van clean for anything we can get, fingerprints, blood, sweat... anything that can tie it to whoever did this to Sasha."

Tamara let out an exasperated sigh.

"What is it?" Tom asked.

"All... this!" she said, flicking her hand from the van to the ambulance as it moved away for the short trip to the hospital. The flickering blue lights of two patrol cars illuminated the space around them. The sun was dropping over the horizon and the surrounding trees saw them plunged into darkness ahead of time. "I don't feel we are any closer to figuring this out. Do you?"

"We have Sasha now... once she's feeling more secure, maybe she will open up—"

"You sound like me two days ago, Tom. Cassie suggested I press her, but I thought *go easy, play it slowly.*"

Tom shrugged. "Who's to say you were wrong?"

"I got her to a safe place and as soon as I tried to speak to her, she ran... and ended up here. Think about it, even if she does talk and points a finger at McInally – which I doubt she will because he's not stupid enough to do this himself – he will deny it, and then it will be months before it gets to trial. Do you think she's going to stick around to testify?"

Tom shook his head. "No, she'll be on the first available flight back to Latvia—"

"And good luck getting her to return for the court date. That's why McInally will be so confident."

They were alone and Tamara allowed herself an uncharacteristic stifled scream of frustration.

"It wouldn't be half as irritating if I didn't feel that we had all the pieces but can't put them together."

"I'm feeling that too," Tom said. "Why?"

"Why what?"

"Why let her go? I mean, if you're brazen enough to snatch her off the street right in front of the police then you must have good cause. Whether she knows something or has something they want, why let her go only a matter of hours later?"

Tamara frowned. "Maybe they bottled it, realised the heat they were going to get and dumped her as soon as they thought about it?"

"Yeah, maybe."

"You don't sound convinced, Tom."

He smiled. "No, sorry. To know where she was they must have been paying attention, looking for her... and watching us. They knew we'd be immediately in the hunt and yet they still took the risk."

"Perhaps she gave up whatever it was they were after," she said, thinking aloud.

"Or she never had what they thought she had in the first place."

"You're not helping with my clarity of thought, Thomas."

He placed a supportive hand on her shoulder and she leaned in to him, resting her forehead on his arm.

"It's going to be a long night, isn't it?"

CHAPTER TWENTY-EIGHT

TAMARA TURNED the key in the lock and entered. The muted sound of the television came to her through the closed door to the living room. She hung up her coat and wandered through to the kitchen, putting her bag down on the table. Glancing at the clock, she saw it was approaching half eleven. She felt shattered, but her brain was so wired there was no chance of sleep coming any time soon.

Crossing to the fridge, she took out the open bottle of wine and, first picking up a glass, she returned to the table. Pouring out a glass, she set about removing the files from her bag and setting them out in a fan around her seat, determined to figure out what she was missing.

The television noise grew louder, accompanied by footsteps on the wooden floor. Tamara's mother, Francesca, came into the kitchen, surprised to see her at the table.

"I didn't hear you come in, Tammy darling."

"Yes, I was purposefully quiet."

If her mother was offended by Tamara's obvious intent to be alone, she either wasn't aware or didn't show it.

"Long day?"

"And getting longer," she said with a half-smile.

"Your father's asleep on the sofa."

"Some things never change," Tamara said, lifting her glass to her lips. The wine was a little dry for her tastes but her mother chose it and anything would do right now.

"May I join you?"

Tamara looked up at her mother. She was on edge about something. Perhaps that wasn't fair. Tamara was well aware that when she was buried in her work, she didn't take well to distraction and her mother was many things – distracting being one of them.

"Yes, of course. Grab a glass," she said, sliding the bottle across the table ever so slightly.

Francesca smiled, got her own glass and came over to the table. Tamara picked up the bottle and filled her mother's glass halfway when it was presented to her. Francesca pulled out her chair and sat down.

"Rough day?"

"You wouldn't believe the half of it," Tamara said, sitting back and raising her own glass once more.

"You can tell me about it, if you like?"

"Thanks, Mum, but to be honest it's already making my head spin as it is," she said, picking up a clutch of crime scene photographs taken at Billy Moy's house. She had already separated the ones depicting Billy's body, being more interested in the rest of the house. There was something about the scene that did not fit in her mind and it had troubled her since Eric's wedding day when she and Tom had first entered.

Seeing as Sasha remained silent on her abduction, as had Rory McInally and his associates, they'd spent the entire evening applying pressure, cajoling, even threatening at times, only to end the day with as many questions as answers. Taking a break from the murder of Aleksandrs Balodis and reviewing Billy Moy's was as much respite as she was likely to get. She needed to see movement on both cases and thus far there was precious little. At ten thirty they'd released everyone currently detained in relation to either case. They had no choice.

The team were annoyed about it, Tom in particular. She was too, but without cause to hold anyone any longer, the decision was out of her hands. She flicked through the photos, as she had done many times previously but nothing leapt out at her.

"Nice place."

Tamara looked up at her mum quizzically. Francesca tipped her glass towards the photograph in her hand taken in Billy Moy's kitchen. The body was just out of shot.

"I mean, it's a little basic for me... rustic even," Francesca said, angling her head to one side to get a better view, "but nice enough. The case you're working on?"

Tamara nodded, staring at the image. She doubted the kitchen had been updated in decades. To her it looked old and tired, but tastes varied. "One of them, yes."

"Is that where you were called to last week, leaving the reception?"

"I'm afraid so. A man was killed in his home."

"Oh, that's awful. The poor chap. Burglary, was it?"

"We don't know. Drug deal gone bad... maybe," she said, adding the maybe as a precaution. Her mother was particularly vocal when it came to gossip, although being new to the area and only visiting – a visit now in its fifth month – she didn't imagine she'd made many friends yet with whom to discuss the news just yet.

"Even so, his family must be devastated no matter what brought such evil to their door."

Tamara shook her head, leafing through the next couple of photos. "Not that you'd know it. He only had a brother, and they were estranged for years."

"Was he not married?"

Tamara glanced at her mother, reading her surprised expression.

"No, confirmed bachelor." She chose not to muddy the conversation by mentioning the voyeurism, allegations of touching an underage girl or the links to cannabis production and probable supply.

"Odd. I would say that place had a woman's touch to it."

Tamara frowned at the obvious gender bias in her mother's mind. Why do women always have to do the cleaning? Then again, more often than not, they usually still did.

"Yes, well, no one's talking and we're struggling to make a breakthrough."

"Do you have suspects that you're looking into at least?"

Tamara tilted her head. "We have people of interest, and between them I dare say we could explain what happened. But, like I said, no one's talking."

"Well, people don't like the police very much, do they, Tammy? I told you that when you first joined. Is that why you and Conrad didn't hit it off?"

"Who?" The name meant nothing to her.

"Conrad... I introduced you to him last week at the reception. Remember? Perfect fit for you, I reckon."

"Oh, yes, of course. Him. I think his wife being there had more to do with the lack of progress, to be honest."

"Wife? Ah... I missed that." Francesca sipped at her wine.

"Hmm... maybe next time do a little more homework before you pair me off with someone, yes," Tamara said dryly. "Actually, perhaps you don't pair me off with anyone... ever again!"

Francesca bridled but said nothing further.

"And while we are talking about the police, people do like the police. They just don't like it when they are the ones who are being policed." She lifted her glass, still managing to point her forefinger in her mother's direction. "And there is a difference." She turned her attention back to the photographs, seeking inspiration.

"... is that okay? I mean, your father is happy to."

Tamara looked up, realising she had been momentarily lost in thought. "Um... yes, I don't see why not."

"Great!" Francesca said, smiling broadly. "Your father will be so pleased. I am, too, obviously but I've been so worried about mentioning it to you."

Her attention was now focussed, unsure of what she'd just agreed to.

"Sorry, Mum. What were you saying?"

"Oh, don't worry, Tammy," Francesca placed her hand on the back of Tamara's. "It won't be for long."

"What... won't be for long?"

"We'll be out of your hair as soon as we find a place. Although, the estate agents back home weren't optimistic about a quick sale..." she inclined her head slightly, "unless we slash the price but we want what it's worth, plus a little more what with prices being as they are in your neck of the woods."

"You're... selling your house in Bristol?"

"Of course. We couldn't afford a place here if we didn't. Not a nice place, anyway. The agents around here have told us there's been an influx of people vacating London this past year and the demand has far outstripped supply, so it might be a bit of a wait."

"Um..."

Francesca patted her hand. "As I say, we'll be out from under your feet in no time. Two to three months. No more than six."

"Six?"

"Hopefully less. That's still okay, isn't it?"

Tamara knew she was frowning and forced herself to lighten her expression, much to her mother's relief. "Yes... yes, of course it is."

"Good. Thank you. I was so worried. The removal men will be bringing some boxes across next week—"

"Removal men?"

"Yes, your father's been supervising them packing up this past week. That's one reason he's so tired. A little is going into storage until we find our own place, but in the meantime, we'll have the rest of it come here."

"Here?" Tamara whispered, looking around and envisaging stacks of storage boxes in every inch of spare space.

"Well, we can't put our antique furniture or my ceramics in storage, can we? It will be a mess by the time they bring it across."

"Yes, a mess. Right."

"I'm so pleased you don't mind, Tammy." Francesca stood up, leaned in to kiss her head, hesitated and withdrew, instead rubbing her back gently as she moved away. Tamara felt like she'd just walked into a bear trap and wasn't likely to get free any time soon. "I've put the delivery details in a note on the fridge for you. I'm afraid your father and I will be out house-hunting, but I'm sure you can be here to see them bring everything in, can't you?"

Tamara looked at the fridge, seeing a sticky note with some writing on. It gave her a thought and she hurriedly flipped through the photos in her hand, stopping at one in particular. Putting the others down, she stared at it, her anxieties about her parents moving in forgotten.

"Tammy? You will be here, won't you?"

Tamara slapped the photograph with her free hand, spinning in her chair to look at her mother, waiting at the threshold expectantly.

"Mum, you are a certifiable genius!"

Francesca smiled awkwardly, fingering her necklace. "I–I... if you say so."

Tamara stood up, quickly gathering her papers together and stuffing them back into her bag. She picked up her wine glass, then thought better of finishing it because she had to drive. Approaching her mother, she put an affectionate hand on her upper arm, leaning in and kissing her cheek. Francesca flinched. After all, she wasn't used to sharing physical contact with her and it caught her off guard. Tamara looked her in the eye, taking her mobile from her pocket and dialling Tom's number.

"Genius!" she said again, raising an expressive hand and stabbing it in the air in front of her mother before hurrying to the front door.

CHAPTER TWENTY-NINE

TAMARA APPROACHED THE FRONT DOOR, unsure of how to announce her presence, bearing in mind it was now past midnight. She needn't have worried, the external light came on and the door opened, Tom swiftly stepping out to meet her. He smiled and gently pulled the door closed behind him.

"I'm sorry, Tom. I know it's late."

"That's okay. Your call got me thinking."

"Did I wake anyone?" Tamara said, looking guilty.

"Alice and I were still up. Saffy is dead to the world now but she has only just gone off."

Tamara looked puzzled. "Why is she up so late?"

"She hasn't seen a lot of me this week. She flat out refused to go to sleep until she'd seen me, and seeing as it's the weekend, Alice said she could wait up. Not that I think she had a lot of say in the matter. You know what Saffy can be like."

Tamara nodded. "Yep, do you think she gets her stubbornness from you or her mother?"

"Well, seeing as she's not biologically mine, it must be her mother!" Tom said as they reached his car. He unlocked it. Tamara pointed to her own. "Yes, I know, but you've been drinking and I haven't."

"Fair enough. Although, I feel obliged to say, I've barely had half a glass."

"Still," he said, opening the door. "Are you sure about this?"

"Yes… and no," she said, frowning and got in.

The drive didn't take long. The roads were empty at this time of night and when Tom turned onto the lane leading up to Billy Moy's house, the thick cloud cover and lack of light pollution in the absence of streetlights saw them picking their way through the darkness with only the headlights to illuminate the way.

Passing Billy Moy's cabin, they continued on the lane. The car bounced and lurched as the quality of the unadopted road deteriorated further. Tom glanced across at Tamara, half expecting her to comment on his inability to pick a less bumpy route, but she was deep in thought. He wondered how confident she was in her theory.

They came upon the house, the last residence on the lane and shrouded in darkness. He looked across at Tamara and she smiled, pointing to the vehicle parked out front.

"Well, that's new."

Tom looked at the car. It was a BMW, less than two years old judging by the plate. There was no sign of the battered old Mondeo they'd seen previously. Getting out, they walked up to the front door, their steps sounding twice as loud as they crunched the gravel underfoot in the dead of night, passing the BMW. It was immaculately presented.

Tamara lifted the cast iron knocker, rapping it against the door three times in quick succession. Unsurprisingly, they didn't get a response. Tom drew his coat around him, feeling the chill of the night air. Tamara repeated the knocking and this time a light flickered on in a window overhead. The window creaked open and a face appeared, leaning out.

"Do you know what time it is?"

Tamara stepped back and looked up at him, brandishing her

warrant card. "Yes, Mr Bartlett, we do. Can you come down and open the door please."

"Oh... it's you," he said, looking back inside. He appeared to say something but it didn't carry to them below. He looked back down at Tamara and then Tom. "I'll be right down."

Several minutes later, a reticent Gary Bartlett, Billy Moy's acquaintance and neighbour, opened the door, reluctantly beckoning them inside. At the foot of the stairs his wife, Jenny, waited for them, nervously toying with the hem of a casual jumper she'd thrown over her pyjamas.

"W–Why are you out here so late?" she asked Tamara.

"I think you already know, Mrs Bartlett."

She looked at Tamara and then Tom, shaking her head.

Tamara smiled. "Okay, you can keep it up for a little bit longer. That's fine."

"What are you talking about, I don't understand," Gary said, his brow creased.

Tamara looked him in the eye. "Well, I'm sure it will become clear soon enough." She took a photograph out of the folder she held in her hand, passing it to Gary. He looked at it, squinting to see the detail in the lack of light provided from a single bulb above them in the hallway. It was an enlarged photograph of the fridge in Billy Moy's house. He looked at it, his eyes darting up to Tamara's. He looked puzzled.

"You expected Billy here, at your home, on the Friday, didn't you? When he failed to show, the two of you," Tamara looked at Jenny, "called in at his place the next day and found him dead."

"Yes, that's right." Gary looked at his wife. She was wide-eyed and fearful. "We've told you this already—"

"Except it wasn't Saturday, was it Mr Bartlett?" Tamara stepped in and put the point of her finger on one of the slips of paper stuck to the fridge with a magnet. "G & J's, Thurs," Tamara read aloud. Gary stared at the photo, his lips moving but no sound emanated from his mouth. "You were expecting Billy a day earlier. Your story is very credible, because it all happened exactly as you said it did except for one thing,"

Gary looked at her, his chest visibly heaving now, "… and that is that it all happened twenty-four hours earlier than you said it did."

Gary shook his head. "N–No, that's not what happened at all."

Jenny Bartlett drew a sharp intake of breath and sank down onto the second from bottom tread of the stairs.

"Where is it, Gary?" Tom asked. "Where's all the money?" He gestured towards the front door, as if they could all see through it to the driveway. "That's a nice car you have parked out there. A significant upgrade on your old Mondeo."

Gary shot Tom a look, not of denial but one of panic. Then he looked at his wife, slowly shaking her head and staring at the floor.

"But… you don't understand—"

"Gary… it's over. I told you not to…"

"Quiet, Jen," he hissed, making ready to argue with his wife, but she wasn't interested and remained looking at the floor of the hall.

Gary chewed on his lower lip, his eyes moving between Tom and Tamara. He dipped his head in silent acknowledgment.

Leading them along the narrow hallway, Gary stopped short of the kitchen, opening the door to the cellar head. He pulled a light cord and the stairwell lit up. He gestured down and Tom indicated for him to lead. Tamara waited with Jenny as the two men descended. At the foot of the stairs, Gary pulled another cord and they were bathed in the light of a solitary, naked bulb. Gary moved to one wall, lined with storage racking, and lifted a plastic crate from the middle shelf, setting it down on the floor at his feet.

Kneeling down and releasing the clasps holding the lid on, Gary took a deep breath and removed it. Tom peered over him. Inside the crate were bundles of used notes, all tied with elastic bands. He looked up at Tom, imploring him with his eyes.

"It was… just there, on the kitchen table. Billy was… he was dead. I checked, honestly I did. He was cold to the touch. But this, this was right there."

"And rather than call us, you thought you should help yourselves?" Tom said. "With friends like you—"

"But Billy doesn't have anyone... I mean, we weren't doing anyone any harm, were we? And we did call you the next day. It's like your colleague said, we did everything we said, only a day later."

Tom eyed the crate. There must be thousands of pounds stacked inside.

"And you mean to tell me all of this was on view in the kitchen?"

"Well... no, not all of it. There was an old shoe box with about a grand in it."

"And where did you find the rest?"

Gary looked sheepish. "Billy had it stashed in boxes in his wardrobe... I don't know why."

"So you took the extra day to search his place for any more cash he had hidden, while his body lay in the kitchen?"

"Hey!" Bartlett said, standing up and finding some courage despite sweat forming on his brow. "I didn't kill him. I swear, I didn't."

Tom grasped him by the shoulder, turning him around and drawing his hands behind his back.

"Consider yourself under arrest, Mr Bartlett."

He yelped as Tom tightened the handcuffs. "You don't understand," he said quietly as Tom led him back to the stairs.

TOM SHUT the door to the second patrol car. Gary and Jenny were both arrested and being transported in separate vehicles back to the station. Gary stared straight ahead as the car pulled away, a reserved expression on his face. Jenny had been tearful from the moment the realisation struck her that she was going to the police station, borderline hysterical.

Tom came to stand next to Tamara. She smiled at him.

"You were right," he said, "and I can see them as opportunistic thieves, unable to turn down the temptation. What I don't see is either of them being cold-hearted killers."

"They're not killers," Tamara said. "And I never thought they were. But it all makes sense to me now."

"Well, please can you make sense of it for me?"

Tamara shook her head, smiling. "You know, it's been staring us straight in the face all along. It's so obvious." Tom sighed, irritated. "Come on. Let's get going. We have one more call to make tonight."

CHAPTER THIRTY

MARY BLOOM OPENED the door to them, bleary-eyed and initially irritated until she realised who it was. The irritation in her expression moved to concern as she opened the door further, seeing the liveried police car and two constables standing behind Tom and Tamara.

"I'm sorry it is so late, Mary, but we really need to speak to Sasha."

Sasha had nowhere else to go once she had been checked over and released from the hospital, agreeing to return to stay with Mary Bloom for the time being. They entered the refuge, Tamara heading upstairs with Mary. Tom waited in the foyer with the police officers. A few minutes later, Tamara descended the stairs with Sasha Kalnina in tow. Together, the small party walked into the kitchen, Mary turning on a light switch and the fluorescent tubes overhead flickered into life. Tamara pulled out a chair, offering it to Sasha who slowly sat down without making any eye contact with them. She placed her hands together in her lap, looking at the table. Tom stood in the background, Mary Bloom by his side.

Tamara took a seat opposite Sasha, lowering her head and almost forcing Sasha to meet her gaze. Reluctantly, she did so.

Tamara put a folder down on the table, opening it slowly. She put a photograph down in front of her. It was a picture they'd received from Interpol of Aleksandrs Balodis. Sasha lifted her head and looked at it, her expression saddened. Tamara placed another picture alongside it. Sasha turned her face away, clamping her eyes shut.

The second photograph was of Balodis when he was found on Hunstanton beach.

"Did you know about it before or after?" Tamara asked.

Sasha took a breath, then looked at Tamara. Her lips parted slightly.

"Because I don't think you knew what was going to happen to Aleksandrs. If you had, then you would have done anything you could to stop it."

Sasha held her gaze, unflinching.

"But as it is, he did it without telling you, didn't he?"

"Who?" Sasha asked.

"The man who loved you... killed the man you loved," Tamara said, picking up another photograph and placing it in front of her in a very purposeful, deliberate manner. Sasha stared at the picture of Billy Moy lying on the floor, the handle of a kitchen knife protruding from his chest. She sat still, motionless, displaying no reaction, staring at the picture. Tamara tapped the picture. "This is an image that would shock even the most hardened of hearts... but you've seen this before, haven't you Sasha?"

She lifted her gaze from the photo, meeting Tamara's eye with a defiant look, one far from the vulnerable, fragile victim that had been on display for the last few days.

"I don't know what you mean."

"Oh, I think you do, Sasha. What was the plan? Befriend a lonely man over the internet... help him to fall hopelessly in love with you and have him bring you to the UK? What did you promise him in return?"

Sasha shook her head.

"Oh, come on, Sasha. We're women of the world, we know how

it works. Men like to have all the power, the influence... to rescue a woman and provide a better life is a fantasy for most men. Top experience the gratitude, the hero worship. I'll give it to you, you're a wonderful actor. You certainly had me fooled."

Sasha glared at Tamara and for the first time demonstrated a steely edge that sat below the visible veneer of fragility.

"Billy must have been incredibly excited to have finally been able to free you from your supposed bonds of slavery. What was Balodis asking for? A thousand a month for your services or was he suggesting a one-off payment to enable Billy to free who he thought was the love of his life? Only he wasn't, was he? You cooked for him, cleaned for him and took care of everything he desired... leaving him at the mercy of his infatuation with you." Tamara sat forward, resting her elbows on the table, hands together and making a tent with her fingers. "What was your price? What was Billy supposed to pay for your freedom that night? But Billy wasn't going to pay—"

"Shut up!"

"He would have gladly paid, wouldn't he? But he didn't have any money. Those huge sums that came through the house from time to time weren't his. They were payments for the drugs that Rory McInally grew on Billy's property. It wasn't Billy's money to give, but you weren't to know that. Not you, and not Aleksandrs. So how much did Aleksandrs ask for? Five thousand? Ten? More?"

"Shut up, damn you!"

"You must have thought your dreams were coming true when Billy agreed to pay. You watched him leave for the meeting that night, fully expecting him to hand the money over to your boyfriend. How shocked must you have been when he returned later, tired, fearful and... excited at having secured your *freedom*?"

"All he had to do was pay!" Sasha screamed at her. "That's all. Then it would have been over—"

"And by the same time the following day you and Aleksandrs would have been away, leaving poor little Billy to figure out what had happened. Would you have told him, pleaded some case for having to return home to care for a sick grandmother? You see, I checked up on the back story you gave us. Heartbreaking as it was, it would appear that both your grandmothers are deceased and have been for quite some time. And as for your poor, dead mother... well, she will be up for parole next year according to Latvian authorities. But I wouldn't hold your breath on seeing her anytime soon. Although, I'll hand it to her, it's a remarkable return from the dead—"

Sasha sat forward and spat in Tamara's face.

"Bitch!"

She sank back while Tamara wiped her face with the sleeve of her coat.

"Now that's the reaction I would expect to see from a woman who is able to stab an unarmed man in the chest. Did he even see it coming? I doubt it—"

"He was happy! Happy to have murdered my Alek..." Sasha said through gritted teeth, waving her arms in the air in exasperation. "It was only money! If he paid... nobody dies this night."

"And that's why they grabbed you off the street, isn't it? They thought you took the money when you left but no, you high-tailed it out of the house and ran. Had you been thinking straight, then you would have taken as much as you could carry and run as far away as you could, but you messed up. No money, no Aleksandrs... and no way to leave the country. Which is why we found you trying to gain entry to the hotel room... in the hope that Aleksandrs had left your passport there and maybe a bit of cash. At least then you would have had a chance to leave before anyone caught up with you."

Sasha glared at Tamara across the table. After a moment, she sat back and folded her arms across her chest. The look of defiance was back. "I want to speak to a solicitor. I say nothing more."

Tamara shook her head. "There's no need to. You can keep your mouth shut for as long as you like. None of this will be hard to prove... now we know what to look for."

Sasha looked indignant, averting her eyes from Tamara's gaze.

Tom beckoned the two uniformed officers into the kitchen and they formally arrested Sasha. She didn't resist, standing and remaining silent as she was handcuffed. As she was led away, she looked sideways at Tamara one last time, and smiled.

Mary Bloom looked horrified at the revelation, Tamara came to stand alongside her, placing a reassuring hand on her forearm.

"I've never met anyone so, so… callous and cold-hearted," Mary said.

"I'm sorry you had to hear that, Mary. The internet is full of people like this targeting people's emotions. If it's not men looking to con money out of vulnerable women, it's women targeting lonely men. Ultimately, they know we're all looking for somewhere to belong, to feel needed."

"But it's all just about money," Mary said quietly.

"The way of the world, I'm afraid."

Mary shook her head, disappointed. "Not for me it isn't."

Tamara smiled weakly, putting an arm around the older woman's shoulder and giving her a gentle hug towards her. "Don't ever change, Mary. You leave the cynicism to us."

To you, Tom mouthed silently.

Tamara resisted a smile but winked.

CHAPTER THIRTY-ONE

ERIC STEPPED out of the front door of the two-bedroomed house he and Becca bought earlier in the year, baby George held in one arm, his head resting on Eric's shoulder. Tom noted that both Tamara and Cassie made approving sounds as the baby came nearer to them. That was a surprise because neither of them seemed particularly interested in having children of their own, and in Cassie's case, it would be a far more complicated process if she did. Tom had to admit George did look handsome in a pale blue Babygro, his shock of dark hair lifting off the top of his head as if it had been purposefully styled.

George appeared to be taking everything in, his large brown eyes seemingly tracking every face as Eric manoeuvred his way to the car with a holdall in his left hand.

"Do you need some help there?" Cassie asked. Eric nodded and passed the baby to her. George didn't mind, nestling into Cassie's upper arm as Eric unlocked the boot and added the bag to the others already packed. Dropping the boot lid, he quickly knelt and casually inspected the underside of the car. "What are you looking for?"

Eric glanced up at Cassie, then the others reading their curious expressions. "I'm just checking, that's all."

Standing up, he offered to take George back but Cassie indicated she was quite comfortable holding onto him for a little longer. Eric went back inside, returning moments later with Becca who was bearing yet another bag.

"Haven't we got enough already?" Eric asked.

"This one's purely for George. We have no idea what the weather will be like up there. What if it's freezing?"

Eric frowned. "It's Northumberland, not Shetland."

Becca offered him a withering look and he relented, accepting the bag from her and proceeding to find room for it in the boot of the car. Becca came to stand with Tom, Tamara and Cassie.

"It's lovely of you all to come and see us off," she said.

Tamara smiled. "We missed the send-off after the reception last week, so this is the next best thing."

Becca turned her attention to George, his eyes closing as Cassie gently bobbed up and down to help him settle.

"You're a natural."

"Aye, it comes with experience," Cassie said, smiling at the child in her arms.

"Well, maybe when it's two in the morning I could call you and you could come over and help him back to sleep in future?"

Cassie laughed. Tom and Tamara stepped back from them.

"Any word from the CPS regarding Rory McInally?" Tom asked.

"The dogs we found out at the site were in a barn owned by a company that we can trace back to him. At least, he is a director of it. There's a fair chance he'll be charged with theft."

"The drugs and the abduction?"

Tamara shook her head. "You know as well as I do that without Billy Moy testifying that the cannabis farm was run by McInally and his goons, there is no chance of tying him to it. As for the abduction, Sasha hasn't fingered any of them for it. They wanted the money from her, thinking she'd stolen it. I'm not even convinced she knew

Billy had all of that money stashed waiting for McInally to collect it. The Bartletts couldn't believe their luck. Whether Sasha's silence is by choice or she just doesn't want to for fear of retaliation, I don't know."

"She could just be bloody-minded. So, McInally gets done for theft... as if he's stolen a load of laptops? That's a maximum seven-year sentence—"

"If convicted, yes. Pets are property, Tom." Tamara shrugged. "I don't like it any more than you do but it is what it is. What did you make of Sasha when you interviewed her about Billy's murder?"

"Calculating," he said. "Very calculating. Now she knows for certain we understand what happened to Billy, she's dropped the shy victim act and gone on the offensive. She's claiming self-defence... Billy bragged to her about killing and disposing of Aleksandrs Balodis, she challenged him and he attacked her."

"A distinct lack of wounds to Billy's body show anything other than an unprovoked assault."

"True," Tom said, "but her solicitor is running with the bruises to Billy's body being the result of an altercation between them."

"We determined that was from his fight with Alan Finney, though."

"Yes, but Finney is playing that down as much as possible. He wants to keep himself and his family out of it as much as possible, so there's every chance Sasha might be able to garner some measure of sympathy from a jury at trial. The timeline could help her with that story. At least she's not denying killing Billy, and I can't see her walking away from it, not once it's revealed in court how she was in a relationship with Balodis and looking to exploit a vulnerable, lonely man, fleecing him for as much as they could get."

"Yeah, a honey trap that cost Billy Moy far more than he would ever have imagined."

Eric came back to Cassie and she handed him George, so that he could strap him into his car seat. Tom and Tamara re-joined them. Once Eric was busy inside the car, Becca leaned in to Cassie.

"Eric told me what you said about talking to me... you know, about the honeymoon?"

"Ah, right," Cassie said, smiling.

"Thank you. I'm pleased he told me what was going on." She looked at the car, Eric was fiddling with the cross straps. "And I think you had something to do with us going away, didn't you?"

Cassie flushed, looking away. "It was nothing. I'm happy I was able to help out."

Becca threw her arms around Cassie, squeezing her tightly.

"Ooookay," Cassie said, smiling and feeling awkward. She eased Becca away from her. "That'll do."

Becca withdrew, still smiling. "Thank you." She then hurried to the passenger side of the car and got in.

Eric stepped away from the car, gently closing the door. "Right, that's us ready to go," he said.

"Make sure the two of you have a good time, Eric," Tom said.

Eric looked past them. "Where's Cass?"

She was nowhere to be seen. She had been with them only a moment before. Tom shrugged, shaking his head. Eric hurried around to the driver's side and offered them a brief wave as he got in. Cassie came from behind the hedgerow running the length of the drive and quickly dropped a loop over the tow bar. Tom raised an eyebrow in query. Cassie just grinned. The car started and they moved off, both Eric and Becca raising a hand from their windows and waving goodbye.

The length of string attached to the car grew taut and several seconds later, Cassie urged both Tom and Tamara to step aside for their own benefit as two dozen tin cans shot out from behind the hedge as if giving chase to the car, clattering down the road and drawing attention from everyone nearby. The car stopped and Eric got out, staring hard at the cans and looking back at them.

Cassie smiled broadly. "Well, the old ones are the best, aren't they?" She glanced between Tom and Tamara before turning to Eric and held her arms out from her sides as if to say she had little choice. "It seemed a shame to pass up the opportunity."

FREE BOOK GIVEAWAY

Enjoy this book? You could make a real difference.

Because reviews are critical to the success of an author's career, if you have enjoyed this novel, please do me a massive favour by entering one onto Amazon.

Type the following link into your internet search bar to go to the Amazon page and leave a review;

http://mybook.to/To_Die_For

If you prefer not to follow the link please visit the sales page where you purchased the title in order to leave a review.

Reviews increase visibility. Your help in leaving one would make a massive difference to this author and I would be very grateful.

FOOL ME TWICE - PREVIEW
HIDDEN NORFOLK - BOOK 10

TIME HAD VERY LITTLE MEANING these days. The enforced routine, stable and consistent from one point of view, coercive and inflexible from the other, made a clock, a schedule or personal plans utterly pointless. It was far easier at night, a time when many found it harder... almost unbearable for some. And it was those simple life experiences that he so often took for granted, no, not took for granted, but in reality never thought of at all; the choice of when to go to bed, what time to put the light out, when to close his eyes.

Some nights were calmer than others. After all, sound carried. The neighbours were prone to arguments; debating how many bricks they could count in their surroundings –then heatedly discussing whose guess was closest to winning the bet – being the latest subject to dominate their focus during lock up. Then there were the others, the ones who should never be incarcerated in a place like this. That stood for half the people on the wing, if not more. They should be elsewhere, undoubtedly held securely in another facility for their own sake as much as for that of others, but not here. Never here.

As for himself, where did he belong? He wasn't offhand or cavalier regarding his fate. He accepted it. And it was terrifying.

Every day was terrifying. And when that door opened, the noise grew louder. The pull onto the landing felt like a whirlpool dragging him down into the abyss or walking into what he imagined quicksand to be like – if it was the same as it had been portrayed in the films of his youth, anyway – but either way, no one was there to rescue him. He was alone and everyone knew it.

His pad mate was okay; unstable and prone to outbursts, certainly, but he was stable and hadn't been violent. At least the aggression had never been directed towards him thus far and for that he was grateful. *Spiral*, as he liked to be called, not his real name – he wouldn't share his real name – could easily be described as a character. *Weren't they all?* He was in for a minimum of fifteen years for aggravated burglary. What the *aggravated* part was related to was anyone's guess. Lying on the top bunk waiting to hear the reassuring drone of snoring coming from below lent itself to growing anxiety after lights out. But it was a respite of sorts, at least. Only then could he close his own eyes and hope to dream of a place beyond these four walls, and the cracked window leaking cold air across his face each night. When it was quiet, he could imagine this was his choice, keeping the room cool with fresh air to aid a comfortable night's sleep.

That didn't happen often.

Spiral, or Dave as he'd been named by everyone else on the landing, not to his face though for obvious reasons of self-preservation, was already comfortably settled into his new regimen. He had done so within a few days. This wasn't his first stay at Her Majesty's pleasure. *Fifteen years.* That was some sentence, one that he could never hope to navigate himself. The thought of it would be too much, undoubtedly overwhelming. The looming thought of what he was facing on top of his already stiff sentence was enough to spark the fear of dread in him. Those moments of peace, night time in the main, was when those thoughts would vividly come to him, when he had the safety of a locked door between himself and those beyond it.

Spiral was remarkably sanguine about his own time. Was it

bravado, false or otherwise? For his part, he kept his head down, and did his level best to stay out of the way. If Spiral would let him then the door to their cell would remain closed, a personal choice to isolate, to put a physical barrier between him and them. If he could lock it, then that would be all the better. Pushing it closed was the best he could do and even then, only if Spiral was at work or circulating during association. Was it better to be completely alone? Every step heard on the grates outside the door made him focus on the threat, and there was always a threat, even if it was only in his head. It didn't mean it wasn't real. Everyone in there had a story, and most of them were horrific.

Footsteps. They stopped on the landing outside. He heard voices and then the door creaked open. A face peered in at him, sitting quietly at the little table he shared with Spiral. It was Liam, at least he thought that was his name. They'd never spoken before. Although that wasn't rare as he hadn't't spoken to many unless he had to.

"You alright, mate?"

He nodded, glancing past Liam to another man standing on the landing behind him looking both left and right. He glanced into the cell and their eyes met.

"What are you staring at?"

"Me?" he averted his eyes from the man at the door, looking at Liam and then the floor. "Nothing. I wasn't staring at anything—"

"You was! What was you staring at?"

He didn't answer, hoping the chance confrontation would go away if he said nothing, sensing Liam take a half step into the cell.

"Spiral around, is he?"

"No… no, he isn't. A–At work… in the machine shop, I think."

He was all but whispering.

"Ah… right. Of course."

He looked up. Liam locked eyes with him briefly. There was something unsaid in his expression, and then he glanced behind him towards his friend at the door, nodded and retreated.

He felt relief. Once they left, he would close the door again. Be safe. Liam stepped out onto the landing and he got up, quickly closing the distance between himself and the door, happy to see the two men move out of sight. Putting a hand on the cast iron cell door, he gently made to close it only to find a figure step into view and force it back open. Hurriedly, he stepped away from the newcomer, backing into the cell. There was something in his hand. What was it, a kettle?

"This is for you!"

The arm came up in a flash, snapping out at him, and the liquid contents of the kettle flew out in his direction. Instinctively, he brought his hands up to protect his face, but it was a fraction of a second too late and he heard screaming – he was screaming – the sound reverberating off the walls around him and he knew then that he was in trouble. He was burning. Boiling water mixed with sugar, what inmates called napalm because the mixture turned to paste, sticking to the skin and intensifying the heat. He didn't hear the alarm sound on the wing outside the cell. He didn't hear the instructions shouted at his fellow inmates to stand back.

He was still screaming.

He was alone. And everyone knew it.

BOOKS BY J M DALGLIESH

In the Hidden Norfolk Series

One Lost Soul

Bury Your Past

Kill Our Sins

Tell No Tales

Hear No Evil

The Dead Call

Kill Them Cold

A Dark Sin

Life and Death *FREE - visit jmdalgliesh.com

In the Dark Yorkshire Series

Divided House

Blacklight

The Dogs in the Street

Blood Money

Fear the Past

The Sixth Precept

Box Sets

Dark Yorkshire Books 1-3

Dark Yorkshire Books 4-6

Audiobooks

In the Hidden Norfolk Series

One Lost Soul
Bury Your Past
Kill Our Sins
Tell No Tales
Hear No Evil
The Dead Call

In the Dark Yorkshire Series

Divided House
Blacklight
The Dogs in the Street
Blood Money
Fear the Past
The Sixth Precept

Audiobook Box Sets

Dark Yorkshire Books 1-3
Dark Yorkshire Books 4-6